The Scars of Us

NIKKI SPARXX

The Scars of Us
Copyright © 2014 by Nikki Sparxx.

ROMANCE THAT *Sparks* YOUR SOUL

For more information
www.facebook.com/NikkiSparxxAuthor
Cover Design: Cover to Cover Designs
www.covertocoverdesigns.com

Photo Credit: Simon Barnes Photography
https://www.facebook.com/HOTSNAPZ

Model: Andrew England

Contents

The Scars of Us

The Scars of Us

Prologue

Kaiya

I've heard people say that time heals all wounds, but I think that's bullshit. All time did was allow the wounds to scar, leaving a permanent reminder of your suffering. The emotional pain might fade away, but a little piece of it always lingered, taunting your happiness, and never letting you forget.

Now love was a different story. I believed love could heal all wounds, but only if you let it; only if you trusted it. Unfortunately for me, I couldn't trust anyone, at least not completely. The one person in the world who I was supposed to be able to trust unconditionally ruined that for me. Now, the only person I could trust was myself, and even that was questionable most days.

Every day, I looked in the mirror, hating everything that stared back at me. Every single feature reminded me of him, of the person he made me to be. I hated what he'd done to me, hated the scars he'd branded on my soul. I wished I could erase them, but they were embedded so deeply into my being that I didn't think even love could heal them.

I never thought I would ever experience love, until I met Ryker. He turned everything upside down the first time I'd laid eyes on him, and neither of us would ever be the same.

Chapter One

Kaiya

I glimpsed at the clock, which blinded me with glaring red light. As usual, my nightmare woke me way before my alarm was set to go off. Exhaling a sigh of resignation because of the ungodly hour, I rose out of bed and ventured to the bathroom.

Unable to look at myself after my reoccurring dream, I avoided turning on the light, not wanting to see my reflection in the mirror. Even a glance at my pale skin, blue eyes, and dark hair would almost guarantee a breakdown that would take hours to recover from. Avoidance was probably not the best method to deal with my issues, but it was one of the only ways I knew how.

After fumbling around in the dark while doing my business, I made my way to the kitchen to make a cup of tea to steady my nerves. Sleep was futile, and lying awake in bed with my thoughts was a disastrous idea, almost as bad as looking at myself in the mirror.

Padding down the hallway of my apartment, I stopped at my brother, Kamden's, open door. Sometimes, I crawled into bed with him when I couldn't handle the nightmares, but I didn't want to wake him tonight. He needed his rest, and I needed to be less selfish. I hated being so dependent on him, but I needed him, more than he would ever know.

Kamden was the only person from my family that I still spoke to, the only person that I remotely trusted. But even after everything he'd done for me, all that he'd sacrificed for me, I still couldn't trust him fully; I'd never be able to trust anyone completely.

Walking the rest of the distance to the kitchen, I began the process of shutting down, blocking out my thoughts, closing out everything around me. Withdrawing into myself was another coping mechanism, numbing myself, pretending that I was fine and didn't care so that my emotions would be unable to break me—they were the enemy. I doubted that I'd be able to function in society otherwise.

After I made my cup of tea, I headed to my office. Immersing myself in my work was easier than addressing my problems and acknowledging my issues. The numbers and figures made sense, and had a purpose, unlike my thoughts and emotions. I had control over the spreadsheets, tables, and documents, dictating everything that happened within them. I needed to have that power, needed to control as much as possible since I was constantly on the verge of unraveling.

After working on several projects for a few hours, I was interrupted by Kamden. "You sleep okay? "he asked, yawning as he leaned against the doorframe.

I gave him a look of disbelief before sarcastically answering, "Wonderful."

"Why didn't you wake me? You know I don't mind."

"It's not fair for me to wake you every night over a stupid nightmare." I replied brusquely, directing my attention back to the spreadsheets on my screen.

Walking over to me, he placed a hand on my shoulder. "Your nightmares aren't stupid, Ky. You can't—"

Cutting him off, I snapped, "I don't want to talk about it, Kamden."

Raising both hands in surrender and stepping back, he softly replied, "Okay, Ky. You know I'm here for you if you need me."

Sighing, I rose from my seat. "I'm sorry, Kam. I didn't mean to snap at you. I'm just exhausted."

"I know. That's why I don't mind if you come into bed with me— you need your rest."

"Not at the expense of yours. I hardly fall back asleep anyway."

Opening his arms to me, he responded, "I want to do all that I can to help you. Always remember that."

I easily fell into his embrace, enjoying the security of his arms. Kamden always made me feel safe, which was a fleeting notion for me most days. "Thank you, Kam."

Hugging me tighter, he replied, "No problem, little sis."

Ringing from down the hall interrupted our exchange. "I left my phone in my room—I better grab it."

Releasing me from his arms, he trotted out of our office. After a few seconds, I heard him greeting our mother. *Great.* His footsteps echoed from the hallway, increasing in volume along with his voice as he neared closer to where I stood.

"Hang on, Mom," Kam spoke into the phone. He pressed his screen before directing his attention to me. "She's asking for you—will you talk to her?"

I gave him a *really* look. "No."

"Kaiya," Kam chastised in an annoyed tone.

"Kamden," I mimicked in the same manner.

He sighed as he pressed his screen again and put the phone back to his ear. "Sorry, Mom, she already left for work," he lied.

I mouthed, "Thank you."

Rolling his eyes, he turned and went back down the hallway as he made small talk with our mom. Following after him, I decided to get ready for work. I almost ran into him when he abruptly stopped in the corridor right before his door.

"What?" he gritted into the phone, his whole body tensing in anger.

I scooted around to face him, locking eyes with his narrowed, enraged ones. His nostrils flared as he inhaled deeply before seething, "You can't be serious."

"What?" I mouthed anxiously. My heart raced, my anxiety peeking from beneath my walls in anticipation of what my mother was telling Kamden.

Jaw clenched, he shook his head.

Shit, this must be bad. Breathe, Kaiya, breathe. You're safe, you're with Kamden—he won't let anything happen to you.

5

Hanging up the phone without another word, he clutched the device in his shaking hand.

"Kam, you're scaring me. What's wrong?"

He blew out a breath of frustration as he ran his free hand over his buzzed head. "You should sit down for this, Ky."

My pulse pounded ferociously under my skin, my blood thrumming through my veins with fear. "What is it, Kamden?"

"Ky, I really think you sh—"

"Tell me, Kamden!" I shrieked, beginning my spiral out of control. My thoughts turned to the darkest of places, to where my nightmares were rooted. *Please no, please don't let it be him.*

Kamden sighed before stating, "Kaleb is being evaluated for release."

No... no, no, no!

Tears poured in rivulets down my cheeks as my lungs seized, my breath leaving me instantaneously at the sound of his name. My legs gave out as my stomach roiled, and my vision blurred. Kamden caught me before I crashed to the floor, and then blackness descended on me.

Light slapping on my cheek roused me from darkness. My eyes fluttered open to Kamden, whose face was creased in concern. His blue-gray eyes locked on mine before he sighed in relief. "Don't scare me like that."

"I didn't plan to pass out," I retorted as I sat up. I shut my eyes tight and pressed my fingers on the bridge of my nose as dizziness spread over me..

Kamden gave me some space, scooting over closer to the edge of my bed. "I told you to sit down, but you're so stubborn."

I scoffed as I rolled my eyes, not acknowledging his comment otherwise. He was right, but I wasn't going to admit that.

Noticing I was in my bed, I scrunched my face in confusion as I asked, "How long was I out?"

"Not long. Ten minutes, maybe."

I glanced at the clock, my stomach dropping at the sight of the time. *Oh shit, I have to get ready for work!*

"Don't even think about it, Ky. I already called your boss and let him know that you're taking a sick day."

"But—" I attempted to argue.

Kamden moved closer to me on the bed. "No buts. You need to rest. You're in no condition to do anything after that incident. Plus, you haven't been sleeping well either. Your boss said that you could work on your projects from home today." His tone was stern, but nurturing, the concern in his voice evident.

"I'm fine, Kam. Really, I am," I said, attempting to get out of staying at home with my thoughts all day, especially following the bomb that had been dropped on me.

Kamden gave me a knowing look as he replied, "We need to talk about this, Kaiya. You can't just avoid everything all the time. It's not healthy." Averting his eyes, I concentrated on a stitch of fabric on my comforter as I picked at it. *He knows me too well.*

"I can't," I whispered as tears began to surface.

Kamden grabbed my hands, cradling them in his larger ones. "Kaiya, look at me. I'm here for you—don't shut me out. I only want to help you, to do what's best for you. Please talk to me."

A rogue tear fell from my lids as I looked up at him. More threatened to follow as I angrily questioned, "How could they let him out, Kamden? After everything he did to me, how could they release him? He's a fucking monster!"

"I know. He's only being evaluated—he's not out yet. I'm going to do everything I can to make sure he doesn't get released. There has to be someone I can talk to at the hospital." His eyes narrowed in determination, his tone resolute as he spoke.

Biting my lip, I nodded as my tears began to flow freely. "He'll find me, Kam. He'll come back for me. What if he—"

Kamden shifted next to me, his body tensing. Gripping my chin, he forced me to look him straight in his eyes. "He'll never touch you again! I'll kill him before I let that happen," he growled in fury. "No matter what happens, I'll protect you, Ky."

Unable to speak, I nodded again. The tears continued to rain down my face as Kamden wrapped his arms around me. Clutching the back of his shirt in my hands, I trembled against him as I sobbed uncontrollably into his chest.

Kamden ran his hand through my hair as he attempted to console me. "Shh, I'm right here, *sorella*. I'm not going anywhere—you're safe with me."

I don't know how long I cried for, but Kamden never complained. Continuing to hold me, he murmured words of comfort, which helped pull me back from the abyss that always attempted to swallow me whole when I thought about Kaleb.

Pulling away, I wiped my swollen eyes with my palms. I looked up at Kam, who smiled softly at me, his face full of understanding. *Thank God for him.* I weakly smiled back, still fighting against the waves of emotion threatening to drown me. Even after eight years, Kaleb still managed to affect me so intensely. I hated it—hated him.

"Are you hungry? Do you want me to make you something to eat?" Kamden asked, his tone tender and loving. *The perfect big brother.*

Wrapping my arms around my legs, I wiped my nose against my pajama bottoms. I probably looked like a horrific mess with puffy eyes and red, splotchy skin. "I don't think I could stomach anything right now. The thought of him always makes me sick."

"Well, let me know when you're hungry. I'll make you something," Kamden offered as he rose up off my bed, making his way towards my door

"Don't you have to go to work?" I inquired curiously, the space between my eyebrows bunching together in confusion.

"I called in, too. I wanted to make sure you were okay for the rest of the day."

"Kam, you didn't have to do that. I'm fine," I lied. I was far from fine, but I didn't want to tell him that. He'd only worry more.

His lips curved up as he leaned against the doorframe. "I don't mind. Let me know if you need anything."

As he turned to walk out, I stopped him, "Kam, wait."

He stuck his head back through the doorway. "Yes?"

"Thank you."

Giving me a genuine smile, he responded, "Anytime, *sorella.*"

Smiling, I watched as he pulled the door behind him, leaving it open just a crack. I couldn't stop the warm feeling that filled me whenever he would use that term of endearment. Since I could remember, he'd called me *sorella,* which meant sister in Italian. Both sides of our family had some ancestry in Italy, and we had learned some words from our grandparents. Kamden was four years older than me, and had always been protective over me. He'd been even more so after the *incident*—especially since he almost didn't make it in time.

Laying back in bed, the warmth from Kamden's words began to fade away as memories of Kaleb came rushing back. Reminiscing about my childhood almost always reminded me of him because he was so interwoven with my past.

Curling up under the sheets, I attempted to dispel the thoughts of *him.* Clenching my eyes shut, I tried to focus on something else, but it was almost impossible since his face was so familiar to me—I'd never be able to forget it, no matter how desperately I wanted to.

Bolting out of bed, I headed to Kamden's room. He was sitting at his desk with his laptop open, staring intently at the screen. Turning in his chair, he directed his attention to me, "Everything okay? Do you need something?"

Gnawing at my bottom lip, I nodded. "Can I lay with you?" I hated asking him to do that, hated being such a burden to him, but having him near me was the only way I would fall asleep after hearing about Kaleb.

"Of course, Ky. Anything you need."

I silently walked over to his bed as he made his way to join me. Lifting the comforter, he slid onto the mattress and scooted back to allow me to slide in next to him before covering us with the blanket. Surprisingly, it didn't take long for sleep to find me in the warm security of Kamden's embrace.

Chapter Two

Ryker

Carefully untangling myself from the naked woman clinging to me, I eased out from under the sheets and got out of her bed. I picked up my clothes from the floor, and slipped them on soundlessly before heading to the door.

Sneaking out, I softly closed the front door, so I wouldn't wake up the woman... *Abby, I think.*

Whatever, her name didn't matter, but I doubted she'd care whether I remembered or not based on the night we'd had.

A slight pang of guilt threatened to surface as I trotted down the stairs from just leaving like that. I shook my head, reminding myself that all women were the same—they couldn't be trusted. I learned that from experience, and I'd be damned if I let myself be manipulated again.

Hopping into my Chevy Z71 truck parked in her apartment complex lot, I checked the time: 3:26 A.M.

Thank God, I don't have to wake up early.

My first class at the gym tomorrow wasn't until two, so I could sleep in. I had some fitness regimens and nutrition plans to work on before then, but I could squeeze them in when I woke up or in between classes if I needed to.

Once I arrived back at my apartment, I undressed and went to bed. My muscles were loose, my body relaxed from my release as I lay on my mattress. The woman from earlier was almost completely forgotten as I drifted off to sleep.

The gym was abnormally packed for a Thursday afternoon when I walked through the doors to start my shift. Our peak times were usually the evenings and weekends, so I was surprised to see so many people. Most of the machines were occupied by a mix of men and women, however, the majority of people were male muscle heads like me. Hardly any weights sat in their spots on the racks that lined the wall, and the clang of all the equipment echoed throughout the building. I also had many new faces in my Intermediate Kickboxing class, including some hot women.

I had to remind myself not to get involved with clients. Hooking up with them was bad for business, especially since I was one of the lead trainers. But it was difficult not to get sucked in by them, given some of the fine specimens that were at the gym regularly.

After my class ended, I went to my office to finish a fitness plan for one of my clients. I had finished most when I woke up that morning, and I just needed to put the final few touches on this last one. The man was an overweight lawyer who was trying to impress his paralegal mistress by losing weight and toning up. *Yeah, right.* The guy got short of breath every time he walked up the stairs to the upper level of the gym. He would need many sessions before he even came close to his goal, which was for him to lose fifty pounds in six months. If he followed the strict diet and exercise plan that I'd set, it could be possible, but it would take a level of commitment that I didn't think he possessed. Most people lacked the drive to stick with a fitness regimen long enough to see results.

Once my client, Harold Banks, arrived, fifteen minutes late, we began the session with stretches to warm up his underused muscles. We briefly talked about one of his newest cases, a woman who had been in a car accident involving a drunk driver, as we stretched. After that, I took him to walk on the treadmill. He had already broken out into a slight sweat from the stretching and stairs, so I set his treadmill on low to start. I chose a medium pace for my machine, wanting to motivate but not discourage my client.

During our run, I noticed an unfamiliar face out of the corner of my eye. A woman, who looked to be my age, maybe twenty-five or twenty-six, hopped on a treadmill two machines away from mine. She seemed to be tuned out to the world around her, not seeking any attention like many of the other women here as her head bopped lightly to whatever was playing in her earbuds. Something about her immediately intrigued me; I couldn't put my finger on what it was, but I wanted to figure it out. I had to stop myself from leaving Mr. Banks to go talk to her.

Her dark hair was pulled up in a high ponytail that swished back and forth as she briskly jogged. Even from this angle, I could see that she had gorgeous eyes, the color similar to that of bright, Caribbean waters.

Images of her beneath me, eyes closed, lips parted as she moaned my name while I filled her with my cock ran through my head. I wanted to run my hands all over her, feel the soft skin of her tits, ass, and thighs under my rough, tattooed hands.

After glancing at me out of the corner of her eye several times, the woman stumbled, gripping the handrails to keep herself from falling and being thrown off the machine.

Jumping off my treadmill, I rushed to her side to help her. Grasping her by the waist, I pulled her up and against me as I turned off the power. Her chest rose and fell rapidly against mine as she struggled to breathe, her hands clutching my shoulders for support. *She feels good in my arms; natural.*

"Are you okay?" The concern in my voice surprised me. *Why did I care?*

Abruptly, she pulled away from me, like she had been stung by my touch. Her face reddened, probably from a combination of embarrassment and adrenaline. Keeping her eyes averted from mine, she meekly replied, "Thank you. I think I'm okay."

Sticking my hand out towards her, I introduced myself, "Ryker Campbell."

Her eyes flitted back and forth from my face to my hand before she timidly placed her hand in mine, peeking up at me through thick eyelashes. Her dazzling eyes mesmerized me as they locked on mine. She gently squeezed my hand as I caressed hers with my thumb. "Kaiya Marlow."

Her skin is as soft as I thought it would be. I wonder if she's that soft everywhere.

"That's a unique name. I've never heard it before. I like it."

Her full lips turned up into a small, shy smile. "Thank you."

We stood there staring at each other for a few seconds, as if in a trance, before I realized we were still holding hands. Kaiya must have noticed too because she pulled her hand from mine as her gaze darted around nervously, her skin flushing deeper as her smile widened. *She's beautiful.*

Heavy breathing from behind me redirected my attention to my struggling client. Sweat trailed from his receding hairline down his reddened face before dripping off his chin. Turning back to Kaiya, I stated, "I have to get back to my client. Are you sure that you're okay?"

"Yes. Sorry for embarrassing myself and interrupting your workout."

Chuckling, I responded, "Really, it was my pleasure. Nice meeting you, Kaiya."

Her voice cracked, catching in her throat as she replied, "You too."

Even though I didn't want to, I reluctantly turned around and went back to Mr. Banks. "Ready for weights, Mr. Banks?"

He nodded enthusiastically as his labored breaths continued. Laughing inwardly, I slowed his treadmill to a stop. He clutched the rails as he caught his breath, then stumbled off and trailed behind me towards the weight room.

As we walked, I looked over my shoulder, my gaze traveling back to Kaiya. She was still standing on the treadmill, unmoving as her eyes met mine, then instantly darted forward again. I smirked as her eyes flitted back and forth several more times before she secured her stare in front of her.

Glad to see I'm not the only one affected.

After Mr. Banks' session ended, I briskly walked back to the cardio

14

room to see if Kaiya was still on the treadmill. Slowing my pace as I neared, I tried to act cool and unaffected as I entered the space. Unfortunately, she wasn't there, and I couldn't stop the disappointment that filled me, my shoulders sagging slightly and my mouth turning down into a frown.

What the fuck is wrong with me ? She's just some girl. They're a dime a dozen.

Shaking off the unexplainable feelings, I focused back on work, turning around and leaving the room without a backwards glance. I didn't need to be distracted by some chick, especially when there were plenty of others that could take her place. I knew I'd be able to find one at the bar later.

My next class was in thirty minutes, so I went to my office to work on some more fitness plans. On my way back, I caught sight of Kaiya talking with one of the regulars at the gym, Kamden.

I'd never seen her with him before, but this was the first time that I noticed her at the gym. They seemed very comfortable with one another, which caused a spark of jealousy to flare within me. *Of course she has a boyfriend. Look at her.*

Tugging on her ponytail, Kamden laughed with Kaiya. Her smile lit up the room, and I couldn't help but wish I'd caused it. *Stop thinking like that!* I veered the other way before I did something stupid I'd regret, like starting a fight in my workplace over some girl I barely knew. *Get a hold of yourself.*

I exhaled a sigh of relief once I entered my office. I set my attention on my fitness plans, class schedules, and workout routines. I actually needed to figure out some new exercises for my self-defense class tonight.

As I attempted to drive away my thoughts of Kaiya, a knock sounded at my door. Turning around, I faced Kamden and the woman that was currently occupying my mind. *Great.*

I plastered my fake, customer service smile on as I greeted them, "Hey, Kamden. How can I help you and your... friend?"

"This is my sister, Kaiya. Kaiya, this is Ryker. He's a personal trainer here at the gym."

Sister? A genuine smile spread across my face. *She's only his sister.* I noticed the slight resemblance between them now, but Kamden's eyes weren't the same color as Kaiya's.

"We've met already," Kaiya said as she tried to hide a smile.

Kamden looked back and forth between us, "When?" His tone was full of confusion, along with some apprehension.

"I slipped on the treadmill, and Ryker was there to rescue me," Kaiya answered as her eyes met mine. The corner of my mouth curved up as her cheeks flushed with color again. *I'd like to make that whole body flush. Over and over again.*

Clearing his throat, Kamden broke whatever haze Kaiya had put me in. He narrowed his eyes, glaring at me as he gruffly said, "I just added Kaiya to my membership. I wanted her to meet some of the staff since she'll be working out here now."

"Great. Please let me know if you need anything," I replied, excited that I would be seeing more of the beautiful woman in front of me. I wondered how long it would take to get her in my bed.

"I will. Thank you, Ryker," Kaiya replied with a shy smile, causing my stomach to knot at the sight.

What the fuck? Snap out of it, man!

"We better get going. See you around," Kamden said as he led Kaiya out. Turning to look over her shoulder, she gave me another coy smile as she walked out the door.

I was unable to fight the grin that spread because of hers. *I'm so fucked.*

Chapter Three

Kaiya

Looking out of the window at the passing traffic, I bit my lower lip to contain the smile on my face. Butterflies performed elaborate, acrobatic routines in my stomach throughout the whole ride home after my encounter with Ryker. No matter how hard I had tried, I couldn't push him from my thoughts. My mind had been preoccupied with the muscular, tattooed trainer ever since I laid eyes on him on the treadmill.

"You're in a good mood," Kamden observed, glancing at me out of the corner of his eye as he drove.

I shrugged my shoulders. "It was good to relax and get out of the apartment for a little bit."

"Well, I'm glad you enjoyed it. Did you like it better than your other gym?"

"Yeah, there's more equipment and space. And I like having someone to go with—makes me feel safe." I replied nonchalantly as I turned my attention to him.

"Good. Aren't you glad I made you call in sick today?" he asked with a smile of satisfaction

Chuckling softly, I punched his arm lightly as I responded, "Yes. Thank you. I needed to relieve some stress."

"Anytime. Let me know when you want to go back."

"How 'bout Saturday?" I asked, trying to hide my excitement. I told myself that my enthusiasm wasn't because of a certain sexy-as-sin trainer, but the knots in my stomach expressed otherwise.

What the hell is going on with me? I never get like this.

When he "rescued" me from careening off the treadmill and injuring myself, I was shocked that his touch didn't make me feel the normal panic I get whenever I come into contact with someone. I actually liked his touch. His strength made me feel safe, and I knew he wouldn't let me fall.

Once we arrived at our apartment, I headed straight for the bathroom. Eager to wash the sticky sweat off my skin, I wasted no time in undressing and turning on the shower. The warm water helped wash away some of the imaginary filth that still clung to me from the news about Kaleb's release earlier in the day, allowing me to relax a little.

I was thankful that Kamden dragged me out of bed to go to the gym. Working out cleared my head, something that I desperately needed in my life. Typically, I worked out at a smaller gym, but Kamden insisted I start going to his after finding out about Kaleb. Even though he'd never admit it, I knew he feared what could happen if Kaleb really did get released.

A shudder ran through me as my thoughts veered back to *him*. Squeezing my eyes shut, I immediately blanked my mind before replacing the horrid images with the first thing that came to my head—Ryker.

My eyes snapped open as confusion set in. *Why did he pop into my mind?* I tried to shake him from my thoughts, but his dark, messy hair, inked muscles, and deep, brown eyes were hard to ignore.

There was no way I could get involved with him, even if it was only a hook-up. I didn't need to get him tangled up in my web of issues. Guys that looked like him didn't fall for average-looking girls like me, anyway. They went after blonde bimbos with fake tans and boobs. At least that's what I told myself.

Sighing, I stepped out of the shower after giving my hair one last rinse. I plodded to my bedroom, avoiding the mirror once again. *Definitely can't look at myself for a while after this morning.*

I quickly dressed before heading to the office to get some more work done before tomorrow. I was the Project Coordinator for a huge marketing and public relations firm in Boston. I handled client invoices, contractor payments, ordered supplies, managed inventory, and created presentations, spreadsheets, and documents for meetings.

Kamden and I lived in the Riverside area of Cambridge, a small town about five miles outside of Boston. After I had graduated from college, we moved out here away from our mother, who lived in Bridgewater, MA.

There was no way I could stay there—not after everything that had happened while in that house.

Don't think about it, Kaiya. Think about something else.

Ryker's face appeared again, but I didn't try to shake his image away this time. Instead, I focused on his gorgeous features, especially his strong jaw line, golden skin, and full lips. Everything about him screamed man, and warmth began to simmer in between my thighs as I thought of him.

Damn, I need to get laid. I'm getting turned on by just thinking about a guy. A ridiculously hot guy, but still.

Grabbing my phone off the bed, I scrolled through my texts until I found the conversation I was searching for. I quickly typed my message before sending the impulsive query.

Me: U busy tonight?

Not surprisingly, I received a response within a few minutes.

Bryce: I think I can fit you in :) same time same place?

I hesitated for a few seconds before typing my reply.

Me: sounds good see you then

Bryce: :)

Bryce was a friend I'd met in college. Despite my standoffish demeanor, Bryce had continued his attempts to break through my walls and befriend me. Eventually, I had given in, unable to resist his good-natured personality and humor. Not to mention, he was extremely attractive—his hazel eyes were set upon a tan face that was framed by tousled, honeyed locks.

I'd never gone into detail with Bryce about my past, and

thankfully, he'd never pressed the issue of my "issues." It had made our arrangement so much easier, and had allowed my need for control to flourish. He had always gone along with everything that I'd wanted, never questioning my stipulations when it had come to sex.

Those rules were absolutely necessary for me to have sex with someone, and most guys wouldn't put up with all of my OCD demands. I had been pretty promiscuous in high school, but after the *incident*, I'd changed. Everything had changed.

I'd spun into a downward spiral, sinking into a depression that encased me, shielding me from the ugliness of the world. Kamden had barely left my side, never relenting as he attempted to coax me out of the hole of despair I had buried myself in.

When I'd emerged, I was irrevocably altered, and I knew I would never be the same again. I had been emotionally scarred beyond repair, left a fractured shell of who I once was—all because of *him*.

Kamden had been the only light in the darkness that constantly enveloped me following what had happened. He and my best friend, Nori, had never let me give up, never let me sink too far back into the chasm deep in my soul. Even now, they still helped keep me grounded, helped keep me tethered to sanity.

Thinking about Nori reminded me that it had been a few days since we'd last spoken. Given the events of the day, I decided to text her to fill her in:

> Me: Bad day today

Nori insisted that I let her know when I had rough days, being the mother hen that she was. She had been that way since we'd become friends in middle school, and I loved her for it, even if it was annoying at times.

My phone chimed with Nori's response:

> Nori: I'm sorry :(want to talk about it
>
> Me: Not ready yet
>
> Nori: Tomorrow night? Girls night?
>
> Me: Maybe

Nori: :)

Even though my reply was noncommittal, we both knew I'd be at her house tomorrow night, ready for a night of dinner and dancing. Dancing was another thing that helped clear my mind. The sound of the music and movement of my body allowed me to drown out everything else as I became one with the beat.

I headed down the hallway to my office to finish some of the spreadsheets I was working on before ordering take-out for Kamden and myself.

When we finished eating, I informed him of my plans. "I'm meeting Bryce at the bar."

I received his typical disapproving look as he responded in a parental tone, "Be careful."

Giving what I hoped was a reassuring smile, I said, "Always."

I'd never explained the details of the arrangement Bryce and I had, but Kamden knew; big brothers always knew stuff like that, no matter how old you were.

When I arrived at the bar Bryce and I typically met up at, I was surprised that he wasn't there yet. He was normally early.

I took a seat at the bar as the bartender walked over to me. "Hey, Ky. The usual?"

"Please." I looked around nervously before directing my attention to my phone, checking if Bryce had sent a message that he was running late, but there was none. *I wonder where he is.*

"And for you?" the bartender asked, peering around me at another customer.

"Jack and Coke," a deep, luscious voice said from behind me.

I stiffened before turning around and coming face to face with Ryker. He unabashedly appraised me, causing heat to simultaneously flood my cheeks and the juncture of my thighs. "Uh, hi," I squeaked nervously. *Fuck, just kill me now.*

Ryker chuckled, obviously amused by my awkwardness. As he laughed, I caught a glimpse of something gleaming in his mouth.

Is that a tongue ring? Oh, God, it is. So fucking hot.

"Can I buy you a drink?" he asked as he moved closer to me, almost pressing his firm body against mine. His arms caged me between him and the bar, causing me to inhale deeply from the sudden proximity.

His scent was amazing, a combination of man and clean. I had to stop myself from begging him to touch me.

"Actually, I, um, I'm meeting someone here," I stammered.

His eyes imperceptibly narrowed; I wouldn't have even noticed if I hadn't been so fixated on his face.

Is he jealous? No way.

"Everything okay, Ky?" the familiar sound of Bryce's voice interrupted.

Ryker's eyes stayed locked on mine, even though my "date" had obviously arrived. His arms remained in place, even when I broke eye contact to look at Bryce.

"Yeah, I'm fine. Ryker's a trainer at the new gym I'm working out at now." I replied, attempting to keep my voice steady, even though Ryker's closeness unnerved me.

Bryce stepped towards to us, keeping his gaze on Ryker as he approached. He warily stuck his hand out in greeting, "Bryce. I'm Kaiya's boyfriend."

What?

"No, you're not!" I impulsively defended. *Shit.* I wanted to slap my hand over my mouth because of my outburst.

Ryker's eyes met mine again as his lips curved up in a sexy smirk. Pulling his arms away, he moved back, taking most of his delicious scent with him. Some of it lingered for a few seconds before fading away I almost audibly sighed from the loss, but stopped before I made a bigger fool of myself.

Get a hold of yourself, Kaiya!

"Maybe I'll catch you at the gym," Ryker said coolly as he grabbed his drink off the bar. Looking at the bartender, he continued, "Put her drink on my tab."

Then, he walked away. *What just happened?* I turned around, not wanting to be caught ogling his retreating form. Grabbing my Cranberry Vodka, I quickly downed it as Bryce stared at me.

"What?" I asked defensively.

"Nothing," he replied with a knowing smile. He turned toward the bartender, leaning on the bar as he ordered another drink for me and a beer for himself.

Rolling my eyes at him, I headed for a booth near the bar while

Bryce waited for our drinks. A few minutes later, he slid into the seat next to me and handed me my drink.

"How've you been?" he asked.

"Pretty good," I replied distantly. That was always my answer, and Bryce knew not to pry. "How about you?"

"I've been swamped at work, but the money's good." Bryce was an investment banker, and earned an envious salary, but he was always stressed out. That stress translated surprisingly well in the bedroom, making our sex intensely passionate as he took his aggression out on me.

After several more rounds of drinks, I was more than ready to head back to Bryce's apartment. I had been torturing myself as I watched Ryker flirt with various women around the bar as they draped themselves all over him. He caught my gaze more than once, giving me his seductive grin every time and causing my stomach to tighten.

"You ready to go, baby?" Bryce whispered in my ear as he trailed his fingers over my thigh. We both had a nice buzz going, making us overly touchy and affectionate. His mouth trailed down the side of my neck, pressing kisses as his hands began to roam over my body.

"Yes," I nearly moaned as I tilted my head to give his lips better access to the sensitive skin of my neck.

Bryce disentangled himself from me before helping me out of the booth. As he led me to the exit, my eyes locked with Ryker's once again. His deep eyes were hardened, his smirk absent from his beautiful lips as he took me in. He paid no attention to the slutty blonde draping herself all over him as he watched me walk away. I couldn't fight the guilt and disappointment creeping into my stomach as we left.

I followed Bryce back to his condo. As soon as the front door shut, I was on him instantly. I tugged at his clothes, needing them off so I could feel his skin against mine. I needed to feel something other than the emotions plaguing me constantly, needed his touch to drown out everything else.

Pushing him down the familiar hallway to his bedroom, I freed his body from his shirt. Even his toned form had nothing on Ryker, whose immaculately chiseled muscles bordered on perfection.

Stop thinking about him!

As we burst through the bedroom door, I fumbled with the belt on his jeans before unbuttoning them as Bryce's lips claimed mine. Our hands urgently worked together to take the rest of each other's clothes off as we fell onto his bed.

Bryce rifled through his bedside nightstand until he pulled out a condom. He eagerly ripped open the wrapper before sheathing his hard length, pressing it against my entrance within seconds.

Ryker's face came into my mind when my eyes fluttered shut as Bryce slowly pushed inside me, groaning as he filled me.

God, I wish it were him inside me right now.

Thrusting at an almost perfect pace, Bryce knew exactly how to please me, knew exactly what I wanted. My eyes closed in pleasure as Bryce's hands threaded in my hair and tugged lightly, pulling my head back to expose my throat.

My lids snapped open as I roughly remarked, "Bryce."

Apologizing, he immediately let go, "Sorry, Ky. I forgot."

Not responding, I tried to focus on the sensations of Bryce stroking inside me. Increasing his pace, he continued to plunge in and out of my slick, hot sex. I could feel my climax approaching as his large cock pounded against my walls. *Almost there.*

I pushed against Bryce, notifying him that it was my turn to take over. I always controlled when I came, needed to have that power over my body. *No one will ever take that power from me again.*

Bryce rolled us until he was on his back and I was mounted on top of him. Beginning to rock against him, I closed my eyes as I pictured Ryker. A moan escaped me as I thought of his luscious mouth, visualizing his tongue ring tracing over every intimate area of my body.

I imagined his rough, tattooed hands caressing my skin as his cock filled me, thrusting inside me over and over, our bodies intimately tangled in hot, sweaty ecstasy.

It didn't take long for me to find release. Normally, it took a while for me to relax and let go of everything, but thinking about Ryker filled me with hot desire. My body trembled as Bryce gripped my hips and thrust upwards, groaning out seconds later as he came.

Once we caught our breath, I lifted myself off Bryce and began to gather my clothes.

Bryce watched me from the bed as he questioned, "Why don't you stay the night?"

I almost ignored the ridiculous question—he knew my rules. Then, I remembered we both had a lot to drink, and it might have slipped his mind.

"You know I can't."

"No, you just won't," he sighed angrily.

This time, I did ignore him. I didn't want to fight with him. What we had was the closest thing that I had to intimacy; I didn't want to ruin that. I cared for Bryce, even if I didn't know how to show it.

Once I finished getting dressed, I said, "I'll call you later, okay?"

"Yeah, okay," he replied sadly as he rose off the bed. Throwing on a pair of gym shorts, he led me to the front door before walking me outside to my car.

"Thank you for a great night." I politely remarked as I pressed a kiss to his cheek.

"No problem. Anything for you, Ky." His eyes were sad as they looked into mine, but he still gave me a smile.

Bryce shut the door for me after I got in my car, then headed inside his condo. As I drove home, thoughts of Ryker still dominated my mind, confusing the hell out of me.

Chapter Four

Ryker

Sitting on the edge of the latest conquest's bed, I ran my hand through my hair. I blew out a breath of frustration as I tried to rid my thoughts of Kaiya. I'd been picturing her while fucking the blonde bimbo that lay next to me.

Why can't I get her out of my head?

Remembering the confusing jealously I felt when I saw that prick with his lips on her neck and his hands all over her body, I angrily stood. I got dressed and quickly left the apartment, not caring if I woke up the girl in the process. I just wanted the night to end already.

Clenching the steering wheel as I drove home, I was still tense, unsatisfied even though I had come while fucking the blonde. I basically had just gone through the motions, too preoccupied to enjoy the other woman. My mind was wired with thoughts of Kaiya, wondering if she was fucking the guy that she left with. *Why do I care?*

Once I got home, I showered, needing to relax. I still didn't understand why she affected me the way she did—she was nothing special.

Yeah, keep telling yourself that.

As the water rained down on me, I thought of her full tits, curvy hips, and long legs. *Fuck, I want to be in between them so bad, filling her with my cock and making her cry out my name.*

Even after the shower, I still couldn't get her off my mind. I kept picturing my hands tangled in her long, brown hair while my mouth tasted those full lips. *Maybe I just need to fuck her so I can get her out of my thoughts.*

Falling into bed, I tossed and turned restlessly, unable to fall asleep. The covers tangled around me as I moved back and forth, constricting my body uncomfortably. Kicking them off, I finally settled and stared at the ceiling. It took what seemed like hours before I finally drifted off, and Kaiya still hadn't left my mind.

Work on a Friday always dragged on and on, especially with a hangover. After Kaiya had left the bar last night, I had gotten wasted with the blonde before we'd gone back to her apartment. I was now paying for it at work.

I'd known better than to get hammered when I had to work the next day, but the whole encounter with Kaiya had fucked with my thoughts. My draw to her perplexed me, and I wanted to know why I thought of her so often.

Forget about her, already.

That would be difficult if I was going to be seeing her at the gym. Kamden frequently worked out, and I assumed that Kaiya would be coming with him, based on her physique. I could tell that she exercised regularly.

Her body is almost flawless. That ass, those tits… fuck, stop it!

I attempted to focus on work, but it was almost impossible with my pounding head. I only had a few personal training sessions scheduled, but I had several group classes for the day, which were going to be hell to get through since I felt like shit.

Later that day, I received a text from one of my friends, Drew:

Drew: Club tonight you in?

Fuck, I had to work tomorrow, but I wanted to get my mind off Kaiya. Maybe the club would be better than the bar had been—lots of women, loud music, and plenty of distractions.

Me: Yeah what time bro?

Drew: My place @ 11

As I knew it would, the day took forever to end. When I'd finally made it to Drew's apartment, I had almost forgotten about Kaiya— almost. She had continued to linger in my mind, but after a few drinks and a woman beneath me, thoughts of her would be gone.

It was midnight when we entered the club. Drew, and two of our other friends, Dane and Logan, headed straight for the bar, and we ordered our first round of drinks.

"Are you stalking me?" a familiar voice giggled.

I turned towards the sound, unbelieving that I'd run into her two nights in a row.

Kaiya stood about five feet away from me. She had on a dark, denim skirt that barely grazed her thighs, and a black, one shoulder shirt that hugged her body like a second skin. Her flushed cheeks and flirtatious smile told me that she probably had a nice buzz going already.

Can I get a fucking break?

"Is this the guy you were talking about, Ky?" a pretty redhead slurred as she bumped into Kaiya, causing her to stumble into me.

Her hands gripped my biceps as mine instinctively grabbed her waist to steady her. Her tits grazed my chest as she struggled to maintain her balance, and I pulled her against me to keep her from falling. "Falling for me again? Do you do this often? Twice this has happened since I met you," I teased. *Damn, she smells good.*

Looking up at me with those entrancing eyes, she smiled shyly, her cheeks flushing more.

She pulled away as she replied, "We're both a little drunk. This is my friend, Nori. Nori, this is Ryker."

"He *is* the guy you were talking about," Nori squealed loudly.

"Nori!" Kaiya responded with a combination of annoyance and embarrassment as she smacked her friend on the arm. Turning back to face me she apologized, "Don't mind her—she's drunker than I thought."

I smirked as I crossed my arms over my chest, "So, I'm not the guy you were talking about?"

"No! Yes… I mean… no." she stammered, her face reddening more.

I chuckled, pleased that I affected her like she had been affecting me. "Where's your boyfriend?" I asked as I moved closer to her, uncrossing my arms.

"I told you he's not my boyfriend," she answered in a slightly exasperated tone as she rolled her eyes.

"He looked like your boyfriend last night."

"Well, he's not. But even if he was, it wouldn't be any of your business." She put one hand on her hip and jutted it out to the side.

"You're right. I'm sorry for prying," I apologized as I took another step toward her. "Can I buy you a drink to make it up to you?"

A smile fought its way onto her lips. "You bought me a drink last night."

I laughed, "I can't buy you another one?"

"I really shouldn't. One of us has to drive home, and Nori's pretty drunk already." she replied as she bit her bottom lip, drawing my attention to it. *Damn, I want to suck that in my mouth, taste her at least once.*

The guys chose that very moment to walk up. Drew interrupted, "Getting started without us?" He checked out Kaiya and Nori. "Who are your new friends?"

"Guys, this is Kaiya and Nori. Kaiya, Nori, these are my friends, Drew, Dane, and Logan."

"Nori. That's a unique name—I like it," Drew commented. *Did I sound that lame when I said it to Kaiya yesterday?*

Nori coyly smiled, giving Drew a flirtatious look. *Well, I guess it works.*

Drew continued, "Can I buy you a drink, Nori?"

Nori giggled in response, "Sure."

Drew sidled up next to Nori before waving down the bartender and ordering their drinks. Dane and Logan had ventured further down the bar, where they talked to two brunettes.

I turned my attention back to Kaiya. "So, can I buy you that drink?"

She looked conflicted, internally debating her options before smiling up at me. "Just one more—Cranberry Vodka, please."

Turning around, I waited for the attention of the bartender. Nori giggled as Drew led her away toward a couch in a dimly lit corner of the club.

Kaiya shook her head and laughed as she watched them. "Maybe I don't have to worry about giving her a ride home."

The bartender came over, and I ordered our drinks, "Cranberry Vodka and a Jack and Coke."

As we waited, I snuck a glance at Kaiya, unable to keep my eyes off her. She darted her gaze away when our eyes met before fidgeting nervously, twirling a strand of her long, brown hair around her finger. Her eyes found mine again, and I could practically feel the connection buzzing between us.

Once we got our drinks, I grabbed Kaiya's hand before leading her through the crowd of people to where Nori and Drew were tangled on the couch making out.

"Oh my God, Nori!" Kaiya laughed.

Either they didn't hear or didn't care, because they continued to devour each other as we sat on the opposite end of the couch.

"I can't believe her," Kaiya remarked before taking a sip of her drink.

"Looks like fun—maybe we should try it," I suggested as I cocked an eyebrow..

Kaiya playfully glared at me while still sipping her drink, which was already halfway empty. "I'm not that drunk."

Teasing her, I called out, "Waitress! I need more drinks over here!"

Laughing, she smacked me on the bicep, "Stop it. I already told you only one more drink—I need to drive home."

"You could come home with me," I seductively suggested.

Desire filled her eyes, but she resisted, looking away as she shifted in her seat. "In your dreams."

"They won't be dreams for long. I'll have you soon," I promised.

"Oh, really? Good luck with that," she replied sarcastically with a clipped laugh.

I placed my drink on the small table in front of us before leaning toward Kaiya and asking, "Is that a challenge?"

Flirtatiously smiling at me, she replied, "Maybe."

Inching closer to her, my leg brushed against hers as I draped my arm on the back of the couch behind her head. She stiffened, but didn't pull away.

I dipped my head next to hers as I gruffly whispered in her ear, "Challenge accepted."

Pulling away slowly, I trailed my lips along her jawline as my hand lifted to brush a strand of hair out of her face. Ever so slightly, she turned her head when I neared closer to her mouth, barely grazing my lips with hers.

The slight touch broke her resistance—she crushed her lips against mine as she pressed her body closer to me, even though we were already almost on top of each other. My hands brushed her bare thighs as I moved her to straddle my lap, draping her legs over mine. Slipping past her lips, my tongue sought permission to thread with hers, which she eagerly gave.

Her taste was borderline addictive. I couldn't get enough as I savored the hot sweetness of her mouth. Her hands roughly ran through my hair as we relentlessly consumed one another.

My hands gripped her ass, pulling her against my growing hard-on. She moaned before abruptly breaking the kiss, hopping off my lap like it had caught fire.

"I'm sorry, I can't," she gasped, her lips swollen and face flushed.

Before I could even reply, she turned and ran into the crowd.

Chapter Five

Kaiya

What the fuck are you thinking, Kaiya? I mentally scolded myself as I left the club. You can't get involved with him!

Replaying the events in my head, I wondered what the hell just happened.

Did that really just happen? Did he really just kiss me? He tasted so good, and that tongue ring—oh my God.

When I got in my car, I immediately locked the doors.. I doubted that Ryker would follow me, but it was almost one in the morning in downtown Boston, and a girl could never be too safe. I sent a text to Nori:

> **Me: Sorry had to leave I'm in the car do you want me to wait for you?**

Sighing, I leaned my forehead against the steering wheel, inhaling deeply and exhaling as I waited for her reply. About five minutes had passed before my phone dinged with her response:

> **Nori: No I'm good r u ok?**

> **Me: Yeah**

I knew I'd hear from her about it tomorrow, but I just wanted to go home and sleep. I wanted to forget about how foolish I had acted. *Damn alcohol.* I was definitely not looking forward to seeing Ryker at the gym tomorrow.

"Kaleb, please stop," I begged as tears ran down the sides of my face.

He didn't respond as he continued to run his hands all over my naked body, covering me with his own larger one. I knew he wouldn't stop. No matter how much I begged, he never did.

He began to remove his clothes, still keeping me pinned with his legs, causing me to sob harder.

"Please, Kaleb, no!"

His eyes already looked detached, like he was no longer there, no longer in control.

I started to squirm and fight beneath him. My fear reached a desperate peak, strangling the air from my lungs and knotting my insides from what I knew was about to happen.

His hand reared back before he swiftly brought it across my face with a biting slap. My cheek stung, but I didn't stop fighting. I couldn't stop, couldn't let things progress any further if I wanted to maintain some semblance of my sanity. I thrashed and kicked beneath him before he pulled out a knife.

I froze as he held it to my neck, daring me to keep fighting him. "Are you going to behave?" he snarled in anger.

I never understood what I'd done to make him so angry with me.

"Yes," I whimpered, afraid to move too much and trigger him.

"That's my girl," he said lovingly, showing a sliver of his normal self before shifting to the hard, evil person I had encountered so often. His personalities changed like the flip of a switch.

His brows furrowed, his muscles tensed, and his eyes went cold again as he hungrily eyed my naked flesh.

He kept the knife pressed against my throat as his free hand traced the curves of my breasts. I trembled from a combination of disgust and pleasure, my body betraying me as it gave in to the sensations from his soft touch.

My cries became louder as he removed the knife, biting down on the handle as

34

he put it between his teeth, His hands trailed over my stomach and chest again before he reached for the hem of his faded, black tee. "Please, Kaleb, don't," I begged, hoping he would stop, even though I knew he wouldn't.

"You made me do this," he mumbled around the knife in his mouth. "By giving away what's mine."

Gripping the bottom of his shirt, he began to pull it upwards. When it came up to cover his face, I used the distraction to get away, pushing him off me before kicking and scrambling out from under him.

I almost made it to the door before he caught me and tackled me to the floor. I screamed as we wrestled on the carpet of my bedroom, obtaining cuts and nicks from the knife as I fought him off.

Overpowering me, he pressed the knife against my throat. "Now I have to punish you. I don't like to punish you, but you leave me no choice."

His eyes hardened as he pushed the knife deeper into my throat. Pain didn't register from the adrenaline running through me, numbing my body as my heart pounded wildly. I only felt the trickle of blood warming my neck, the only indication that I had an injury.

"No, Kaleb, please stop. I'm sorry!" I screeched desperately, my body rigid with fear and panic.

Just then, the door flew open, and Kamden charged in. His face was masked in rage as he ripped Kaleb off of me. The knife flew out of his grasp, clanging as it fell to the hardwood floor. Both men dove for the knife, struggling for it as they rolled repeatedly with their hands clasped tightly around the weapon.

Blood trailed down my neck as I sobbed at the top of my lungs. My screams ripped through my injured throat as I curled into myself, clenching my eyes shut as I prayed for everything to be over.

I sprang up in bed, gasping for air. Sweat dripped from my skin as I continued the screams from my nightmare.

Kamden rushed in seconds later, enveloping me in his arms on my bed. "It's okay, Ky—it was just a dream. He's not here. You're safe," he cooed, trying to comfort me.

Chest heaving, I drew in ragged breaths as tears rained down my face. Instinctively, I reached for my neck and checked to make sure there wasn't an open wound. I felt the familiar raised scar but nothing else—no blood, no gash.

My eyes rose up to meet Kamden's, pausing on the long scar

across his chest before our gazes locked.

"I'm sorry. I'm okay, you can go back to bed," I said, barely above a whisper.

"Are you sure? I can stay if you want," he offered, wiping the tears from my face.

Even though I didn't want to be selfish, I knew I'd never fall back asleep without him. "Please," I murmured.

Kamden softly smiled as he slipped under my comforter. Turning on my side, I propped my hand under my pillow as Kamden draped his arm over me.

Even with his familiar embrace and warm breath on the back of my neck, I couldn't fall asleep. Choking back a sob from the images that I couldn't get out of my head, my body involuntarily shook with fear.

Kamden turned me over so that I faced him before he rubbed my back softly, slowly lulling me to sleep in the safety of his arms.

Kamden had let me sleep late before finally waking me up to get ready to go to the gym. My mind was conflicted over the idea, both loving and hating the fact that I was going to see Ryker.

Once we walked into the gym, I thought I was going to throw up from the nerves that had built up in anticipation of seeing him.

What am I going to say to him? Will he even talk to me again?

I didn't see Ryker as we walked into the cardio room, and relief and disappointment simultaneously flooded me. I hopped on an elliptical, not wanting to have another freak accident like last time, as Kamden headed to a treadmill across from me.

I put my earbuds in before starting up on the machine, letting the music block out the world around me. I didn't even notice Kamden come up next to my machine until he tapped my arm.

I reflexively startled, my body jerking before I focused on him. Pulling my left earbud out, I asked, "What's up?"

"I just wanted to tell you that I'm going to the weight room."

"Oh, okay. I'll be here."

As he left, I saw him stop to talk to Ryker. *Shit.*

Ryker glanced in my direction, and I immediately darted my eyes away.

My eyes kept finding him as he continued to talk to my brother. After they finished, he headed towards me, no doubt wanting an explanation for last night. The knots in my stomach intensified the closer he came, and I had to stop myself from running away.

You'd definitely look like a crazy person then.

I pulled out my earbuds when he reached me, preparing for the inevitable. "Hey," I lamely greeted.

"Hey, yourself. What happened last night?"

Sighing, I averted my eyes from his as I replied, "I'm really sorry about last night. It was a mistake, and I—"

"A mistake?" he interrupted as he crossed his arms over his broad chest, obviously offended.

I swallowed the huge lump that had grown in my throat before I answered, "It's just that I can't get involved with you—with anyone." *Even though I want to.*

"Why not? If you're worried about commitment, don't. I'm not the commitment type," he replied flippantly.

"Oh, so, you just want a one night stand?" I asked incredulously. When he cocked his eyebrow up with a smirk, I continued, "No, thanks." Rolling my eyes, I started to put my earbuds back in so I could ignore him. *Did he really think I was that easy?*

"We'll see about that," he smugly responded before playing with his tongue ring. My eyes immediately went to his mouth. *Fuck me.* "Have a good workout."

Baffled, I watched him stride away, wondering what the fuck just happened—again. Placing my headphones back in, I resumed my exercise as I tried to forget about Ryker. *Yeah, good luck with that.*

Thoughts of having sex with him filled my head, and I seriously contemplated having a one night stand with him. *Maybe that would get him off my mind.* My mind warred as it debated the pros and cons, and unfortunately, the cons outweighed the pros. I'd have to tell him all of my rules before we even got naked, and he probably wouldn't want to have sex with me after that since most guys didn't want to fuck with rules involved. I was lucky that Bryce was so understanding, otherwise I'd be stuck with a vibrator to get off.

But the thought of Ryker's body pressed against mine, of feeling him inside me, of tasting and touching every inch of his skin, was almost enough to change my mind—*almost*. I had to stay in control, not be ruled by my emotions; I couldn't let them overtake me. Opening myself up to Ryker, even just to have sex, could have irreparable consequences that I was incapable of dealing with.

Once I finished on the elliptical, I went in search of Kamden. As I passed some of the exercise rooms, I saw a flyer that read:

Kickboxing/Self-defense classes
Sundays, Tuesdays and Thursdays at 7:00 P.M.
Sign up at the front desk

Maybe I should look into that, especially since Kaleb might get released.

I shook my head, immediately attempting to dispel my thoughts and block out my emotions before they started to take over. I couldn't afford a public breakdown, especially in front of Ryker. *I'd never be able to come here again.*

Kamden was doing squats when I walked in, but he stopped when he saw me.

"You finished?" he asked, wiping the perspiration from his brow with a towel. He handed it to me when he was done.

"Yeah, but I can wait for you if you're not ready." I took the towel from his hand, which was soaked with his sweat. *Gross.*

"I only have a few more reps."

"Okay, that's fine. I'm going to get some water."

As I waited, my eyes scanned the room anxiously. I tapped my foot nervously on the floor as I looked around. I told myself that I wasn't looking for Ryker, but that was a lie. I wanted to see him one more time before we left, but I didn't. *It's probably better this way—the less of him, the better. Now if only I could get him off of my mind.*

Once we got home, Kamden's phone rang. "It's Mom," he informed.

"I'm not here," I said, dropping my purse on the table by the door and heading toward the bathroom to shower.

Rolling his eyes, he answered the phone, "Hey, Mom. No, Kaiya's not here." He paused for a few seconds before angrily snarling, "What?"

The tone in his voice stopped me dead in my tracks. *Oh no. What now? He couldn't have gotten out that fast, could he?*

My heart beat furiously beneath my chest, fear clenched my lungs, making it almost impossible for me to breathe as a panic attack began to take hold. *Breathe, Kaiya. In, out, in, out. Don't have another breakdown.*

"No, Mom, it's not great! He should be left to rot in there forever for what he did to Kaiya!" he yelled before abruptly hanging up his phone.

It began ringing a few seconds later, but Kamden rejected the call. He smiled sympathetically as his anger began to recede, and his eyes softened when they met mine.

Pushing my emotions down, locking them away inside me, I numbed myself, preparing for the worst.

"Just tell me," I impatiently insisted.

Kamden sighed before speaking, "Kaleb's release was approved, pending a six month observation period."

Fear tried to take hold of me again, clawing at my walls, but I forced it down. I needed to be stronger if I was going to survive this whole ordeal. "Can we stop it?"

"I'm going to try. I want to go up there as soon as possible, and I think it would be best if you came with me."

"Kamden, I can't." Shaking my head, I wrapped my arms around myself for comfort. "I can't be that close to him."

"You know that I wouldn't ask you unless I thought it was absolutely necessary. I think that if you remind them what happened, tell them how much what he did has affected you, I doubt they'll give the final approval on his release."

I sighed. "I'll think about it. I can't guarantee anything though. I can barely keep it together with him miles away."

"You're stronger than you think, Ky." He placed a hand on my shoulder. "I know you can do it," he voiced confidently as he gave me an assuring smile.

Uncomfortable focusing on myself, especially when it involved

Kaleb, I changed the subject, "I need to shower. I'm all sweaty."

Turning around, I didn't give Kamden a chance to make me talk about the issue any further. I heard the phone ringing again when I entered my bathroom.

Stripping my clothes, I avoided the mirror as I stepped into the shower. I kept my body turned away from it the entire time, letting the water rain over my skin, hoping it would wash away the emotions trying to break through.

After I stepped out of the shower, I made the mistake of looking in the mirror. Dangerously drawn like a moth to a flame, I inched closer to my reflection, knowing the aftermath would be disastrous. Even though it was my face, all I could see was *him* staring back at me—his eyes, his nose, his mouth, his… everything.

Shuddering, I gripped the counter, trying to pull away, to disentangle myself from the trap I'd fallen in, but the damage was already done. My heart thumped wildly in my chest as I struggled to breathe. My lungs familiarly tightened in anxiety. I couldn't think, couldn't talk myself down, when all I could see was him.

Taunting me, he smirked menacingly as he vowed, "I'm coming for you, Kaiya. This time, I will have you."

"No. No, no, no!" I shrieked in horrified panic. Fear heated my skin, strangled my veins, and rooted itself deep within me as Kaleb responded with intermittent yeses and maniacal laughter.

Impulsively, I grabbed my blow dryer before repeatedly bashing it against the mirror, causing it to splinter and crack. I angrily screamed as I continued, making my throat burn until it became raw. Small pieces of glass began to shoot outward from my blows as I spiraled out of control, hammering him with all my force. Stinging pain registered on my face, but I was too beyond gone to care.

"Kaiya, stop! Stop!" I heard a voice yell before large, strong hands gripped my arms. The blow dryer clanged to the floor as I fought against whoever was holding me, throwing myself back into a bulky mass before slamming us into the wall.

Squirming against the body, I struggled as I tried to kick, punch, and scratch whoever was holding me.

"Kaiya, it's me! It's Kamden. Stop!" he yelled urgently.

Kamden?

Chest heaving with ragged breaths, I looked back at the fractured mirror, seeing Kamden's distorted reflection holding me. I began to relax against him once I realized I was safe—that it wasn't *him*.

Kamden eased his hold on me before gently rubbing my arms.

Slowly turning around to face him, I rasped, "I'm so sorry, Kam."

"Don't apologize. You have nothing to be sorry for. I threw too much at you at one time." Looking toward the mirror, he continued, "I'll have to get that replaced."

"Maybe it's better if you don't," I suggested. When he gave me an inquisitive look, I explained, "I try to avoid looking at it all the time anyway."

He nodded before cautiously lifting his hands up to my face. He turned it side to side, examining my skin. "Let's get you cleaned up— you've got some cuts."

As he walked to the sink, I raised my hand to my face, tenderly touching the areas that were now starting to burn with pain. Blood dotted my fingers when I pulled away, and I couldn't believe how fast I had lost control.

Kamden came back before leading me to the toilet. He sat me down before kneeling in front of me with cotton balls, peroxide, and antibiotic ointment.

"This is going to sting," he warned.

I flinched slightly as he gently cleaned my wounds, and once again, I was awed by how amazing he was. *I don't deserve him, but God knows I need him.* I would've never survived everything without him.

When he was finished, I began to clean up the mess of bloody cotton balls and glass shards on the floor while Kamden went to grab the broom. As I looked at the fragments on the floor, I thought of how much they resembled me—shattered pieces of what they once were. I didn't want to be like that, didn't want to be a broken shell anymore. I wasn't going to keep letting Kaleb dominate my life—I was going to take control.

When Kamden came back, broom in hand, I stood and faced him. "I'll go."

"What?" His eyes scrunched in confusion before searching my face.

"I'll go with you to the hospital. I want to do everything I can to make sure he doesn't get released."

"Are you sure? After that episode, I don't thi—"

Interrupting, I replied, "I want to. I want to take control of my life. I don't want to be afraid to live anymore. And I want to take self-defense classes at the gym—I want to be prepared in case he does get released. I want to be able to fight back."

Smiling proudly, his huge grin lit up his stormy eyes. "Okay, *sorella*. I'll be with you every step of the way. Anything you need."

Returning his smile, pride swelled within me as I hugged him. *You can do this. You will do this.* And with that, I took the first step to becoming whole.

Chapter Six

Ryker

Shock didn't begin to express how I felt when Kaiya walked into my self-defense class on Sunday night. Class didn't start for another fifteen minutes, and she was the first one there. Her eyes reflected the same surprise that I felt as her body stiffened in uncertainty, like a deer right before it bolts away from danger.

"Hey," I greeted. "Welcome to Self-Defense."

"You're the instructor?" she asked in disbelief.

"I am," I grinned.

Mumbling something indiscernible, she set her gym bag down on the hardwood floor against the wall before making her way toward me. As she neared, I saw small cuts on her face, and I couldn't explain the anger that filled me at the thought of someone hurting her.

"What happened to your face?" I all but spat. *Calm down.*

Her eyes widened, my question taking her off guard. "Why do you care?" she retorted defensively.

Why does she have to be so stubborn? "Just tell me. It's suspicious that you want to start my self-defense class after getting those cuts on your face." *Yeah, that's the only reason I want to know.*

Her face relaxed as her features returned to normal. "Uh, my cat scratched me."

Her voice lacked confidence. I didn't believe her for a second, but I didn't want to press the matter. If I wanted to get closer to her, have any kind of chance with her, I needed to gain her trust. I couldn't push her away by interrogating her, even though I really wanted to know what happened.

"I think you need a new pet," I joked.

She gave me a small smile as she fidgeted nervously with her hands. But without missing a beat, she changed the subject, "I've never taken a class like this before. Can you tell me what to expect?"

"Well, we start off with warming up on the bags," I answered, gesturing to the standing punching bags along the walls of the room. "I demonstrate different combinations you can use, and you perform them on the bags. Having the foundation of knowing basic punches and kicks will help you in any situation because you can't predict what an attacker will do. I want to give you as many tools as possible to help you defend yourself, and kickboxing is a great platform for that.

"Then, we have an open request forum. I take requests from the class and show techniques on how to defend yourself in specific situations, which you will then practice with me or one of the other instructors."

Her eyes widened apprehensively, showing fear from my words. I had to stop myself from trying to comfort her. *Why do you care?*

"Everything okay? You look conflicted."

"Maybe this isn't for me—I don't like to be touched, especially by strangers."

Interesting; she didn't seem to mind me touching her the other night. Well, until the end. I wonder what the story is behind that. I shoved my concern for her away as I stated, "If you don't like to be touched, you need to know ways to prevent it from happening, to protect yourself from the people that don't care what you want."

Uncomfortably sighing, she asked, "Can you work with me? I don't think I'll be comfortable with anyone else." Her eyes widened, her cheeks flushing red as she stammered, "Only because I already know you. Not because I want you to touch me or anything."

I chuckled before replying, "Whatever works for you—I want you to be comfortable. If you're not comfortable, then you're less likely to come back."

She nodded before exhaling a heavy breath. "I'm really nervous."

"Don't be—we'll take it slow. I try to give specialized attention to all the students based on their strengths and weaknesses. I'll help you every step of the way."

A small smile graced her beautiful lips, causing my stomach to tighten.

"Thank you. I really appreciate it," she said softly.

"No problem—just doing my job. Go ahead and get stretched out before we get started." I turned to walk away, but stopped and asked, "Do you have gloves?"

"I didn't know I needed them. Can I still take the class without them?"

"Yeah, I have some. They're old and worn, but they'll work until you get some of your own," I said as I walked to the small closet in the corner of the room. Rifling through my storage of kickboxing supplies, I found some gloves that I thought would fit Kaiya's small hands.

When I exited, Kaiya was bent over, touching her right foot gracefully with her fingers as she stretched. Her ass was to me, and I couldn't help but imagine entering her from behind, sinking my dick inside her pussy as I pounded against that sweet ass.

Fuck, stop. Focus—you're about to teach a class.

I cleared my throat before I spoke, my voice slightly cracking, "Here are the gloves."

Straightening, she turned and took the gloves from me, barely brushing her fingers against my palm. "Thanks."

Giving her a slight nod, I turned away and walked back to the supply closet again, trying to distract myself from thoughts of Kaiya and sex.

Minutes later, the other students began to trickle in, along with the other instructors, Mark and David. They were there to give the students real life models to practice with, ensuring they became accustomed to what a typical man's body feels like when they attack since a man's weight and strength were huge factors in overpowering women. All the techniques I taught would be almost useless if they didn't have training utilizing them against a man.

After I had demonstrated the first combo, I walked over to Kaiya to see if she needed help while the others started. She attempted the maneuver, but her form was off. Way off. She'd probably never been in a fight before.

"I'm doing it wrong, aren't I?" she asked, blowing a strand of her hair off of her face in frustration.

I laughed lightly, "Not completely. You're doing a lot of things right, but your form is a little off. Let me show you again."

Repeating the combination again, I said the moves aloud for her to hear. "Jab, punch, palm strike, elbow, elbow, knee, front snap."

"What's the difference between a jab and punch?"

"Well, a jab is basically just a quick punch using your front hand. A punch is thrown from the back hand, and has more power than a jab," I demonstrated as I answered her.

"Okay, jab is front hand, punch is back hand," she said, copying my moves.

"You got it. Let's try the combo again."

As I showed her once more, I could see her mimicking me out of the corner of my eye.

"Remember to always keep your hands up to protect your face when you're not punching. One good hit to the head and it'd be over for you."

Bringing her fists up in front of her face, she asked, "Like this?"

"Yes. You also need to twist your body when you punch—it gives you more momentum, thus giving you more power. Try again."

Doing as I requested, she executed the combo, hitting the bag more forcefully.

"I do feel more power that way," she commented enthusiastically.

"With any method of self-defense, just a small adjustment usually can make a huge difference, whether it be positive or negative. Any mistake could result in injury, while perfect execution of a technique could save your life."

"I'll make sure to remember that. Thank you."

"No problem. Switch legs and keep going, alternating each time."

Nodding, she changed her stance to her left leg before starting again. Each time she completed the combo, her movements became more fluid, her hits delivering more power as they connected with the bag. I couldn't stop the smile that spread as I watched her. The determination was evident on her face as her eyebrows furrowed in concentration. Plus, the fact that she was getting all sweaty and flushed turned me on—a woman was so sexy when she worked out.

Once we finished several more combinations on the bags, we switched to freestyle techniques.

"Five Minute Freestyle! Give it all you got!" I announced.

Everyone knew what that meant, except Kaiya. As everyone started pummeling their bags, I walked over to her, surprised to see that she was already punching and kicking her own bag.

Her eyes locked with mine, causing her to miss landing her punch and stumble slightly. Her already flushed cheeks reddened more as she gave me an embarrassed smile. "I don't know what I'm doing."

"You're doing great. Just keep doing the moves you learned today however you want for the next five minutes. Don't stop, no matter how tired you are."

She turned her attention back to her bag before slowly repeating several of the combinations I had taught today. I couldn't wait to see her once she got more comfortable, once she let go and allowed that warrior to break through that I glimpsed every so often when she argued with me.

Once the five minutes were up, I gathered the group on one of the mats. "Awesome workout, everyone. Before we start the self-defense techniques, I want to introduce Kaiya. She just started working out here and is testing out our class. Please give her a warm welcome."

The other students greeted Kaiya, who blushed profusely from the attention while glaring at me playfully. She waved her hand to everyone as she shyly said hi.

Redirecting everyone's focus back to the class, I asked, "Anybody have an attack you'd like to practice defense against? Even if we've already learned it before."

One of the older women raised their hand. "Can we practice when a guy traps you on the ground? That still scares me, and I think we can never have enough practice with those escape techniques."

Murmurs of agreement flowed through the class, except Kaiya, who remained quiet and still. When our eyes locked, I could see the apprehension and anxiety in her strained face.

"Okay, everyone pair up with your usual partners," I said before making my way to Kaiya. "I need to catch you up on some basics before we start the escape techniques, okay?"

Nervously nodding, she replied, "Okay, sure."

"Before we start anything, there's one thing that I must stress.

Always protect your face—do not get knocked out. Most attackers will immediately try to punch you and knock you out before anything else. If you're unconscious, they can do whatever they want to you—kidnap, rape, or murder you. Got it?"

She gulped before meekly replying, "Yes."

"Okay, the first move I'm going to show you is called the Shrimp. You mu-"

"The Shrimp?" she laughed, interrupting me.

"Yes, the Shrimp. Let me finish," I chastised playfully before continuing. "You must master this move before we can start any other techniques. Lie down."

Surprisingly, she did as I requested without argument. *That's a first.*

When she was flat on her back, I instructed, "Bend your knees. Good, now, when you're being attacked, you need to determine which direction you are going to try to escape from. If you want to go to the right, your right leg is going to remain planted to the floor, along with your left shoulder. If you want to go to the left, then it's the opposite—got it?"

"Yeah, I think so."

"Which way do you want to practice first?"

"Um, the right."

"Okay, keeping your right foot on the ground, I want you to push your body back with it, twisting while picking your left foot off the ground. As you slide backwards, keep your left shoulder pressed to the ground while lifting your right shoulder up until it is directly above the left. Your body should form the shape of an L. We refer to this as shrimping out. I'll demonstrate first, then you're going to try."

I modeled the technique slowly several times, showing both directions before directing Kaiya to try. She executed the move very sluggishly at first, but after multiple attempts on each side, she finally was able to fluidly carry out the maneuver.

"Congratulations, you've mastered the Shrimp." I smiled, slightly teasing her.

Returning my smile, she asked, "What's next?"

"Now, I'm going to walk you through the steps to get away when an attacker traps you on the ground."

Lying down on the floor, I continued, "Get between my legs and press against me as close as you can."

"Wha… what?" she stammered, her cheeks flushing pink.

She's so sexy when she blushes.

"Kneel in between my legs." I paused, waiting for her to do as I said. "Now, scoot up and press your pelvis against me." *Fuck, it's so hard to be professional with her this close to me. All I want to do is rip her clothes off and fuck her.*

Giving me a skeptical look, she slowly inched her way towards me until we were barely touching. I sat up and gently grabbed her by the hips, pulling her flush against me. Her lower body was cradled by the inside of my thighs, and her knees were framing the outside of my hips. "Like this," I stated.

Her blush deepened as our eyes locked. Having her pressed against my dick caused it to start to harden.

"What now?" she asked, her voice cracking slightly. I didn't know if she was turned on or just responding to the sudden feel of me.

"Now, place your hands outside my shoulders. This is the most common form of attack against women, and it usually escalates from this position, so it's best to stop it as soon as possible. The first thing you want to do is brace your hands against your attacker's shoulders, keeping your arms straight, like this." I demonstrated. "This hinders their movement, and prevents them from coming down on your body. Notice how off balance you are?"

"Yeah, but you're like ten times stronger than me. How am I supposed to keep a man off me that's stronger and heavier than me?"

"You only need to keep them off you for a brief time. Once you have them in this position, use the Shrimp technique." I modeled, pushing into the formation and propping my elevated foot against her hip. "Let me show you again."

I demonstrated the move again before moving on to the next step. "Now, keep your foot on their hip as you slide your hands down to your attacker's elbows, like this," I said as I grabbed her elbows. "Next, twist back to the center, bringing both knees up and pressing both feet against their hips. The typical reaction for an attacker is to pull away, so when they do, slide your hands down to their wrists, bring your feet up, and kick the shit out of them. Then, run away and find help."

I sat up, and we both pulled apart. "Any questions?"

"Where should I kick?"

"Anywhere— the groin, stomach, and face are the most vulnerable and effective targets to kick. Are you ready to try?"

Exhaling, she gave me a quick nod, "Yeah, I'm ready."

"I'm going to walk you through everything, so don't worry. Lie down and open your legs," I instructed.

Briefly hesitating, she did as I requested.

"I'm going to get between your legs now, okay?"

When she nodded, I scooted up, placing my knees on the outside of her hips as I draped her legs on my thighs and pressed up against her. My mind briefly transported us to my bed, where she would be naked, open and ready for me, waiting for my dick to slide inside her.

Concentrate on the technique. You'll have her soon.

"Now, I'm going to try to come down on you. Stop me by bracing your hands against my shoulders." I started to move my upper body down toward hers, and she threw her hands up, stopping me by grabbing my shoulders. "Good, now shrimp out and place your foot on my hip."

That move was more difficult for her to execute, so we practiced it several times until she felt like she got the hang of it before moving on to the next step. The constant contact and rubbing had hardened my cock more, but Kaiya didn't say anything. I knew she felt it by the way she tried to adjust when it pressed against her, causing her face to redden.

"From here, slide your hands down to my elbows and move back to the center while bringing both knees up and putting your feet on my hips."

"Like this?" she asked as she trailed her hands down to my elbows and propped her feet on me. Her touch was light as her skin grazed mine.

"Yes, now slip your hands down and grip my wrists as I pull away. I'm going to move my head to the side so you can practice kicking upwards. Go ahead and kick."

We practiced the routine a few more times, and Kaiya moved more fluidly each time. I could tell she was becoming more comfortable with me as her body relaxed throughout the exercise. As class ended, I gathered everyone on the mat again before I closed. "Great class today, everyone. I love the enthusiasm, and I want to thank you for your active participation. Remember, we can't predict exactly how an attack will happen, but practicing these techniques will definitely help in any situation. Always fight back—punch, kick, scream, scratch, anything to protect yourself. See you Tuesday."

Everyone filed out of the room, except Kaiya.

Glancing shyly as she approached me, she said, "I just want to thank you for working with me. Like I said, I don't do well with strangers touching me."

"No problem. See you Tuesday? For the next class?"

Biting her lower lip in contemplation, she didn't say anything for several seconds before she replied, "Yes. I'll be here Tuesday."

"Great, I'll see you then."

She turned to walk away, but I stopped her. "Wait." I wanted to keep talking to her. Something about her intrigued me, maybe the fact that she didn't just give into me like other girls.

"Before you go, let me give you my number, in case you need to get a hold of me for class or something." Reaching my hand out, I gestured for her to give me her phone.

Rolling her eyes, she questioned, "Do you give your number to all your students?"

"Only VIP ones," I joked. I didn't normally give out my personal number to students, but I wanted an excuse to get Kaiya's. I kept my hand out, and she finally placed her phone in my palm. Keying my number in, I called my phone so that I'd have her number, too.

As I gave her phone back, I said, "Let me walk you to your car."

"You don't have to do that—I'll be fine."

"Just let me walk you to your car," I insisted.

"Fine," she huffed before smiling.

So stubborn.

As we walked, I took the opportunity to try to get to know her better, hoping that would help in my quest to get her in my bed. I ignored the fact that I was interested in her, that I actually wanted to know more about her.

"So, do you and Kamden live together?"

"Yeah, just me and him. We've lived in our apartment together since college."

"Any other family?"

Her skin paled as her eyes widened. "No."

Okay, not a good topic. Maybe we have more in common than I thought. "What do you do for work?"

Her face relaxed, and color began to return to her cheeks. "I'm a Project Coordinator for a marketing and public relations firm in Boston."

"Sounds boring."

She looked offended, but laughed. "Thanks. Not everyone gets to work out for a living."

"It's pretty awesome," I admitted. We were nearing the exit doors, so my time with her was running out. "What do you like to do for fun?"

I opened the door for her as she answered, "I love to go dancing."

"I'll keep that in mind when I ask you out."

She laughed again; this had to be the most I'd ever seen her do so. I was getting somewhere, finally.

"Anything else that might help my chances?"

She stopped by a black, Acura TL before leaning against it, facing me.

"You don't want to get involved with me," she said with a half-hearted smile.

"Oh, yeah? Why not?" I replied as I stepped closer to her. *Always fighting me.*

Her eyes watched me warily. This close to her, I could see so many different hues of blue and green that made up the unique shade of her eyes. They really were beautiful. "I just... I have a lot of issues."

"Don't we all?" I asked in a rhetorical tone. *I know I do.*

She chuckled softly, "Not like mine."

"You tell me yours, I'll tell you mine." *What am I saying? I don't want to her to know about my past—do I?*

"That's never going to happen," she replied matter-of-factly, an unspoken challenge present in her eyes.

"Never say never." I smirked while backing away. "Goodnight, Kaiya."

I didn't need to say anything else that I might regret, like telling her my whole life story. *Why does she make me feel so different? Why do I want to open up to her?*

Shaking her head, she smiled as she got into her car. As I turned around, I couldn't help but think, *Tuesday can't come fast enough.*

Chapter Seven

Kaiya

My body still thrummed with adrenaline from a combination of class and touching Ryker. It amazed me how just being close to him made me feel so alive, like I hadn't really been living until I met him. Honestly, I really hadn't.

Kaleb had made me afraid to live, afraid to trust anyone. But with Ryker, I felt there was a chance that I could open up to him, and that scared the living shit out of me. *If I couldn't even trust Kaleb, how could I trust Ryker?*

Shaking the thoughts from my head, I started my car to drive home. I didn't want to think about anything negative when I was feeling so good, when I actually felt... happy. I knew completing one self-defense class wasn't very significant for most people, but it was huge—absolutely huge—for me. One of the many steps I needed to take to reclaim my life and eliminate the power Kaleb had over me.

My stomach growled as I walked into my apartment, so I headed straight for the kitchen to look for something quick to throw together for dinner.

As I rifled through the refrigerator, I heard Kamden call out, "I ordered a pizza—figured you wouldn't want to cook."

His voice had increased in volume as he walked from wherever he was in the apartment into the kitchen. When I closed the refrigerator door, I turned to see him standing in the doorway. "How was class? Everything go okay?" he asked with concern.

"Yeah, everything went fine," I shrugged. "I was a little nervous at first, but Ryker worked with me one-on-one to make sure I was comfortable," I continued as I searched for the pizza, which I found right on the counter next to the refrigerator. *So observant.*

"Ryker's the instructor?" Kamden questioned. He sounded a bit bothered by the idea.

"Yeah," I said, my focus mainly on the pizza box as I stalked towards it. Opening the cabinet above it, I grabbed a plate and put two slices on it before putting it in the microwave. When I turned back around to look at Kam, I noticed his furrowed brows and tense jaw. "What?"

"Nothing, just be careful with him," he warned with a cautionary look in his eyes.

I voiced my thoughts aloud, perplexed by his warning, "Why?"

"I notice how he looks at you, Ky. He's a total womanizer, and I don't want you to be another notch on his bedpost." He crossed his arms as his voice took on that over-protective, brotherly tone I knew so well.

Wow, I so don't want to have this conversation. Thankfully, the microwave beeped, giving me the perfect opportunity to escape. As I removed the plate, I said, "Don't worry, Kam. I'll be fine—I'm not interested in Ryker." *Keep racking up those lies.*

"I'm serious, Kaiya," he sternly remarked, authority obvious in his words.

Placing the plate on the counter, I turned around to look at him— arms still folded tensely over his chest, eyes narrowed, mouth set in a tight, thin line. *He's really upset over this.*

"Kam, do you really think I'd be getting myself involved with someone, especially now? I'm barely holding myself together."

The angry expression on his face eased, his features softening as he walked toward me. "You're doing great, *sorella.* I didn't mean to get upset at you. I just don't want you to get hurt."

"I know, but you have nothing to worry about. I'm not planning to get involved with Ryker, okay?" For some reason, those words caused my chest to tighten uncomfortably. *Do I want to be with Ryker?* I couldn't deny the attraction to him, or the fact that I wanted to jump him every time I saw him, but did I want to be with him?

My stomach grumbled, interrupting my thoughts.

Kamden laughed. "You better eat—that thing sounds hungry."

I smacked him on the back as he turned to walk away. Picking up a slice of gooey, cheesy goodness, I opened my mouth to take a bite as Kam turned back around. "I'm really proud of you, Ky."

I stopped mid-bite as another genuine smile spread across my face. *I must be setting a record today.* "Thank you, Kam."

Wordlessly, he exited with a matching grin on his face.

After finishing my pizza, I went to my room and decided to call Nori and update her on everything that had happened since the club. She'd called and texted me a few times after that day, but I'd had yet to get back to her.

"Hey, girl. What's up?" Nori greeted when she answered.

"Hey. I wanted to apologize for bailing the other night."

"Don't worry about it. What happened?"

"Things moved too fast, too soon. I don't know what I was thinking." I fell onto my back on my bed with a sigh.

"Don't be so hard on yourself. He's a hot guy, I mean really hot guy, and you got caught up in the moment."

"I can't get involved with him, Nori. You know that."

"Why not? You can't let your past rule you forever, Ky."

I sat up, shaking my head in disbelief. I couldn't believe what she was saying, but she had a point. "I know, but a guy like Ryker wouldn't be interested in me—I have too much baggage."

"I'm not saying for you to get in a relationship with the guy. You have heard of having a good time, right? Nothing wrong with a little fun for once in your life. He doesn't need to know about your issues for you to have sex with him."

"I love how you think." I laughed.

"That's why I'm your bestie. Seriously though, you deserve to have some fun."

I blew out another breath as I lay back down. "Yeah, I guess." Wanting to change the subject, I brought up my class. "Hey, I started taking a self-defense class."

"That's awesome! I'm so proud of you, Ky."

"Guess who the instructor is?" I asked, biting my lower lip as I stifled a smile.

"No way! Ryker?" she shrieked, sounding like a teenage girl.

"Yep. I couldn't believe it. He gave me his number after class was over."

"Shut up! I think fate is trying to tell you something," she squealed giddily.

"Yeah, it's trying to torture me," I replied in exasperation. Having Ryker as my instructor didn't help in my efforts to try and stay away from him, even though I was seriously reconsidering that now.

Nori giggled, "I'll take that kind of torture any day. That man is delicious."

"He really is," I sighed dreamily. "It's been so hard to resist him."

"I can imagine. I don't think I'd be able to."

"Kamden says Ryker's a man-whore. He wants me to be careful around him," I said, deepening my voice to imitate his as I spoke.

"Of course he's going to say that. He's your older brother."

"Yeah, I know." I hesitated, doubting myself. "But what if he really is?"

"Who cares? That's what condoms are for," Nori responded as though it was obvious.

I snorted. "Nori!"

"What? You're not looking for commitment, and I doubt he is either. It doesn't matter if he's a man-whore. Sex is sex, and he looks like he'd be damn good at it."

"You're such a bad influence," I joked as I rolled over onto my stomach.

"Hey, you only have one life. I guarantee you'll regret it if you don't sleep with him at least once."

Would I? "Yeah, I probably would. He's the hottest guy I've ever seen." I paused, gnawing on my bottom lip in contemplation. "I don't know if I can do this, though. I haven't been with a guy, other than Bryce, since everything with Kaleb."

"I know. And, you don't have to do anything if you don't want to. I just want you to be happy; I don't think I've seen you as happy as when I've caught the two of you together, and when I've heard you talk about him."

"Really?" I asked, holding back a smile.

"Really. It's good to see you smile so much, and hear the happiness in your voice. Ryker may be just what you need to finally move on. And if not, at least you would get some really great sex out of it."

"Maybe. I'm not promising anything, but I'll keep an open mind. I better get ready for bed; I have an early day at work tomorrow—our weekly Monday morning meeting," I groaned unhappily.

"Ugh. Okay, text me tomorrow?"

"Okay, bye."

"Bye."

After hanging up with Nori, I got ready for bed. Kamden had removed what was left of the mirror sometime today, so I was relieved not to have to deal with that mess.

My phone chimed while I brushed my teeth. When I finished, I went to my bed to pick it up. When I swiped my passcode in, I saw that Ryker had sent me a text:

Ryker: sweet dreams

A smile spread over my face as I texted him back:

Me: you too :)

As I lay in bed, thoughts about my conversation with Nori kept me awake. Should I really get involved with Ryker? Does he really want me? Would I be okay with just a one night stand? Could I handle it?

The only thing that I was able to determine was that if I decided to go through with it, I would take things slow concerning Ryker. Neither one of us wanted a relationship, and I definitely wasn't ready to have sex with him, no matter how much I wanted to. So if it was going to happen, it was going to happen on my terms.

When I finally fell asleep, it was to images of Ryker's heavenly body over mine.

Let's just say that I really hoped that dreams came true. I needed a cold shower after the imagery from last night. I slept all the way until my alarm went off, which was unheard of for me. Usually I'd wake up from a nightmare.

Even though I had worked from home on Thursday, and went back to the office on Friday, I was behind on my work, swamped with documents and spreadsheets. Mondays were typically the busiest day of the week, especially since we had our weekly meeting to discuss happenings throughout the whole company.

Once I got home, I couldn't wait to go work out and relieve some of the tension from the day. I dropped my keys and purse by the door before trotting to Kamden's bedroom. Tapping on his open door, I peeked in. "Hey, you want to go to the gym?"

His eyes rose to mine from his laptop. The screen illuminated his handsome face. *Thank God he doesn't look like me.*

"Yeah, I was waiting for you. I need to talk to you about something first, though," he stated while closing his laptop.

Great, what now? "Okay," I said as I walked in and sat on his bed. He swiveled his rolling chair to face me before saying, "I set up an appointment to speak with the head of the hospital."

My mouth suddenly became dry from his words. I swallowed deeply before asking, "For when?"

"Six weeks from today— April 28. Do you still want to come with me?"

My first instinct was to say no, but I thought about my goal, about the baby steps I had made so far. "Yes. I want to do everything we can to keep him in there. I don't want him to be released."

Pride shined in his blue-gray eyes as he smiled at me. He turned and rifled through some documents on his desk. "Great. I think we still have the paperwork from the attack somewhere."

"I don't know—I haven't looked at them since we filed them. They should be in the filing cabinet unless you took them out."

"I'll look for them. Go ahead and get ready for the gym," Kamden said as he continued to search through the mess of papers on his cluttered desk.

I hopped up off his bed before going to my room to change. Fifteen minutes later, we were out the door on the way to the gym. Nervous, excited energy bounced through my veins as I anticipated seeing Ryker. *Play it cool, you're supposed to take things slow, remember?*

The drive to the gym seemed to drag on as my nerves continued to build up, making me feel like a kid on a sugar high. I practically skipped into the building, but my mood deflated when I realized Ryker wasn't there.

I didn't want to seem like a stalker by asking for him at the front desk, so I just assumed it was his day off—Monday probably wasn't a peak workout day. *Oh well, I'll see him tomorrow at class.*

Brushing off the disappointment, I headed to my usual elliptical. Kamden went straight to the weight room, but he joined me in the cardio room to finish up his workout before we left.

When we got home, I decided to call Nori again, needing to talk to her about what Kamden and I discussed before we went to the gym. After dialing her number, I cradled the phone between my shoulder and ear as I took out some of the leftover takeout from the other night. I could hear the surprise in her tone—I typically didn't call her two days in a row. "Everything okay, Kaiya?" she answered.

I chuckled, "Yes. But I have something to tell you."

"You did it, didn't you? That was fast, you whore," she teased, giggling.

My eyes popped in shock as I pulled two plates from the cabinet. "No, I didn't, Nori! I can't believe you think I'm that easy."

"I don't, but he's hot, and he seems very determined to have you from what you told me."

I sighed, a little disappointed. "I didn't even see him today." Pausing, I cleared my throat. "But that's not why I called. Remember I told you about Kaleb possibly being released?"

"Yes," she said, her playful tone from a second ago gone.

Setting the plates down, I went to sit at the breakfast bar. I released a deep breath before explaining, "Well, Kamden and I are going to the hospital to try to stop it. I wanted to see if you would come with me. You know, for support."

Without hesitation, she answered, "Of course, Ky. When?"

"April 28, six weeks from today."

"I'll ask for the day off when I get to the office first thing in the morning."

"Thank you, Nori. You don't know how much it means to me that you'll go." I let out a sigh of relief. I'd need as much support as I could get to get through all this.

"Aw, it's no problem, girl. I'd do anything to keep that bastard committed."

"Yeah, you and me both. I'll call you with more details later—I just got home from the gym, and I need finish dinner and shower."

"All right, talk to you later. I'm really proud of you, Ky."

"Thanks," I smiled. "Bye."

"Bye."

I exhaled another deep breath, easing more of the tightness in my chest. *You can do this. You're stronger than you used to be.*

I made a plate for Kamden and heated it in the microwave, but I didn't feel like eating anymore. Talking about the meeting and Kaleb caused unease to settle in the pit of my stomach, so I decided to skip dinner and take a shower.

As I walked to the bathroom, I repeated my phrases to myself, afraid that fear would try to take root inside of me because of the upcoming meeting about Kaleb. It would be the closest I've ever been to him since the *incident,* and that thought terrified the weak, fragile part of me.

The warmth of the water helped erase the tension in my muscles. Working out had cleared my head, but after talking about the meeting with Nori, thoughts of Kaleb started to creep to the forefront of my mind again.

Shoving the thoughts back, I continued to chant my mantra and focus on the water trailing over my skin. Closing my eyes, I tipped my head back and let it pour over me as I let go of everything else.

Once I finished, I felt so much better. The weight of the situation had been alleviated, even if it would only be for a short time. I knew that as the date approached, it would be increasingly difficult to cope with everything.

Exhausted, I quickly dressed in my pajamas before falling into bed. Sleep found me quickly, pulling me under its veil seconds after my head hit the pillow.

"Kaleb, I don't like when you touch me like this." I flinched as he ran his hands over my skin.

"Why? You're mine, and I'm yours. I should be able to touch you wherever I want." Both his hands and voice were possessive and harsh as he continued to touch me.

Mom and Dad have always said that Kaleb was supposed to take care of me, but this feels wrong. Good, but wrong.

"Doesn't it feel good when I touch you like this?" Kaleb asked, interrupting my thoughts.

We were in my bedroom, on my bed with the door locked. Mom and Dad never questioned when they came up and found the door that way. Kaleb lay next to me, pressing his body up against my side. His fingers stroked my breasts before trailing down my stomach, eliciting a shudder from me.

"You're so beautiful, made just for me," he murmured against my ear before sucking my earlobe in his mouth.

"We shouldn't be doing this," I weakly protested as I squirmed beneath his venturing hand. My friends never talked about their brothers touching them this way, but his mouth was on my neck, and the combined sensations were making it hard to think.

"Why? You love me, right?"

"Of course I love you, Kaleb, but—"

"Then, you'll let me do this. And you won't tell Mom and Dad."

His fingers had reached their destination, slowly caressing me and making me forget why I was objecting when it felt so good. My head lolled back against the pillow as Kaleb continued to touch me. Something that felt this good couldn't be wrong, could it?

When he was finished, I immediately covered myself with the blanket, clutching it to me as he stood up from my bed. He licked his fingers, like he did every time, and disgust began to replace the pleasure tingling through my body once the haze began to recede.

I fought the tears that threatened to spill over, not wanting him to see me cry. It would only make him angry, and he hurt me when he was angry—I didn't want him to hurt me more than he already had.

He walked toward me, leaning on the bed as he pressed a kiss to my forehead, causing me to cringe in response. "I love you, Kaiya."

As a tear escaped each of my lids, I quickly swiped them away before he pulled away and saw. "I love you, too," I replied, avoiding his gaze.

I didn't move until I heard the door shut. Then, I bolted out of the bed and into my bathroom, barely reaching the toilet before throwing up.

Once I finished vomiting, I hopped in the shower, turning on the water to the hottest I could stand it before scrubbing my skin until it was red, almost raw. Tears poured off my face, sobs wracking my body as I stayed there until the water ran cold.

Sitting up in bed, my eyes snapped open to darkness, the only light coming from my alarm clock. Sweat clung to my skin as I threw the covers off me, feeling as though they were suffocating me.

Much like my dream, I sprang out of bed to throw up in my bathroom. Disgust still permeated my body, my stomach still nauseated despite vomiting. Shakily, I stood, stripping my clothes before turning on the shower.

Stepping in, I turned the handle almost all the way to the left before scouring my skin in the scalding hot water as I cried. My body burned as the heated drops pelted me, feeling like molten lava dripping down my flesh. Sobs shook my body as tears trailed down my face and mix with the spray falling over me from the shower head. Nothing I ever did could totally erase the dirtiness that still remained whenever I had a flashback. *How could he do that to me? How could I let him? Why didn't I make him stop? God, I was so weak! I'm still weak!*

Slumping to the tile floor, I set my forehead against my knees, wrapping my arms around my legs. I sat there until the shower ran cold, letting the frigid water numb my skin. *If only I can get it to numb my brain and emotions, too.*

Chapter Eight

Ryker

Kaiya was more uptight than usual during class on Tuesday night, if that was even possible. She angrily hit and kicked the bag aimlessly, and I could tell that something was bothering her.

Sweat dripped down her face as I approached her. "Is everything okay?"

"I'm fine," she snapped, keeping her eyes trained on the bag, panting angrily as she continued to fiercely attack it. As I watched her, I noticed that she was holding her breath.

"Breathe, Kaiya," I urged, moving closer to her. "You need to breathe or you're going to pass out."

Her hands fell to her sides as she stepped away from the bag and took deep breaths. She began to pace in a small circle in front of me as she steadied her breathing.

"Are you sure everything is okay?" I asked again as I handed her water bottle.

She took the bottle, greedily drinking before taking more deep breaths. "Yeah, I just... I had a bad night last night, and it carried over into today."

I furrowed my brow. *I wonder what happened.*

"Well, take it easy, alright? I don't want you to overexert yourself."

She nodded before focusing back on the bag and repeatedly kicking the shit out of it.

There's that warrior.

After the kickboxing segment of class, I decided to work with Kaiya on different strikes since she was still so tense—she definitely needed to keep hitting something.

"I'm going to teach you where you should target different hits. First thing I'm going to show you is strikes that are best for the face—avoid directly punching someone in the face because you'll more than likely break your hand. Only use elbows, hammer-fists, and palm strikes when you are hitting the face."

I modeled a palm strike on one of our dummy bags, which had the upper body of a man, instead of the regular, cylindrical punching bag. I wanted Kaiya to target the specific areas of the body we were working on. I then repeated the same with elbows and hammer-fists, stopping for Kaiya to practice each one. I loved watching her body move and seeing sweat glisten over her skin. *Fuck, I want to feel that body beneath me.*

I didn't notice that Kaiya had completed the last move until she cleared her throat. When our eyes met, she smiled shyly and asked, "What next?"

Smooth. She caught you checking her out. Concentrate. Playing cool, I ignored that she had noticed me looking at her. "You can also use a double palm strike on an attacker's ears, which will completely knock off their equilibrium. Aim for right here," I instructed as I demonstrated on the dummy. "Right outside the ear. Slam as hard as you can."

We continued working on different strikes, and Kaiya's anger began to slowly fade as she released it on the bag. I didn't focus on her technique that much because I could tell she needed to blow off some steam, so I just let her. I knew she'd been hiding something beneath her guarded exterior, and whatever it was affecting her tenfold today.

When class was over, I stopped Kaiya as she was about to walk out, catching her at the door. I pulled her to the side as the remaining students squeezed past us and left. "Hey, you want to grab a drink? You seem stressed today."

"I really shouldn't," she replied as she pulled her bottom lip between her teeth, her tone indecisive.

"You always give me that lame excuse. Just one drink—you earned it after kicking the shit out of that dummy," I said with a grin.

She rolled her eyes as she fought a smile. "Should you be taking your students out on dates?"

"Oh, so this is a date?" I teased, raising my eyebrows as my smile spread.

"No! I... you know what I mean." She blushed as she darted her eyes away from mine.

"Yeah, you want me to take you out on a date." I smirked knowingly.

"No, I don't," she blurted as her eyes widened in embarrassment.

"Oh, really?" I challenged as I played with my tongue ring, knowing it unnerved her. I always caught her staring when I messed with it.

As I expected, her eyes darted to my mouth, and her lips parted slightly. With a knowing chuckle, I asked her again, "So, do you want to grab that drink or not?"

Her eyes snapped back to mine. "I need to shower."

"Do you need help? I'd be happy to assist you," I offered as I continued to toy with the barbell in my tongue.

Her gaze darted back and forth from my mouth to my eyes as she stammered, "No... I... I can meet you after I shower."

Yes. Smiling confidently, I suggested, "Phoenix Landing? In an hour?" Phoenix Landing was a popular, central bar in Cambridge, so I figured it was a safe choice.

Her words were rushed as she replied, "Sounds good. I'll see you there." Tucking a strand of stray hair behind her ear, she gave me a flustered smile before turning to leave. "Bye."

"Bye," I returned with a laugh.

Glancing over her shoulder as she walked out, her lips curved up more as our eyes locked. *I'm going to taste those lips again tonight.*

Rushing to close up, I quickly wiped down everything and locked up since my class was the last one of the night. I was anxious to meet up Kaiya, hoping to get another step closer to getting her in my bed. I blocked out the thoughts that passed through my head of actually wanting to spend time with her, ignoring that I wanted to get to know her. *No relationship—just sex. You don't have to get to know her to have sex with her.*

An hour later, I was waiting for Kaiya at the bar, leaning my back against it with a Jack and Coke in hand. After fifteen minutes had passed, I thought she had changed her mind and wasn't going to show. *If she's not here by the time I finish this drink, I'm leaving.*

As I took another sip from my glass, I glanced over toward the door. My lips involuntarily spread in a grin as I watched Kaiya walk in, wearing some tight jeans and a strapless, white top. Her hair flowed down her back before ending in big, loose curls, and I pictured myself wrapping my fingers in it while I bent her over and fucked her. Searching the room, her eyes roamed before locking on mine. A shy smile spread over her lips as she made her way toward me, those luscious hips swaying with each step. *She's so fucking hot.*

When she reached me, I snaked my arm around her waist, bringing her closer to me. I felt her muscles tighten beneath my touch, but she didn't resist otherwise.

Bringing her between my legs, I inhaled her sweet scent, a mixture of strawberry and vanilla, as I kissed her cheek. Her hands lightly pressed against my chest as I pulled back. "I thought you weren't going to show for a minute there."

"Me too. I almost didn't come." Her gaze darted down before coming up to meet mine as she shifted nervously.

"Well, I'm glad you did. It would've really hurt my ego if you didn't," I said as I rubbed my hands along her sides.

"I'm sure your ego is strong enough to survive," she replied dryly as she moved away to sit on the barstool next to mine.

"I don't think it stands a chance against you," I joked.

"Do women really fall for that?" she asked as she fought a smile.

"Most of the time. But they're not always the brightest."

Kaiya slapped me on the bicep as her eyebrows rose and her mouth opened in shock. "Ryker!"

"What? I'm being honest. Woman want honesty, right?" She stared at me, mouth agape for a few seconds before she shook her head and laughed.

"What do you want to drink? Cranberry Vodka?"

She thought a few seconds before replying, "No. Apple Martini."

"Damn, that bad of a day?" I commented before turning and

getting the attention of the bartender. Once I ordered us a round, I focused my attention back on Kaiya, determined to figure her out.

"Do you want to talk about it?"

Her body stiffened slightly as she sipped her drink. "No. I don't want to think about it—I just want to forget."

I know that feeling. "I know plenty of ways to help with that."

Her lips tipped up. "I'm sure you do. I've heard about your reputation."

This is going to be good. I took a swig of my drink. "Oh, really? What have you heard?"

"Basically, you're a man-whore," she replied bluntly as she swirled her martini, avoiding my gaze.

I laughed. "I'm not going to lie—I've had my fair share of women."

Kaiya gave me a perplexed look before replying, "Thank you for being honest. I thought you'd lie about it."

"Why? I am who I am. I'm not going to pretend be anything that I'm not."

"I respect that. Not the being a man-whore part, but that you're true to yourself."

I took another drink, enjoying the warmth of the liquor as it slid down my throat. "How are you liking class?" I asked, attempting to redirect the topic away from my personal life. *Not ready to talk about that yet.*

Kaiya took another sip, leaving only half of her martini. "I like it. Everything can be a little overwhelming, but I'm willing to work through it."

"You'll get the hang of it. Why did you decide to take self-defense?"

Visibly swallowing, she cleared her throat before taking another long gulp, leaving only a small sip in the bottom of her glass. "Old demons."

"Care to elaborate?" I didn't know why I asked, I already knew she'd say no.

"No." She threw back the remainder of her drink before standing. "I'd better go. Thanks for the martini."

"Why don't you stay for another? I won't ask any more personal questions. Scout's honor." I said as I put my fingers together to make the hand gesture.

She snorted, "I doubt you were a Boy Scout."

"Why? Is it the tattoos?"

"No. I just can't picture you as one. You don't seem like the type that follows directions well."

"I don't. I was thrown out for kicking my scout leader."

She laughed. "You didn't."

"I did—guy was a prick."

Kaiya continued to laugh; she definitely didn't smile or laugh enough, and I wished she did more of both. When our eyes met, I repeated my earlier question, "Can I get you another drink?"

Even before she responded, the smile she was fighting gave me my answer. I ordered another round of drinks from one of the bartenders, then turned my attention back to Kaiya. Our gazes locked as a blush began to creep up onto her cheeks, painting her porcelain skin with pink.

"You're so beautiful," I said, just above a whisper as I leaned towards her. Her eyes focused on my lips as they neared hers, which parted in anticipation, as if waiting to reacquaint themselves with mine after so long.

Closing my eyes, I brushed my mouth against Kaiya's, enjoying the silkiness of her lips.

Her hands rested on my chest before sliding up and around my neck as she brought herself closer to me, pressing our bodies together. Winding around her, my arms enclosed her against me as my tongue intertwined with hers.

Fuck, she tasted so good—I could get lost in her for days, oblivious to everything else but consuming every part of her sweetness. One of my hands trailed up her back before cupping her head, tangling my fingers in her hair as the kiss intensified.

"You have a tab? Or do you want to pay cash?" the bartender interrupted, causing Kaiya to abruptly pull away from me.

Asshole. Glaring at the bartender, I grabbed the drinks. "I have a tab—Ryker Campbell."

Handing Kaiya her drink, I couldn't help but notice her swollen lips. My cock hardened more as I thought about Kaiya sucking me with those lips, taking my dick deep into her mouth before letting me sink myself into her pussy. *Fuck, I have to have her.*

As we drank, we told each other stupid bar jokes that we had heard over the years. Kaiya giggled loudly, her eyes glassy as she swayed slightly in her seat. Her cheeks had deepened to a light shade of red and she wore a drunken smile. She was definitely tipsy. "I should go. I have to work in the morning," she said halfheartedly.

"Why don't you come home with me?" I suggested with a crooked grin as I pulled her barstool between my legs.

"I can't," she replied as she leaned forward, bringing her face only inches from mine.

Closing the distance, I barely grazed her lips as I asked, "Why not? We both know you want to."

Pulling back a little, she put some distance between our mouths. "Those old demons I mentioned earlier—they haunt you forever." Before I could respond, she continued, "You don't want to get involved with me."

Resting my hands on the outside of her thighs, I rubbed my thumbs against them. "You've said that before. I know what I want, and I'm looking right at her."

She smiled sadly. "If you knew me, you wouldn't want me."

"Why don't you let me decide that for myself instead of fighting me all of the time? You don't even give me a chance to get to know you."

"I have to fight—it's the only way I can protect myself. I need to go," she snapped before grabbing her purse off the bar.

"Kaiya, wait," I called after her. Ignoring me, she pushed through the crowd, continuing to walk toward the door before exiting. I wanted to go after her, but I wasn't the type to chase a woman. My pride wouldn't allow that, so I just let her go, forcing myself to stay at the bar.

I ordered another drink, along with a straight shot of Jack. I downed it as a sexy brunette walked up next to me, her tits almost popping out of her skin-tight dress.

"Want some company?" she asked before biting her bottom lip seductively.

She wasn't what I wanted, but I didn't want to sit around sulking about Kaiya, so I pulled her onto my lap. "Sure, baby. Wanna get out of here?" I asked before tracing my tongue along her jawline.

"Yes," she practically moaned as she tilted her head. *Too easy.*

After I paid my tab, I followed the girl back to her place. We barely made it in the door before she started stripping her clothes off and getting on her knees in front of me.

Unbuttoning my jeans, she pushed me back against the wall next to her front door. She pulled my cock out before eagerly sucking it into her mouth, skimming it lightly with her teeth.

Grabbing her hair, I pushed my dick deeper into her mouth before starting to thrust in and out. I tried to lose myself in the sensations, but all I could think about was Kaiya and how I wished her mouth was around me instead.

Pulling out, I turned the woman around as I knelt behind her. I took a condom out of my wallet before rolling it over my cock and sinking myself into her, making her moan loudly in pleasure.

Gripping her hips, I imagined I was pounding into Kaiya instead of some random girl. I closed my eyes, envisioning her silken skin, perfect body, and beautiful face as my dick repeatedly stroked inside her.

My hips smacked against her ass as my pace increased, the image of Kaiya bringing me closer to release with each passing second.

Crying out, the woman's pussy tightened around me, her body trembling its climax before she lay slack on the floor, ass still up as I plunged deeper into her. My fingers dug into her hips as I slammed her harder against me, seeking my own release.

Groaning, I stilled as I came, panting heavily to regain my breath. Once I did, I pulled out from the unnamed woman.

She rolled over and spread her legs, opening herself to me. "Want to go again?"

My dick had already started to go down once I was reminded that she wasn't Kaiya. I slid the condom off me as I said, "Nah, I'm good."

She looked offended as I stood up before throwing the condom away and buttoning my jeans.

"What?" she angrily asked, her mouth setting in a hard line as she closed her legs and sat up.

"I said that I'm good," I replied as I turned and reached for the doorknob. I didn't even wait for her reply as I opened the door and left.

Chapter Nine

Kaiya

Bryce had been more than happy when I'd called and asked if I could come over. Even though I'd wanted to take Ryker up on his offer at the bar, I'd been too scared to go through with it. So instead, I pushed him away. *Chicken shit.*

As I put my clothes back on, Bryce commented, "I've missed you, Ky."

What's with him lately? He's never been so affectionate. "We saw each other last week," I reminded, my response cut and dry as I avoided his penetrating gaze.

"I know, I've just missed you," he said with sincerity as he sat next to me on the bed. He tucked a strand of my wild, sex hair behind my ear before caressing my cheek.

What do I say to that? "Thanks." It sounded more like a question than an expression of gratitude.

"Thanks?" he chortled without humor.

Squeezing the bridge of my nose with my fingers, I replied, "What do you want me to say, Bryce?"

He stood angrily as he said, "I don't know, maybe that you missed me too."

But I haven't. I've been too consumed with Ryker to think about anyone else. "I'm sorry—you know I don't do feelings well." I really didn't.

Sighing, he rubbed the back of his neck. "I know. Don't worry about it."

After Bryce walked me to my car, I drove home, thinking about the events of the night, wondering why I couldn't have just let go and lose myself in Ryker like I'd wanted to.

I didn't see Ryker again until class on Thursday. He wasn't at the gym on Wednesday when I went after work. I hated the gnawing feeling in my chest from not seeing him, and I thought I was going to explode once it combined with the knots in my stomach from the anticipation of finally seeing him again at class.

When I arrived, he was hitting one of the bags. Sweat glistened over his skin as he fluidly moved, doing intricate combinations while simultaneously delivering substantial force. His muscles bulged as he used them expertly, and I found myself drawing closer to him, enthralled by his power and grace.

Seeing me out of the corner of his eye, he stopped before turning, his lips curving up in a cocky grin, "Like what you see?"

Um, yeah. Ignoring his comment, I responded, "I'm just trying to see the correct form so I can get better. I suck at this stuff."

"Yeah, you're pretty terrible," he replied jokingly as he leaned against the bag. When I glared at him, he continued, "You just started—you're not going to be an expert from the get go. But honestly, you've been doing great."

I felt my cheeks heat—*seriously? Get a grip.* "Thanks," I replied before pausing. "I'm sorry about the other night."

He chuckled, "I think I'm having deja vu."

I smiled. "I'm just not good at this—whatever this is."

"A beautiful woman like you shouldn't have any trouble with guys."

Yeah, and they shouldn't have issues because of their brother molesting them either. "I'm not like other women. I've already warned you that I have issues."

"And I thought I made it clear that I didn't care." He pushed off the bag and came toward me. "I want to get to know you, Kaiya."

"I'm not looking for a relationship," I stated firmly, locking my eyes with his as I crossed my arms over my chest.

Ryker's lips tipped up in that sexy smirk. "I guess we have something in common then."

"I don't just want a one night stand, either," I blurted, surprised that I had voiced what I wanted. My stomach knotted uncomfortably as I waited to hear his response.

Those deep, beautiful eyes of his studied me, and I wished I could hear what he was thinking. "So, you want something between a one night stand and a relationship, huh?"

I sighed, "I don't know what I want. This is all happening so fast for me." *I want you, though.*

He kept our eyes locked as he said, "Well, when you figure it out, let me know. I don't want to keep pressuring you if you're not ready." His tone was sincere, but I still didn't trust his words.

"Thank you for understanding." The skeptical side of me wondered if he was trying to play me, telling me what I wanted to hear so that I'd give into him. But the smaller part of me, the optimistic side, hoped that it wasn't just an act. "What are we working on today?"

"I'll probably work with you again on the techniques we've done, but I also want to show you some blocks and other moves to keep you from getting in those situations."

I get to have that body pressed against me again? Yes, please. "Okay, sounds good," I replied, hiding my excitement.

As I turned to walk away, he asked, "Hey, do you want me to help you with some punches before class starts? I can give you some one-on-one attention."

Yes! Yes! "Sure, that's fine. I bought some gloves," I said, trying to pretend I wasn't jumping for joy on the inside as I pulled my new gloves out of my bag.

"Great, put them on and meet me at the bag."

I set my stuff down by the wall before slipping my gloves on. I don't know why, but just putting them on made me feel powerful and in control, like I could take on anyone. Even *him*.

When I came up to the bag, Ryker surprised me by walking around and standing behind me. Stiffening, my heart skipped a beat before going into overdrive, thumping wildly in my chest as I nervously asked, "What are you doing?"

"I'm going to show you how your body needs to be moving with each strike," he replied unaware of the panic overtaking me. He was so close that I could feel the heat from his body at my back. Pressing his large, muscular chest against me, he ran his hands over my arms, causing goose bumps to break over my skin.

For some reason, I wasn't scared like I would normally be if someone was this close to me. I was nervous as fuck, but not afraid. Excited, but not afraid. I still couldn't understand why Ryker was different, why he made me feel so many things other than fear. The only thing I knew was that I liked it.

His gloved hands covered mine as he instructed, "Relax—you're always so tense. Kickboxing is very fluid and is all about moving your body the right way."

Bringing our joined arms out by my sides, he shook them, trying to loosen my taut muscles. Then, he brought our hands up in front of my face as he positioned our bodies in the traditional fighters' stance. Extending our right arms out towards the bag, he said, "Do you feel how we're twisting slightly when we throw this jab? Every move needs to be like this, using your body as a power source. Our muscles are made to work together, just like when we lift something heavy or do other everyday tasks."

As he pulled my hand back in front of my face, he twisted our bodies more as we threw a punch with our left hands, slightly pivoting our hips inward. Feeling his sweaty, firm body pressed against me, especially the lower half, was so distracting; I could barely focus on what he was saying. "Kaiya?"

"Huh? What?" I felt like I was under some sort of spell.

"Did you feel how we used more movement with the punch over the jab? Whatever side is behind will require more force to correctly execute."

I couldn't speak, not with him flush against me like that, so I just nodded. We continued working that way until other members started entering for class. By then, my body was sticky with heat from a combination of hitting the bag and Ryker's proximity to me. All I could think about was how his bare body would feel tangled with mine.

Once we started kickboxing, I started to let myself go as I worked on the combo Ryker modeled. I loved hitting the bag—absolutely loved it. Even though I wasn't very good yet, it was an amazing outlet for my stress and anxiety, not to mention my anger. It felt good to release it, free myself from all my negative emotions, at least for a brief time. They always slithered back, snaking their way inside and tainting my soul with their poison.

After the kickboxing segment of class was over, Ryker and I practiced the technique that he taught me the week before. I wasn't as uncomfortable since I was becoming accustomed to his touch, so I was able to execute the maneuver better.

Constantly touching him electrified my skin, intensifying the sexual tension that was already present between us. My mind and my body warred—my body wanted to give in to Ryker while my mind protested, fearing that inevitably, I would be hurt by him.

I didn't trust my body, especially since it betrayed me so many times in the past. I knew that I needed to follow my head when it came to Ryker, to be smart and not give into my emotions and desires so easily.

Ryker broke through my thoughts, "Let's work on a common variation of this move since you seem to have this one down." He lay down on his back before continuing, "Straddle me."

"Excuse me?" I stammered nervously, feeling my cheeks heat.

"Straddle me. I'm going to show you how to escape if an attacker pins your arms to the floor."

I hesitated briefly before climbing on top of him. His body felt so right beneath me.

"Now, pin my hands by my head."

Doing what Ryker instructed, I leaned over, clasping my hands around his thick, tattooed wrists and pinning them to the ground.

"First thing you're going to do is simultaneously bring up your right knee while shooting your left arm upwards, like this," he said before modeling.

I felt his knee prop against my ass as he made me lean forward by jerking his left arm upwards. "Now, you're going to roll to the right and pin your attacker."

Swiftly rolling, Ryker had me pinned beneath him in seconds. "Once here, you can use the strikes I taught you last week to attack them. Elbows would probably be best from this position."

Even though he was wearing loose shorts, I could still feel his semi-hard, yet still impressive erection pressing into my lower abdomen, muddling my thoughts as arousal flooded me. *Focus, Kaiya.*

Ryker smirked at me; I was pretty sure that my desire was written all over my face. "You want to try? I already have you pinned," he pointed out as he lightly pushed his hips against me and pressed down on my arms.

Heat simmered between my thighs from the slight movement, from having Ryker's flawless form hovering over me. My eyes trailed over the intricate tattoos exposed from his tight muscle shirt, which spanned his chest and spread over his arms all the way down to his hands. I had to fight the urge to trace them with my fingers.

Ryker cleared his throat before huskily saying, "If you keep looking at me like, I'm not going to be able to do what I said earlier."

My gaze snapped up to his, and his eyes reflected the desire I felt. I wanted him so badly, wanted to tell him how I felt, but I couldn't. I had too much baggage that he didn't deserve to deal with; no one did. My voice cracked as I said, "Sorry. What do I do from here?"

"Jerk your left arm up while bending your right knee and putting it against my back."

I doubted that I would be able to move my arm, especially since his were double the size of mine and his muscles were so big.

Jerking my arm above my head, I caused Ryker's weight to shift forward as his arm went with mine, bringing his face only inches from my own. My eyes focused on his lips, the ones I had tasted only a few nights ago, and had thought about every night since.

Ryker's grip tightened on my wrists as he gruffly reminded, "Don't forget your knee."

Shit, concentrate! I brought my right knee up, pressing it into Ryker. "Now use that leg to roll us over."

Pushing with my right leg, I tried to roll us, but couldn't; Ryker was so much heavier than me. "I can't," I sighed agitatedly.

"Yes, you can, Warrior. Put those hips into it—use your whole body."

Doing as Ryker said, I bucked my hips, using my entire body for momentum as I pushed against him. Slowly, I was able to roll us over until I was mounted on top of him again. A smile spread over my face as I impulsively put my arms up in the arms and squealed, "I did it!"

Embarrassment took over my happiness as I brought my arms down, the heat that was in my core now rushing up to my face. I looked down at Ryker, who had a proud smile on his face as he chuckled, "Awesome job."

"Thank you," I mumbled.

We practiced a few more times, and the longer Ryker was touching me, the more my resistance crumbled. I probably would have let him fuck me right there on the mat in front of everyone by the time we finally finished. Not really, but I was seriously contemplating it.

After class ended, Ryker walked me out to my car. Leaning against the driver's side door, he praised, "You did really good today."

"You're just saying that," I replied as I rolled my eyes.

"No, really, you did great. You're progressing well—it usually takes people weeks to really get the techniques down."

"Well, thank you," I smiled. Our eyes met, and Ryker was looking at me with that sexy smirk that tightened my core while setting it on fire.

Uncomfortably squirming under his gaze, I spoke, "I better get going. I'll see you Thursday."

Ryker leaned in, and my lips parted in response to his closeness. I closed my eyes as I waited for his lips to meet mine, but instead I felt them on my cheek as he brought me into him and whispered, "Goodnight, Warrior."

As he pulled away, my voice embarrassingly cracked, "Goodnight."

Ryker stifled a laugh as he backed away, his eyes never leaving mine until he turned around and jogged back to the entrance of the gym.

As I sat in my car, I wondered how long I could resist him, if I would be able to at all. I didn't want to, but I couldn't think of an outcome that ended well. One of us would end up hurt, most likely me, no matter which way I looked at it. No one wanted damaged goods anyway.

As I started the car, I sighed and made my decision. It was best for both of us if we didn't get involved. No one would get hurt, and it was less complicated if I was going to continue taking classes. No matter how much my body wanted him, my head knew better, knew what was best to protect me from more pain. Now if only my heart would understand.

Chapter Ten

Ryker

Kaiya had been coming to class for a few weeks, and her technique and form had improved greatly. But when we practiced certain defense maneuvers, her body stiffened and her grip was tight, her apprehension evident in her tense muscles and wary eyes.

She had become more guarded, keeping some distance between us and pulling away when I touched her for too long. I tried giving her the space I had promised, but it was getting harder with each passing day.

The sexual tension between us had increased over the weeks. Every detail of her silky skin had been committed to memory from touching her so much, making me want her even more. Since Kaiya was only comfortable working with me, that meant constant, close contact, which I didn't mind at all, but she was always resisting, always fighting me, both in class, and in my personal advances. I could see the desire all over her face, especially in those eyes, but she always fought it, fought what I knew we were both feeling. *My little warrior.*

I hadn't realized I had so much self-control—I wanted Kaiya more than I had ever wanted another woman. Her resistance only made me want her that much more. Any other girl would've been in and out of my bed by now, but Kaiya was different—I couldn't do the same with her that I did with other women. That confused and irritated the shit out of me. My patience was running thin, and I wasn't going to keep playing games with her. *I'll have her soon.*

After working on the bags, I asked the group about what self-defense technique they wanted to work on. One of the students raised her hand. "Can we work on getting out of a choke?"

The other students voiced their agreement, but Kaiya stiffened. Her eyes widened, and her lips tightened as our gazes locked.

"Okay, get with your usual partners." While everyone else split up on the mats, I walked over toward Kaiya, keeping my eyes fixed on her. "Everything okay?"

"I don't know if I can do this." She looked away as she reached for her neck. She stopped herself and pulled her hand away before looking up at me. "I don't like having my throat touched."

My eyes went to her throat. A thin scar spread about two inches long against her pale skin. I had to be looking at it just right to see it, or else it would be undetectable in the natural creases and curves of her neck. *How the fuck did she get that?* I knew she wouldn't tell me what had happened, so I didn't ask... yet.

Rubbing her arms, I leaned down a little so that my face was in line with hers, forcing her to bring her downcast eyes to look at me. "We can take it slow. I'm only trying to help you learn how to defend yourself—I'm not going to hurt you." *I'd never hurt you.*

Even though she nodded, she still looked uncertain as she took a deep breath and shook out her hands.

"You can attack me first, and I can show you how to get out of it, like always."

"Okay," she replied softly. The other instructors had already started with the rest of the students, so I prepared to demonstrate the techniques with Kaiya. I lay down on the mat and patted my abs. "Get on me."

She glanced around nervously, biting her lip before finally straddling me, framing my torso with her legs. Even though we had done this several times before, she was still embarrassed and self-conscious. She nervously looked down at me as her cheeks turned pink, and I wished we were doing this without clothes on, just like I wanted to every time. "Now, choke me."

"What? No!" she exclaimed. "I... I can't do that to you." She crossed her arms over her chest.

"Just do it—you don't have to squeeze hard. I'm going to walk you through the steps to get out of the hold." I reassured as I softly rubbed the sides of her thighs.

Slowly, she brought her delicate hands down to my neck before applying slight pressure. "Too hard—can't breathe!" I gasped as I pretended to choke.

Inhaling a sharp breath, she instantly jerked her hands to away as her eyes grew wide. My body rumbled with laughter, and her eyes narrowed as she smacked me on the shoulder. "That's not funny, Ryker!"

I continued to laugh as Kaiya crossed her arms across her chest again, trying to stifle a smile. Once I stopped, I apologized, "I'm sorry. I was trying to get you to loosen up. I promise I'll behave. Choke me again."

The smile she'd been fighting broke through as she leaned over to grab my throat again. *I wish she smiled more.* She squeezed my neck, bringing my attention back to the exercise. "The first technique I'm going to show you is using your forearm. Bring it up and over, parallel to your chest," I said, modeling as I talked. "Then, slam it down across their forearms and push. Usually when someone is being choked, the attacker is just out of reach. This move will make them come closer to you, so you can grab them, like this, and force them off you." I easily tossed her off me onto the mat.

"Yeah, it's easy for you—I'm lighter than you." She rolled over and sat up as her eyes looked over my arms. "Plus you have all those muscles. How am I supposed to overpower you? Or any guy for that matter?"

"Let me show you again, and I'll explain how. Get back on me," I instructed as I lay back down.

Straddling me again, she closed her hands around my neck. *Fuck, I love how she feels on top of me.* Images of her riding me, head tipped back and eyes closed as she moaned my name played through my head.

"Ryker?" Kaiya softly spoke, snapping me from my thoughts. Our eyes locked and her lips curved up, drawing my attention to them. *Damn, I want to kiss her again.*

"Sorry." I cleared my throat. Bringing my arm up, I braced it against hers. As I pushed against them, I asked, "Feel how your weight is forced to shift when I do this?" When she nodded, I continued, "I'm not pressing that hard, so even if your attacker is stronger, the pressure will still affect their balance and move them close enough for you to grab something."

Pushing harder, I forced her arms to bend, bringing her closer to me. Our faces were only inches away from each other; I had to stop myself from closing the small gap to touch her lips, wanting to taste her after so long.

Her breath hitched as our gazes met; her eyes always revealed so much, even when she tried to hide everything away. Fear and longing swam in those bright, blue eyes, and I wanted to lose myself in them— in her.

Breaking the haze we were in, she darted her eyes away and hoarsely asked, "What next?"

What were we doing again? Oh, yeah. "You grab anything you can to help you push them off of you—face, shoulder, arm, clothes, anything."

"And if I can't get them off?"

"Then, you kick, bite, scratch, punch, whatever. Do everything that you can do to defend yourself. Usually, that will catch your attacker off guard, allowing you to get them off of you," I stated firmly.

Kaiya squirmed against me, and I realized that my free hand had found her hip. Slowly pulling away, I grazed the tips of my fingers over the skin exposed from her tank top riding up.

Shuddering a shaky breath, she pulled away before dismounting me. I propped myself up on my elbows. "Ready to try?"

"I think so," she replied. Her tone was unsure, but her eyes held a look of determination.

"We'll take it slow. Lay down." When she complied, I continued, "I'm going to get on top of you, okay?"

We locked eyes as she nodded. As I straddled her, I assured, "I'm not going to hurt you."

"I know," she softly replied with a small smile.

I'm making progress here.

"I'm going to put my hands around your neck now. Do what I just demonstrated to escape, okay?" I studied her face, waiting to make sure she was ready.

She gave me a clipped nod. "Okay."

I kept my eyes fixed on hers as I gently placed my hands around her neck, applying light pressure. My thumb brushed over the small, raised scar, causing anger to swarm me like a pissed off hive of bees. *I'd like to meet the asshole who did this in a dark alley.*

Kaiya began to implement the technique from beneath me, but she couldn't throw me off. After several attempts, she huffed in frustration. "See, I told you that I wouldn't be able to get you off of me."

"Remember to use your whole body," I suggested with a chuckle.

Her eyes furrowed in determination as we attempted the maneuver again. Once she forced my arms to bend, she used her hips to try and vault me off of her while pushing them up into my crotch. My cock began to harden, especially when she started moving side to side, trying to get me off of her. *Fuck, how does she do this to me?*

Stilling beneath me, Kaiya's eyes widened, and her creamy skin flushed as she panted heavily. "I'm not doing it right."

"Oh, you're doing something right," I winked.

Softly giggling, she redirected the topic back to the maneuver. "You know what I mean. I'm not getting you off."

"Not yet, but if you keep doing that you will." I said suggestively as my eyes roamed over her face.

Her lips quirked up even though she ignored my comment, keeping her focus on the training. "What should I do?"

I wanted to continue playing with her, but she was really trying to execute the move, so I focused back on my job. "As you buck your hips, use your arms to help you. Push me off at the same time you're pushing up with your hips. Use that momentum together in the direction you want to throw me. Let's try again from the beginning."

Sitting up, I waited for her to readjust before starting the routine over. This time, she was able to throw me partially off of her. I landed on her right side, my legs still over hers.

"If this ever happens, which is likely since you're so small, you need to go crazy once you're in this position. Do everything you can to hurt your attacker—hammer-fists, kicks, knees, elbows, anything. Do whatever it takes to push them the rest of the way off of you. Again," I firmly said, going back into instructor mode, trying to keep my attention off her sweaty skin and how it would feel as I fucked her.

We practiced the move a few more times, and I couldn't help but notice how she tensed every time I placed my hands back on her neck. I really wanted to find out why, to make sure no one was hurting her.

As I helped her up off the mat, I asked, "What happened to your neck?"

Jerking her hand away, her face tightened with anxiety as she snapped, "None of your business."

Turning away, she began to storm off towards her stuff. *Shit.* Following her, I said, "Don't be upset. I just want to make sure no one is hurting you." When I caught up to her, I pulled her to a stop and placed my hands on her shoulders. I lowered my head to look into her eyes, hoping she would see my genuine concern. "You'd tell me if someone was hurting you right? Even if it was Kamden?"

Shock replaced some of the anger in her eyes as she sighed in defeat. "I'm sorry. I just…" She looked away, shaking her head. "I can't talk about it. But no, no one's hurting me, especially not Kamden." She grabbed her bag and turned to walk away again. "Thank you for your concern, though."

Grabbing her hand, I stopped her. "I want you to know that you can come to me if you need help, okay? Not just as your instructor, but as a friend, too."

A warm smile spread over her lips. "Thanks," she replied softly as she squeezed my hand.

I pulled her closer to me, to where her tits pressed against me. A strand of hair had fallen loose from her ponytail, and it dangled in her face. Reaching to tuck it behind her ear, I caressed her cheek with my palm. Her eyes closed as she leaned into my hand, but she snapped them open and quickly pulled away.

Letting out a heavy breath, I dropped my hands to my side. "Why do you fight me so much? Why won't you just give in to what I know you're feeling?"

Her lips tightened into a frown, and her eyebrows furrowed. "I can't," she said barely above a whisper.

"Can't or won't?" I challenged, my voice thick with frustration.

Her eyes watered as she opened her mouth to speak, but she snapped it shut instead. She turned around and rushed out of the room, pushing past some of the other class members.

Fuck! Why does she have to be so stubborn? Clenching my fists, I punched the bag nearest to me, sending it into the wall about three feet away. I ran my hands through my hair, pacing as I debated whether or not to go after her. We were both too upset for anything to end well, so I decided against it. *Damn it.*

I didn't see Kaiya again until Tuesday, but we had texted back and forth a few times on Monday, after both of us had apologized for our actions during class Sunday.

Tonight, I was really excited, not only to see Kaiya, but also because I planned to have the students spar, which we hadn't done in a long time. I had been waiting until Kaiya demonstrated she was ready, and since she had made so much progress, I thought she could handle it.

Once all the students arrived, I announced, "Today's class is going to different. All we're going to do is spar."

There were a few groans along with some enthusiastic cheers. I had the other instructors hand out the sparring equipment as I grabbed some for Kaiya and myself before walking over to her.

She looked at me nervously. "Are you sure I'm ready for this?"

"Yes," I responded confidently. "But if you're not comfortable, we can work on something else or watch the others spar." I set the rest of our equipment down and then looked up at her for confirmation.

"No!" she blurted. "I mean, I want to, I just don't know what to do."

"We'll take it slow. A lot of things will come naturally since you've been practicing. Let's get you suited up," I said as I picked up a chest protector. "This is a hogu—it'll protect your chest and stomach from any hits."

Slipping it over her head, I turned her around to tie the straps behind her. *I'd like to tie her hands to my bed and fuck her senseless.* Grinning stupidly at the thoughts, I moved around in front of her, making sure the hogu was positioned correctly. She looked up at me and smiled. "What?"

I shook my head and chuckled, "Nothing." I bent over to pick up her head gear and handed it to her. After she pulled it on, I helped adjust it, making sure it fit comfortably.

Once she had everything on, including shin guards, her gloves, and a mouthpiece, I put my own equipment on. As we stood in the center of one of the mats, I instructed, "Use everything you've learned so far. I'm going to let you hit me for the most part, but if you let your guard down, I'm going to take advantage, okay?"

She nodded, but I could see the anxiety in her eyes. As I walked closer to her, I assured, "Hey, you know I'm not going to hurt you, right?"

Her response was muffled by her mouthpiece, "I know." She nodded once more. "I'm just nervous."

"Are you sure you want to do this? It's okay if you don't want to."

"I want to," she replied with confidence, a determined gleam in her eyes.

That's my girl.

Moving back a few steps, I gestured with both hands for her to come to me. "Let's see what you got."

Hesitantly, Kaiya advanced towards me, keeping her hands in front of her face like I had taught her. She threw a few punches that I easily blocked, but she nailed me with a roundhouse to my thigh. "Nice hit," I praised.

She attempted to hit me with another roundhouse, but I deflected it with my own leg, causing her to stumble slightly. Recovering quickly, she came at with more jabs and punches, but I was able to block them. She lowered her hands from her face to her chest, obviously tired from the constant movement—sparring was exhausting for anyone.

Jabbing her lightly in the forehead, right where her head gear went across, I reminded, "Hands up! Always protect your face."

Her hands shot back up right before she swung at my stomach. I jumped back to avoid her hit. "You need to get closer for shots like that. Get some water and I'll explain more about your technique."

After we both got a drink, I sat with Kaiya on the mat to let her catch her breath before we started the next round.

"You're doing great. The only thing I noticed is that you're not close enough for some of the hits you're attempting." I took a long swig of my water and watched as she brought her bottle to her mouth. I quickly looked away, not wanting to focus on her plump lips and remember how they tasted. "You'll tire yourself out by throwing and not landing them."

Sweat dripped down her face as she nodded. "Got it."

"Hey, loosen up. Have some fun—I'm giving you a chance to beat the crap out of me. I don't let just anyone do that."

"I feel so special," she remarked sarcastically, fighting a smile.

I tugged on her ponytail and nudged her playfully. "Smart ass."

Slapping my arm away, she laughed and pushed me back. "Jerk."

I chuckled before taking another swallow from my bottle and standing. "Ready for round two?"

When Kaiya nodded, I reached down to help her up. We took our defensive stances, and I motioned for her to come at me again. She came in closer before executing the basic one, two, three combination of jab, punch, jab to my stomach, but I blocked with my arms before pushing her away.

Her eyes narrowed in determination as she advanced towards me again, throwing an elbow to my face that I batted away with my forearm. She threw a jab to my chest and kicked me below the ribs with a roundhouse.

Grabbing her leg, I trapped it against my side before stepping closer to her, bringing our bodies together. Ignoring the feel of her against me, focusing on how to help her technique, I said, "If this ever happens, you need to start punching anything you can to make them let you go, but don't pull away—you could break your leg."

Kaiya's breathing was ragged as I kept her trapped against me, enjoying having her pressed against me. Reluctantly, I let go before backing away slowly. Kaiya took advantage of my lowered hands by throwing a hook to the left side of my face.

"Nice." I grinned.

A smile lit up her face, showing her pink mouthpiece. Bringing my hands back up, I waited for her to attack me. After she threw a few punches, her hands fell to her chest again.

I threw a back-fist to the side of her head. "Hands," I reminded. "One good hit, and you're done for. Remember the first thing I taught you: never get knocked out."

We went a few more rounds before I decided to work with her on defending against standing attacks. I had Kaiya remove her equipment, but I kept mine on so she could use more force when hitting me during the escape techniques.

"Many times, an attacker will come up and grab you from behind, trapping your arms and putting you in a bear hug. I'm going to show you some ways to escape while disabling your attacker. Come up behind me and wrap your arms around me."

Doing as I instructed, she grabbed me from behind, pinning my arms to the side.

"First thing that you want to do is crouch down, leaning over a little so that it's harder for them to lift you up. Most attackers will try to throw you or slam you to the ground—you can't let that to happen."

I bent down. "Now, you're going to stomp on their instep then shift to the right side, giving you some space to throw a hammer-fist into their groin with your right arm, like this. This should cause them to either completely let go or at least loosen their grip on you, allowing you to throw some back elbows into their stomach."

I softly elbowed her in the stomach a few times before turning. "Once you're in this position, I would recommend a couple of knees to the groin, and some elbows to the face, even a knee to the face because they'll probably be hunched over. Put all of your force into your hits so that you can knock them out. Want to try?"

After she nodded, I came up behind her, pinning her arms to her sides as I brought her body against mine. Her ass pushed against my crotch as she leaned over, and even though I was wearing a cup, I couldn't keep thoughts of bending her over and fucking her from behind out of my head.

She shifted then threw a hammer-fist into my crotch. I loosened my hold on her as she started to elbow me in the stomach before turning and kneeing me in the nuts twice. *Thank God for cups.*

Elbowing me, she connected with the side of my face, which thankfully, was protected by the head gear. Elbows were one of the worst hits to take, especially to the nose or mouth.

We practiced a few more times before I ended class. Everyone was drenched with sweat as we discussed their feelings about sparring, most of which were positive. Tired smiles lined everyone's faces as they talked about what they practiced.

As everyone left, I started gathering the equipment to sanitize before I closed up. "You need some help?" Kaiya asked.

"Sure. I just need to clean this stuff," I said as I grabbed the gym's disinfectant spray and some paper towels from their station in the corner of the room.

After we had sanitized everything, I put the equipment back in their containers before putting them up in the closet. "Thanks for helping me."

"No problem. I'll see you Thursday." Kaiya smiled as she headed for the door.

"Hey, you want to grab something to eat? My treat for your help," I offered.

She turned back to face me. "I can't—Kamden waits for me for dinner."

"Oh, okay. Maybe some other time," I replied coolly, trying to mask my disappointment.

Our eyes met as she nibbled her bottom lip. "Tomorrow?" she suggested, quirking up an eyebrow in question.

My lips curved into a grin, "Just tell me where and when."

"East Side at seven?"

Is she serious? I couldn't fucking believe it—Kaiya was actually agreeing to go out with me. "I'll see you there."

Her skin began to flush as she replied, "Okay. See you tomorrow."

Hastily, she turned and exited as I finished closing up. My stomach knotted itself as I thought about tomorrow night—I hadn't felt like this about a date in a long time. I had given up trying to make sense of how Kaiya made me feel—all I knew was that I wanted more, anything she would give me.

Chapter Eleven

Kaiya

Oh my God, did I really just do that? I couldn't believe how impulsive I was—what was I thinking? I was supposed to be keeping my distance from Ryker, not going out on dates with him. *But one date can't hurt, can it?*

My resistance was wearing down, especially when he was trying so hard to give me the space I asked for. I knew it couldn't be easy since we were always touching during class. I could see and feel his desire when we practiced all the techniques he taught me. And I'm sure he could see mine written all over my face.

I felt like I was going to throw up all day on Wednesday since I was so nervous about seeing Ryker that night. None of the figures on my computer screen at work were making sense, my mind too caught up in thoughts of him for me to get anything done. I decided to text Nori and get her thoughts on everything:

> Me: Ryker is taking me to dinner tonight :)

> Nori: Finally! I was waiting for you to grow some balls and go out with him

I laughed aloud as I text her back:

Me: Idk if this is a good idea :/

Nori: Stop overthinking like you always do just have fun :)

I smiled at her text but didn't reply back. I tried to focus back on work, to keep my mind off dinner, but it was almost impossible. My phone beeped, and I thought Nori had text me again, but it wasn't her:

Ryker: Can't wait for tonight ;)

There was no use trying to fight the goofy smile that took over my lips. Impulsively, I sent the first thing that came to mind:

Me: Me neither :)

Now I'm definitely not going to get any work done.

I anxiously sat on Nori's bed as she helped me with my make-up for my date. I had told Kamden that I was going to dinner with her, not Ryker. I knew he wouldn't approve, and I didn't want to get a lecture from him, not when I was feeling so good.

"Stop moving," Nori scolded as she applied my eye shadow.

"I'm sorry, I'm just so nervous. I don't think I can do this," I said as I started panicking. My palms started sweating as I wrung my fingers together.

Nori stopped what she was doing and put her hands on my shoulders. "Calm down. Deep breaths—in, out, in, out."

Doing as she said, I slowly inhaled and exhaled until I felt calmer.

Nori looked at me with concern. "You don't have to do this if you don't want to, Ky."

"You don't think I should?"

"No, I think you should. You've been giving that poor guy blue balls for weeks now."

"Nori!" I exclaimed as I smacked her arm.

"What? You have."

"I know." I let out a deep breath. "He's been pretty understanding, but I'm just scared I'll get hurt. If Kaleb, my own brother, my own blood, hurt me, then how can I possibly believe that Ryker won't?"

"You don't know for sure, Ky. You can't punish everyone for Kaleb's actions. He has mental issues. Look at Kam—he's never hurt you and never will, same with Bryce. There are some good men out there."

Absorbing Nori's words, I contemplated what she said. Even though she was right, my defense mechanisms wouldn't fully accept it. I could never completely trust anyone, her and Kamden included.

With pursed lips and a raised eyebrow, she shook the eyeshadow brush in my face. "So, am I finishing your make-up or not?"

Smiling, I nodded. Even with all the conflicting thoughts running through my head, I couldn't deny that I wanted to see Ryker. Maybe I could let everything go and just have fun for one night. Unlikely, but a girl could hope.

I was about ten minutes late, as usual, and Ryker was waiting just inside the doors. Dressed in a nice, black dress shirt and dark jeans, he had his sleeves pushed up, exposing the tattoos on his forearms.

Our eyes met as he gave me his trademark smirk. Heat flooded my entire body as I took him in, and I wondered why I kept resisting him— he was absolutely gorgeous and made me feel so many amazing things that I'd never felt before. *Because you're crazy, that's why.*

As I approached, he brought me into his arms as he pressed a soft kiss to my cheek. "You look beautiful," he complimented.

"So do you. I mean handsome—you look handsome," I stammered. *Great start.*

His chest rumbled with laughter as he kept me against him. Keeping my hand in his, he pulled away and led me to the hostess stand.

When the hostess directed her attention to us, she gave Ryker a flirtatious smile. "I was hoping she wouldn't show—my shift ends in fifteen minutes."

Jealously sparked through me as my eyes narrowed and my hand tightened around Ryker's. *Bitch. I'm standing right here.*

Ryker released my hand to wrap his arm around the small of my back, drawing me into his body. He pressed a kiss to my temple, causing her smile to fade as he said, "She was just running late, right, baby?"

Giving her a smug smile, I leaned into Ryker, placing my hand on his chest. "Two, please."

Her eyes thinned as she huffed and grabbed two menus. Ryker chuckled as she angrily stomped in her heels while leading us to our table.

"What a bitch," I said after she walked away.

Ryker laughed, "Jealous, huh?"

Yes. "No! She was just rude."

Ryker gave me a knowing look before directing his attention to the menu. The waiter arrived to take our order after a few minutes, then left to get our drinks.

Ryker grinned. "I have to admit, I was surprised you suggested this."

You and me both. "One of my rare impulsive moments," I joked.

"I like the impulsive side of you. You should let her out more often."

The waiter came back with our drinks, giving me an opportunity to change the subject. "We always talk about me. Tell me about you."

He propped his elbows on the table as he looked at me. "What do you want to know?"

"Anything—what about your family?"

"My parents died when I was in high school."

Shit. "I'm sorry. Do you have any other family?"

"I have a brother, but we don't talk," he replied coldly, his jaw tensing in anger.

I'm sure he can't be as bad as Kaleb. Fuck, don't think about him—change the subject. "How long have you been a personal trainer?"

The anger in his face receded as he answered, "A few years—I went to school for it, and was lucky enough to get a job right after I graduated."

"That's awesome—I can tell how much you love it."

"Yeah, it definitely has its perks. I basically get paid to work out."

And it shows. I smiled as I thought about his flawless muscles, how they felt when I touched them while we practiced, and how hot he looked when they gleamed with his sweat.

The waiter brought our food, interrupting my delicious thoughts about Ryker, who slyly grinned at me, as if he could tell that I was thinking about him. Blushing, I directed my attention to my food to avoid his heated gaze.

After we finished eating, we had a few more drinks before Ryker paid our bill. Once we reached my car, he wound his arms around my waist, pulling me flush against him as he kissed my cheek. "Goodnight, Warrior."

Unable to control myself, I turned my face, connecting our lips. My mind reminded me that this was a bad idea, that I'd just end up hurt, but I blocked it out, enjoying the feel of Ryker's hot mouth on mine.

I almost moaned when his tongue parted my lips, missing his taste after so long. His hands came up to cup my face as he pushed me back against my car.

Nibbling my bottom lip, he gruffly whispered against my mouth, "Come home with me."

I almost said yes—almost. Lord knows I wanted to, but that scared, broken part of me took hold, making me break away from Ryker as I breathlessly replied, "I can't."

Ryker's face fell, then set in frustration. His voice raised in anger as he stepped away from me. "That's what you always say, Ky. And we still end up like this every single time."

"I know, and I'm sorry. You just don't understand." I sighed as I hugged myself. *No one ever will.*

"Help me understand, then. I know you feel what's between us, so tell me what the problem is," he demanded as his eyes locked on mine.

"Me! I'm the problem! I'm too fucked up for this; for you!" I yelled, gesturing towards him before dropping my arms to my sides.

His eyes softened as he closed some of the distance between us. His voice reflected the gentleness in his eyes as he said, "Ky, no-"

I cut him off as I felt tears rimming my lids, "I have to go."

Once inside my car, I couldn't contain the tears anymore, and I ended up crying all the way back home. Thankfully, Kamden was asleep, so he didn't see my puffy, red eyes and blotchy skin. I didn't want to explain to him why I was crying after dinner with Nori.

As I lay in bed, my mind taunted me, *I told you this was a bad idea.*

Fuck off, I replied as I closed my eyes, hoping sleep would find me sooner rather than later.

Going to class the next day probably wasn't the best idea, but I didn't want to give up on all the progress I had made. I just needed to suck it up and stick with it, no matter if I had to suffer with my emotions. Plus, even though I had ruined things with Ryker, I still wanted to see him.

Things were more tense then normal between us, which I had expected. I didn't know how he could look at me, let alone touch me after how I treated him.

We practiced all of the escapes that he'd already taught me, reviewing everything to make sure I remembered the moves. I wouldn't have been able to focus on any new techniques with everything running through my mind, so I was glad that we were doing things I already knew.

Once class was over, Ryker asked me to stay behind. "I want to talk to you. I'm going to lock the doors—I'll be right back."

I wanted to leave, but he deserved an explanation for last night. I needed to just break things completely off with him, maybe ask to work with one of the other instructors, even though I didn't want to. *It's best for him. You'll just bring him down with you.*

When he walked back in, he surprised me by saying, "I have a proposition for you—if you can get one good hit on me, I'll leave you alone."

My head cocked in confusion as I stared at him, contemplating what he had just said. *Would he really leave me alone? Did I want him to?* I had just been telling myself to break things off, but I really didn't want to. "Just one hit?"

"Just one. And a good one, not some weak shit. Are you up for it?" His eyebrow raised in question.

My heart screamed no, but the fear rooted inside me said yes. I didn't want him to quit pursuing me, but I doubted that I'd ever be enough for him; he didn't deserve someone as fucked up as me. So, I went with what was familiar, what I knew, pushing him away. "Yes."

The smirk that was on his face fell slightly, but he played it off as he took up his fighting stance, holding his hands up to protect his face as he chuckled. "Good luck."

Narrowing my eyes, I mimicked his pose. He always wanted a challenge, so I planned to give him one. Or at least go down trying.

"Ready?" he questioned as he pulled off his shirt, exposing those immaculate, inked muscles. My eyes instantly traced over them, admiring every inch of his perfection. *Fuck.*

When I nodded, he advanced on me instantly, landing a soft slap to the right side of my head, toying with me. "Hands up!"

I picked my hands up, but I knew they'd be falling again soon. I always forgot to keep them in front of my face when I got caught up doing combos, and I tended to drop them more when I was tired.

Aimlessly, I threw punches and kicks at Ryker, all of which he dodged or blocked easily. After several attempts, I finally landed something, grazing his jaw with my fist. He cockily smiled in response as he pushed me out of the way, throwing me off balance as he got me with a light side kick.

Stopping, I struggled for air while wondering how he sparred so effortlessly, seemingly unfatigued while I was the opposite. I was utterly exhausted from just a few minutes.

Ryker's legs swept mine out from under me, causing me to slam to the mat on my back. The impact stung my exposed skin, the force from the fall reverberating through my bones and causing the air to vacate my lungs.

Covering me with his firm, sweaty body, Ryker mounted me, pinning me to the mat as my chest heaved with heavy breaths. "Are you finished?" he gruffly asked.

My heart pounded wildly but not from fear or panic. Ryker was like a pure shot of adrenaline mixed with lust that ramped up my entire being.

I struggled against him, not wanting to concede defeat. I had only been coming for about two months, so I didn't know that many defensive tactics to aid in my efforts, at least not with sparring.

Ryker grinned as he trapped my hands above my head on the mat. "Why do you insist on fighting what you feel for me? I know that you want me."

"No, I don't," I panted. That was a huge lie, maybe the biggest I'd ever told. I wanted Ryker more than I'd ever wanted anything before, and that scared the shit out of me.

"Oh, really? You don't want this—want me—to fill your pussy?" he challenged as he ground his ample erection against me.

Closing my eyes, I bit my lip as I stifled a moan. Ryker's firm body pressing against mine was like gasoline to the fire he always set within me, and I was so close to letting the flames consume me.

Ryker's hot mouth met my neck, causing the moan I'd been withholding to escape. His tongue slowly trailed over my skin before he brought his lips to hover over mine. "Admit it, Warrior. You… want… me."

Clouded by desire, I breathlessly groaned in response, "Yes."

He softly grazed my lips with his as he gruffly asked, "Yes, what?"

Voice laced with need, I replied, "Yes, I want you."

My words set off a passion within both of us. Ryker crushed my mouth with his, eagerly devouring me as his hands roamed over my body. His tongue parted my lips before tangling with mine, the barbell in his mouth adding to the amazing sensations from his kiss.

Instead of fighting him like before, I melted into him, wanting to feel him all over and in me. My hands ventured over the hard planes of his flawless muscles as he mercilessly kissed me, one hand tangled in my hair, the other skimming under my muscle shirt.

His fingers traced over my fevered skin, causing a slight shudder to run through me. All of my thoughts, insecurities, and compulsions were erased by Ryker's skilled mouth and hands. The only thing I could focus on was the divine sensations he elicited in me as he flooded my senses, making me lose all control in a completely different way.

His hands continued up my body, pushing my shirt up as they explored my skin. Breaking our kiss, he pulled the tank top over my head before reconnecting our mouths, which couldn't get enough of each other.

Finding the waist of his shorts, my hands tugged on them, needing to remove the remaining barriers blocking his skin from mine. I wanted to feel every inch of him all over me, wanted him to continue to drown out everything else with his touch.

Ryker growled as he swiftly removed his shorts before pulling at mine. "Fuck, baby, I've wanted you for so long."

Maneuvering my body, I allowed him to easily slide my shorts and panties down while I lifted my sports bra off.

His naked body was flush against me within seconds, his thighs opening my legs as his shaft pressed against my slick entrance. I moaned from the contact, wanting and needing more of what only Ryker seemed to be able to give me.

Slowly pushing into me, he blissfully filled me inch by inch with his massive cock. Arching against him, he sank even further into me, the entirety of him still not able to fully fit inside me. We both groaned as he seated himself within me, my pussy tight around him as he began to stroke inside me.

My nails dug into Ryker's shoulders as he nipped and sucked on my breasts. Each thrust was like heaven, giving me an immense pleasure that I'd never experienced before.

Wrapping my legs around his hips, I pulled Ryker deeper within in me, causing him to emit a sound that was a cross between a growl and a groan. "God, Kaiya. I've wanted you so badly, wanted to feel your sweet pussy clench my dick."

I moaned in response to his words, unable to think straight, let alone say anything comprehensible. He continued to relentlessly pound into me, bringing me closer and closer to ecstasy with each exquisite thrust.

Perfectly caressing my walls, his cock sent me into orgasmic oblivion. Tremors of bliss flowed through my body as Ryker extended my climax with his perfect strokes. Seconds later, he pulled out before streaming his warm release all over my breasts and stomach. The feel of his cum on my body added to my arousal, making me want him inside me again, filling me over and over.

As we both regained our breath, Ryker grabbed his sweaty shirt off the mat before wiping his cum off my fevered skin. Immediately I became anxious as realization of what we'd just done sank in. *Oh my God, I just broke all of my rules. We didn't use a condom. I'm on the shot, but still. How could I lose control like that?* "I have to go," I stammered as I abruptly stood, grabbing my clothes off the floor.

I awkwardly dressed as I continued to rush towards the door. *Shit, shit, shit. Wait until you get in the car to break down—don't let Ryker see you. Breathe, breathe, breathe.*

"Kaiya, wait. Where are you going?" Ryker called after me as I flew out the door of the kickboxing room.

Please don't follow me. I all but ran towards the main entrance but was stopped by the locked doors. *Fuck!* I pushed against them, even though I knew Ryker had locked them when everyone left. We were the only ones still there.

Tears began to drip down my face as I realized I had to face Ryker. *He's never going to want to see me again. Why do I have to be such a freak?*

Pressing my forehead against the cool glass of the door, I exhaled a shaky breath as I willed back the tears. *In, out, in, out. Breathe, breathe, breathe. Just tell him the truth.* Tell him the truth? What the fuck was I thinking?

Ryker interrupted my thoughts as he placed a hand on my shoulder. His soft voice surprised me as he asked, "What's going on, Warrior?"

Swallowing the huge lump in my throat, I apologized, "I'm sorry, Ryker. I can't do this. We shouldn't ha—"

Interrupting me, his harsh voice was a stark contrast to the gentle one from a moment before. "Hey, don't worry about it. I got what I wanted. I told you I'd have you once, remember?"

My head snapped from the glass toward him, not believing what had just come out of his mouth. My jaw gaped open, my brain unable to form the words needed to express the emotions roiling within me. "You fucking bastard," I finally seethed as I slapped him. Hard.

Ryker's eyes thinned to tiny slits as his nostrils flared in anger. Silently unlocking the door, his muscles tensed, making his tattoos bulge as he held the door open.

Neither of us said anything else as I exited the gym, and I couldn't help but feel as if I left another broken piece of myself at his feet when I walked out that door.

Chapter Twelve

Ryker

What the fuck just happened? I stood staring at the doors to the gym, wondering what the fuck went wrong. Things went to shit in less than two seconds. I couldn't believe what she'd said after we just finished having sex, especially when it ranked up at the top of my list. I thought she was blowing me off until I saw her face.

Those watery eyes and tear-stained cheeks made me regret what I'd said. Every. Fucking. Word. It was all bullshit anyway. *Why did I have to be so fucking stubborn?*

I didn't understand what caused the pain in her eyes, but I knew what I'd said made it worse. I wanted to apologize, to take back the lies I defensively spewed out; anything to remove the hurt on her face. But, I couldn't, my words stuck in my throat for fear of her rejection.

Then, my warrior broke through. Anger replaced the sadness and mixed with the pain that always seemed to linger on her face. Her eyes hardened, and her lips thinned as she slapped me.

Yeah, deep down, my girl's a fighter.

I wanted to find out everything that made Kaiya who she was, to peel back every intricate layer and uncover what lay beneath her guarded exterior.

I knew her standoffish demeanor was a front that she put up to protect herself. What I wanted to know was from what. Obviously, someone had hurt her—I recognized that type of pain; the kind that embeds in your soul, and never goes away. I endured that scarring pain every fucking day.

I wanted to erase some of hers, even if it was only a sliver. I would take what she'd give me, if that was anything at all after what had just happened. *Damn, I fucked up.*

I couldn't help what I had said, especially when her words reopened old scars. "I can't do this."

That phrase had changed everything, altering my whole life when it was said to me four years ago.

"Ry, we need to talk."

"About what, babe?"

She exhaled a heavy sigh. "I don't know how to say this…" she trailed off as a sob broke through.

"What's wrong? Is it the baby?" I asked with concern as I took her hand in mine.

Jerking her hand away, she stood and clenched her fists. "I can't do this anymore!"

Confused and worried, I questioned, "Baby, calm down. What are you talking about?"

"This! Us! I can't stand the lies anymore!" She threw her hands out to the side.

"Lies? What lies? I've never lied to you before." I had no clue what she was referring to.

"The baby's not yours!" she blurted.

The air caught in my lungs, my heart stuttering in my chest from her words. "What?" I whispered as tears began to burn my eyes.

Her own tears trickled down her face as she coldly repeated, "The baby's not yours."

And to twist the knife she had plunged in my heart, she added, "Ethan's the father."

Fuck her. And him. The both of them could rot in hell. It was because of them that I was the way I am—hollow and numb, just going through the motions of everyday life without giving a fuck about anyone else. I never thought that I'd let another person in, but Kaiya was different. She made me want to feel again, to experience life again, kindling a long dead fire inside me. Now, I'd gone and fucked it all up.

I thought that having her once would be enough to satisfy my desire for her, just as it had with all the others. But, it didn't; if anything, it had made me want her more. Her sweet sex had become my drug, addicting me the moment I sank my dick inside her.

I watched her angrily storm off to her car before she got in and sped out of the parking lot. Locking the door, I tried to stash away my thoughts of her, unable to process anything with the smell of her still on my skin.

I was off the next day, so hopefully I'd be able to make sense of all the mess after I slept, but I had a feeling that I wouldn't be getting much sleep tonight.

As I had expected, I slept like shit. Tossing and turning all night, I was unable to get Kaiya off my mind. Memories of her moaning my name, digging her nails into my skin, and feeling her soft flesh against mine as her pussy clenched my cock taunted me as I tried to sleep.

Even though it was my day off, I was still going to the gym. I needed to release the pent up frustration from last night. I knew Kaiya wouldn't be there—she never worked out on Fridays, so I wouldn't have a chance to apologize to her. I'd tried calling and texting her, but she didn't answer any of my attempts. I was hoping to run into her at the club later where we had first kissed—she and Nori went there most Fridays. But I wasn't sure if she'd go after what had happened last night.

I was wound up even after working out, the stress of last night still weighing me down. *Why did I have to say those things to her? She'll probably never want to see me again.*

I sent a text to Drew to see if he wanted to go with me to the club:

Me: Club tonight?

After a few minutes, he responded back:

Drew: I'm down what time

Me: Your place 11

Drew: Cool

When I got to Drew's apartment, he opened the door and offered me a beer. "What's been going on with you? Still talking to Kaiya?"

I took a long swig of my beer and let it slowly roll down my throat before saying anything. "I kind of fucked it all up last night. She won't return my calls or anything." I sat down on the couch. "I'm hoping to see her tonight."

Drew popped the top on his own bottle as he leaned against the counter in the kitchen. "You really like her, huh?"

Taking another drink of my beer, I swallowed deeply. "Yeah—she's not like all the girls we run game on all the time."

"You think she'll be at the club tonight?" Drew asked as he came and sat on the end of the couch.

"I don't know. Kaiya says she and Nori go there almost every Friday, but I don't know if she'd want to go out after last night—she was pretty upset."

"Even if she doesn't, we can still get drunk and hook up with some hotties, right?" Drew said as he punched my bicep.

"Yeah," I replied halfheartedly before taking another long pull of my beer. I didn't feel like hooking up with anyone else; I just wanted Kaiya. *Don't be such a pussy. She can be replaced.*

I almost laughed at myself. I'd never find anyone else quite like Kaiya. She wasn't like the sluts that threw themselves at me all the time—there was more to her than that, something deeper that she didn't let anyone see.

After finishing off a six pack of beer, we left Drew's in separate cars. We arrived at the club a little after midnight. The club was so crowded that you couldn't turn around without brushing up against someone. Music blared as we waited at the bar to order drinks, and I searched the room for Kaiya. Within seconds, my eyes zeroed in on her. My jaw twitched and my fists clenched—she was completely wasted, dancing all over some guy in the middle of the dance floor.

My blood boiled as I angrily stalked through the crowd, making my way to where she was grinding herself against him.

Lightly grabbing her arm, I pulled her to me as I glared at the asshole dancing with her. "Fuck off," I seethed, holding back from knocking him out right there on the dance floor.

I turned my attention to Kaiya, who was swaying in her heels. I cupped her chin and forced her to look at me. "What do you think you are doing?" I growled.

Her glazed eyes narrowed as she angrily slurred, "Why the fuck do you care? You got what you wanted already, remember?" She weakly shoved my chest.

Fuck. I knew she wouldn't let what happened go so easily, but I didn't think it would have affected her that much.

My grip on her eased as I softened my tone. "Kaiya, I—"

She pulled out of my grasp, basically falling into the dickhead's arms. "Leave me alone, Ryker."

The bastard smugly grinned at me as he wrapped his arms around Kaiya, resting his hands on her ass. I balled my fists as I took a deep breath so that I didn't end up strangling the guy. I kept trying to tell myself that she wasn't mine, that I had no claim on her, but everything in me screamed that she was.

Fuck this shit, I'm leaving. I pushed through the crowd towards the exit, getting cussed at as I forced people out of the way.

When I reached my truck, I hesitated as I was about to get in. *Don't let that asshole punk you out and take your fucking girl from you. Go back in there and get her.*

My eyes scanned the room when I went back in. Kaiya and the tool she was with were in the same spot on the dance floor. As I wound through the mass of bodies, the guy leaned over to whisper something in her ear, then led her towards the back of the club.

Increasing my pace, I followed after them, shoving people that got in my way. *Fuck this shit.* I'd drag her over my shoulder if I had to; I wasn't going to let her do something I knew she'd regret.

As I reached the door, I stopped. *What are you doing? You're acting like some stalker. If she wants to hook up with some guy in the back alley of a club, then let her—she's not your problem.*

I tried to turn around, to walk away, but I couldn't. She meant more to me than that. I'd only wanted a one time fuck, but she changed things, made me want something more.

I pounded my fist against the door and cursed, "Fuck!"

As I warred with my thoughts, dull voices from outside interrupted my internal debate.

"Come on, baby, you know you want it," the jackass urged.

Really, guy?

"No. Stop, please," Kaiya pleaded, the desperation in her voice snapping something within me. Sounds of a struggle followed, and both fear and rage consumed me at the thought of someone hurting her, constricting the air in my lungs as my heart beat increased. I shoved open the door, sending it to slam against the wall as I stepped into the alley. Darting my head from side to side, I searched for Kaiya in the dim lighting behind the club, but I couldn't find her. *Where are you, baby?*

I heard shuffling to my left, along with the guy's voice again. "You've been all over me all night—I know you want it."

Following their voices, I rushed in the direction that Kaiya was speaking now. "Get off me!" she shrieked before I heard a slap.

I could see them in the distance now, on the other side of a dumpster. *Real classy, asshole.*

"Oh, you like it rough, huh? I'll give it to you rough, then."

I was about thirty feet away when he slapped her back, which sent me into a rage-filled run. *I'm going to kill that motherfucker!* Kaiya began to scream as he covered her mouth with one hand, pushing her back against the wall while using the other to grope all over her body. *I'm almost there, baby.*

Then, my warrior bit him. *Good girl.* He pulled away instinctively before rearing back again to hit her, but it was too late—I was already there.

Tackling him to the ground, I immediately began punching him, bashing his head into the asphalt with my fists. He tried to fight back, but with the combination of my training and his drunkenness, he was no match for me. Fury took hold, overpowering any other emotion as I continued to beat him until I couldn't recognize his face beneath the blood and bruising.

Then, I remembered Kaiya. Standing up, I turned to face her—she was huddled against the wall, arms tightly around herself, crying. As our eyes locked, we both began to move towards each other until I wrapped her in my arms.

Burying her face in my chest, her sobbing intensified. I held her tighter, pressing kisses to the top of her head. She clutched the back of my shirt in her hands as her body shook against mine.

"Shh, it's okay, now—I've got you, baby," I whispered into her hair.

"I'm sorry," she apologized through her sobs, the sound muffled against my chest.

"You have nothing to be sorry for—I'm the one who should be sorry. I shouldn't have said what I said last night, shouldn't have hurt you like that. I fucked up."

Looking up at me, she propped her chin on my chest as tears continued to stream down her face. Even with her smeared make-up and blotchy skin, she was the most beautiful woman I'd ever seen.

"Thank you for saving me."

I brought my hands to her face, stroking the tears off her cheeks with my thumbs as I looked into her eyes. "I'll always save you, Warrior. You just have to let me."

Her bottom lip trembled as she nodded. Her hands came up to cover mine as my mouth came down on hers. Unlike our other kisses, this one was gentle, but not less passionate—electricity surged through me as my heart rate up kicked up, just like it did every time.

When we separated, I placed my forehead against hers. "Ready to go?"

She pulled back, looking up at me with reddened eyes. "Yeah, I have to find Nori—she drove." Her voice was hoarse and knotted with emotion.

"I can give you a ride home."

She briefly hesitated, unsure as always. Reaching toward her, I waited for her to put her hand in mine. She threaded our fingers together while giving me a small smile as we started to walk towards the end of the alley.

Once we got in my truck, I could tell she was still shaken up. She trembled as tears rimmed her eyes, and a few escaped every so often to fall down her cheeks.

After starting the truck, I placed my hand over hers, hoping I could calm her some. "Hey, it's okay, it's over. Please don't cry anymore."

She squeezed my hand tightly. "You don't understand. I... I just..." she hesitated, cutting off her words.

"What, baby?"

Her eyes closed as she took a deep breath. "This just brought back so many bad memories."

Bad memories? "This has happened to you before?" I asked angrily.

"Not exactly," she sighed before pausing. Her eyes opened and met mine as I waited for her to continue. "I... I—" a sob broke through, cutting off her words as she shook her head.

"Kaiya, baby, tell me." I urged.

Our gazes locked, her eyes searching mine as tears streaked her cheeks. Stroking the back of her hand with my thumb, I said, "You can trust me, Warrior."

She continued to hold my gaze before speaking, her voice cracking, "I... I... I was abused when I was little."

"What? For how long?" I asked, my anger building back from her words.

Tears were raining down her face as she choked through her sobs, "As long as I can remember. He... he wouldn't stop. No matter how hard I tried... he always touched me. It didn't end until... until I was seventeen."

My body was on fire with rage, even more so than minutes ago when I saw that asshole hit her. Someone had hurt my warrior for years, making her live in fear.

"Who?" I gritted through clenched teeth.

Her skin paled, making the slap mark on her face stand out even more. I softly caressed the area on her cheek as her eyes closed and she exhaled a heavy breath.

"I can't," she whispered as she shook her head.

Even though I wanted to, I didn't question her further. She'd already opened up to me more than she ever had before, and she'd been through enough for the night. "You don't have to tell me now— whenever you're ready, I'll be here."

"Thank you," she murmured softly as she gazed down at our joined hands. "Oh my God! Your hands!"

Grabbing both of my hands gently, she inspected them before looking up at me sadly. Most of my knuckles had split open, and blood splattered the skin.

"It doesn't hurt, not yet anyway. This is a perfect example of why you should never punch anyone in the face. I just couldn't control myself."

She softly smiled as she pressed her lips to my fingers, careful to avoid my injuries.

How could anyone want to hurt someone so perfect?

Once she finished, she leaned over the center console to lay her head on my shoulder, keeping one of my hands linked with hers.

"I need your address for the GPS."

"19 Pleasant Street."

By the time we got to her apartment, Kaiya had fallen asleep. Carefully reaching to lift her in my lap, I cradled her in my arms as I stepped out of the truck. *Shit, I don't know her apartment number.* "What's your apartment number, baby?" I asked softly.

Stirring slightly, she mumbled, "Sixteen."

Once we made it to her door, I pushed the button for the doorbell. After several seconds, the door opened to a surprised Kamden. When he focused on Kaiya in my arms, his expression morphed from shock to anger as he reached for her. "What the fuck did you do to her?"

Stepping back, bringing her closer into my body, I said, "I didn't do anything. We need to talk."

He must have seen something in my face because he moved from the doorway to let me in.

"Where's her room?"

"I'm not letting you in her room," he stated gruffly.

"Then, I guess I'm holding her until we finish talking," I retorted as I looked down at her, sleeping peacefully. She was like an angel, and I couldn't believe someone had hurt her for so long.

When my eyes went back up to meet Kamden's, his anger seemed to have receded some. His jaw was no longer tense and his eyes softened as he gazed at Kaiya.

"Her room's this way," he sighed.

I followed him down the hallway to the door at the end. After we walked in, Kamden pulled back the comforter so I could lay Kaiya down. As I covered her, I pressed a kiss to her temple and brushed the hair back from her face. "Goodnight, Warrior."

She drowsily smiled as I pulled away. I shut the door before following Kamden back out into the living room.

"Care to explain what happened?" he asked, his eyes glaring as he crossed his arms over his chest.

"Some guy got too handsy at the club tonight. I took care of him."

He sighed in relief. "Thank you." He fell back onto the couch and covered his face with his hands. "I don't know what I would've done if something happened to her."

"Sounds like a lot has happened to her already." I stood in front of him and folded my arms over my chest. "Care to explain that?"

His gaze snapped up to mine as his body tensed. "You don't know what you're talking about!" he spat.

My fists clenched. "Was it you? Were you the one that abused her when she was little?" If he was, I was going to kill him.

He sucked in a breath, eyes wide with disbelief before furiously responding, "No! I would never do that to her!"

"Who was it, then?" I gritted.

"It's not my place to tell you—Kaiya will tell you when she's ready," he replied firmly.

We both silently stared at one another for I don't know how long before Kamden finally spoke, "Thank you again for protecting her."

I nodded, then headed for the front door, but stopped. Turning back around to face him, I asked, "Will you have her call me? I want to make sure she's okay."

He hesitated, shaking his head. "Look, you seem to have feelings for Kaiya, but I don't think you two should see each other anymore."

I squared my body, pushing my chest out. "Last I checked, Kaiya is a grown woman, and you aren't her father. She can make her own decisions."

He stood up with authority and stared me down with a death glare. "And last I checked, you're a womanizing asshole. I don't want my sister getting involved with you."

"Too late." I shrugged. "I'm going to see her, whether you fucking like it or not."

"Oh, really? We'll see about that." There was an obvious challenge in his tone.

"Yeah, we will," I responded. I turned and walked out the door, slamming it behind me. I was going to see Kaiya, and there was nothing Kamden or anyone could do to fucking stop me.

Chapter Thirteen

Kaiya

Noise from the kitchen woke me, and I winced from the throbbing pain in my cheek and head. *Why did I drink so much? I can't believe how stupid I was.*

As I slowly sat up in my bed, I thought about how Ryker not only came to my rescue, but listened to me when I needed someone—he actually seemed like he cared, despite what he had said to me the night before. *What changed?*

I dreaded facing Kamden—Ryker had to have brought me home, and I wondered what happened after that. *Did Kamden question Ryker? Did they talk about what happened at the club?*

Slowly, I trudged to the kitchen, where Kamden was making breakfast.

"Hey." I plopped down at the breakfast bar, preparing for the inevitable.

As Kamden turned to face me, his eyes focused on my cheek, then immediately set in anger as he stalked over to me.

"Did Ryker do this?" he growled as he gently grabbed my chin, tilting it to look at my face better.

"No!" I snapped, pulling back from him. "Ryker saved me from the guy that did—he stopped him." I looked away and wrapped my arms around myself.

Kamden placed his arms on my shoulders, looking at me with concern. "Tell me what happened."

Tears stung my eyes as I remembered last night. *Thank God Ryker was there to save me. I don't know what would've happened if he hadn't come after me.*

"I acted stupid—I got drunk and was all over this guy." My voice was barely above a whisper as shame and embarrassment got the better of me. "He wanted to take things further, and I didn't want to. He didn't like that, and got physical."

When I looked up, Kamden's nostrils flared in anger as he took a deep breath and gripped the side of the counter. "And?"

"Ryker intervened—he beat the crap out of the guy and brought me home."

"You told him about Kaleb?" He sounded irritated and confused as his eyes searched my face.

My muscles tensed slightly at the accusation. "Not everything. I just told him that I was abused when I was little. Not who."

"He thought it was me—I thought he was going to kick my ass." His stern expression and tone told me he was serious.

"What?" I laughed nervously.

"Seriously—he asked if it was me. He was pissed."

"Really?" *I can't believe he cared.*

"Yeah. I told him to stay away from you." Kamden crossed his arms.

"What?" I exclaimed angrily as I stood. "Why did you tell him that?"

"He's not good for you, Ky. He—" He relaxed his stance as he moved towards me again, but I held my hand up to stop him.

"That's not your decision, Kamden!" My voice rose as I narrowed my eyes at him. "It's my choice whether I want to see him or not!"

Kamden paused, giving me a perplexed look as a grin attempted to curve his lips. "You really like him, don't you?"

Did I? "I don't know… he makes me feel different." I sighed as I locked eyes with him. "Alive… like I'm not just a hollow shell anymore."

"Well, he didn't sound like he was going to listen to me, anyway.

He wants you to call him." He smiled knowingly at me.

My lips tipped up, but almost immediately fell. "I can't believe he wants to talk to me after last night. I was all over that guy right in front of him, and I yelled at him in front of all the people in the club." I blew out a breath of frustration as I buried my face in my hands and groaned.

"I don't like the guy, but he obviously has feelings for you. He wouldn't have wasted his time otherwise. Ryker has no problem getting women."

That was an understatement. Ryker had told me that he had lost count of how many women he'd been with, and never slept with the same one twice. *I wonder if he'll be the same with me.* After Thursday night, I would've said yes, but given the events of last night, I wasn't so sure anymore.

"I know. I'm going to get some ice for my cheek and call him."

After grabbing a bag of frozen vegetables, I went back to my room and dug my phone from my purse. *Fuck, it's dead.* Plugging it in to the charger, I powered it up before dialing Ryker's number.

"Hey, Warrior."

A warm tingle spread through me at his words, causing a smile to spread over my face—I loved when he called me that. "Hey." I lay back on my bed, keeping the phone to the opposite side of where I was holding my makeshift icepack to my cheek.

"How you feeling?" His tone sounded genuine, like he actually wanted to know.

"Fine. My cheek and head hurt, but I'm okay. How are your knuckles?"

Ryker's laughter sounded into the phone. "You're the one who got attacked last night, and you're worried about me. They're fine, baby."

"Good." I paused for a few seconds, nibbling my bottom lip. "I'm really sorry about last night."

"Me too, for everything." He sighed into the phone. "Let's just forget about it and move on. Can I see you today?"

Some tension eased in my chest—he still wanted to talk to me after how I acted. "What did you have in mind?"

"Lunch? I don't have to go into the gym until two today. I can pick you up or meet you somewhere."

"You can pick me up. In an hour?" A goofy smile spread across my face as I stifled a girly squeal.

"I'll see you then. Bye, Warrior."

"Bye."

After I hung up, I rushed to shower and get ready in time before Ryker got there. We had a lot to discuss, especially the things he'd said to me after we had sex Thursday night—I hadn't forgotten them. Their harshness still stung me, and they were such a contrast to his actions last night that I was left totally confused.

I dressed in a deep purple sundress, then applied some foundation to the bruise on my cheek, but it didn't help much. The purple of the welt almost matched the color of my dress and looked terrible against my pale skin.

Ryker texted me when he was downstairs, and I peeked my head into Kamden's room to tell him about my plans.

"I'm going to lunch with Ryker. I'll be back later."

Kamden gave me a disapproving look as he cautioned, "Be careful."

I rolled my eyes. "I will."

Ryker was waiting for me at the bottom of the stairs. He looked amazing, as always, in a tight blue V-neck shirt that emphasized his muscles. He gave me his sexy grin until I got closer, then his eyes focused on my cheek. His eyebrows creased in anger as his smile morphed to a scowl. "That fucking bastard," he mumbled below his breath.

When I reached him, he pulled me into his chest, cradling my face as he examined the bruise like Kamden had earlier.

"I'm fine." I pulled away, uncomfortable with him looking at me so closely, afraid he would see what lay underneath if he looked too long.

"Ready to go?" Ryker asked as he joined our hands.

Giving him a small smile, I nodded. He led me to the passenger side of his truck, opening the door and helping me get in the raised cab.

"Where do you want to go?" Ryker asked when he got in.

"Hmm. What about Cafe Luna?" I suggested.

Cafe Luna was a quaint brunch spot that Nori and I went to occasionally. They had delicious paninis and breakfast, including a spicy chicken chorizo and black bean omelet.

"Wherever you want, baby," Ryker said as he started the truck.

It only took us about ten minutes to reach the restaurant. Ryker once again threaded our fingers together after helping me get down from his truck. *I really like this side of him.* A smile took over my lips as I glanced at him, but I quickly darted my gaze away when he caught me looking at him out of the corner of his eye. *What are you, like twelve? Quit being such a girl.*

We were seated in a booth right next to a huge window overlooking the street. People hurried past us on their cell phones, some talking on them as others stared at the screen while trying not to run into anything.

The waitress came up to our booth and took our drink order. After she brought our drinks and jotted down what we wanted to eat, I impulsively asked Ryker, "Did you mean what you said the other night?" I couldn't keep the question inside any longer—it had been nagging at me the whole drive.

The muscles in his jaw tensed as he swallowed. "No."

"Then, why did you say those things to me?"

He didn't say anything for several seconds, and I was afraid he was going to get up and leave me there, not wanting to deal with my bullshit anymore.

"Fear." He reached for his glass of water before taking a long drink.

Fear? What was he afraid of? "Fear?" I repeated, wanting him to clarify.

He gave a quick nod as he set down the glass. "I thought you were blowing me off."

"So, you decided to blow me off first?" I raised my eyebrow and rested my arms on the table.

"Look." He sighed. "I know I made a mistake, and I'm sorry I hurt you. I… I have issues." He leaned in, grabbing my hands and locking eyes with me. "I've been fucked over in the past, and it's hard for me to trust someone after what I went through." He sat back and shrugged his shoulders. "We all have our own demons."

"Yeah, but some demons are worse than others." I stared at my glass, tracing a finger along the rim.

"That doesn't make them any less easy to deal with for the person that has to live with them."

He had a point. Just because I felt my demons were worse, didn't mean that Ryker's weren't hard for him. I didn't even know what his were to be able to judge. I wouldn't feel right asking him to tell me since I kept so much from him all of the time.

I nodded in understanding. "So, where do we go from here?"

"I'm not sure." He released a heavy breath. "All I know is that I want to keep seeing you. That is, if you still want to."

"I want to, but I'm scared." I gnawed on my lip as I looked over his face. "What if you hurt me?"

Abruptly, he stood before coming to my side of the booth and scooting in next to me. He draped an arm around my shoulder, pulling me into him. He used his other hand to tilt my chin to look in his eyes.

"Honestly, Warrior, I'm scared, too. I haven't felt this way about someone since… well, a really long time. I promise I won't hurt you if you don't hurt me."

My heart fluttered. I wasn't completely sure I could trust him, but I was willing to take the chance. Life wasn't meant to be lived in fear, and I felt that moving forward with Ryker was taking another step to becoming stronger, to becoming whole.

Instead of answering him with words, I brought my lips to his, hoping that was enough of an answer for him. I wasn't good at expressing my feelings, but I hoped that the kiss demonstrated how I felt, showed that I was trusting him not to crush what was left of me.

When we finally parted, he said, "So, was that a yes?"

I laughed. "On one condition—no other girls."

Making a skeptical face, he teased, "I don't know if I can do that."

"Then, I guess I'm leaving," I joked, pushing him away from me.

Wrapping me in his arms, he chuckled. "I was just kidding." He brushed his lips over mine. "No other girls."

I pulled back and gave him a deal breaking glare. "Promise," I demanded.

Cupping my face, he held my gaze. "I promise—no other girls."

"You better not hurt me or I'll be forced to use my fighting skills on you." I lightly jabbed him in the stomach as I giggled.

"No, please don't," he playfully pleaded, acting fearful of my non-existent threat. We both laughed before he brought his lips to mine again, sending warmth through my entire body before it pooled between my thighs. My stomach tightened as his tongue entered my mouth, joining with mine to deepen the kiss. *Damn, he kisses so good.*

Throat-clearing caused us to break away from each other, but not before Ryker pressed one last soft kiss on my lips. We both directed our attention to the waitress, who held a tray in her hands.

"I'm sorry to interrupt, but your food is ready," she said politely.

Blushing with embarrassment, I avoided her eyes as she set our food on the table. When she left, I looked at Ryker, who chuckled at me and shook his head.

Once we finished eating, Ryker drove me back home. He made plans to take me to dinner once he got off work, and I couldn't fight the foreign feeling of happiness that overtook me. *Maybe Ryker is good for me.*

When I entered the apartment, Kamden came out of his room and asked me a million questions about Ryker and our date. Okay, maybe not a million, but way more than necessary.

After his interrogation, I tried to escape to my room, but he stopped me as I was walking down the hallway.

"Do you remember about Monday?"

"Monday?" I said quizzically. *What's Monday?* After a few seconds of contemplation, it hit me. *Our appointment. Kaleb. Fuck. Shit. Fuck.* "Fuck. I can't believe it's already here," I groaned.

"You okay?" Kamden asked with concern, rubbing his hand up and down my arm.

My stomach tightened uncomfortably. "Yeah, just nervous. I better call Nori and remind her."

"Let me know if you need anything—I know this is going to be tough for you."

"Thanks, I will," I replied before turning and heading into my room. Taking my phone out of my purse, I dialed Nori. She answered after the second ring. "What the fuck happened last night, Ky? You didn't return any of my fucking calls or texts. I was worried sick."

Shit. I forgot that I just left without a word—she sounded pissed. I sat on my bed as I apologized, "I'm sorry. My phone died, and it just slipped my mind this morning."

"Well, what happened? Is everything okay?" Her voice lost some of the venom that had been in it.

I explained everything that happened at the club last night, but I started with Ryker and I having sex on Thursday. I hadn't told her about it because I was so upset, but she needed to know everything to understand the events of last night. Nori didn't say anything for several seconds, then finally spoke, "So, how was it? I bet he was amazing."

That was an understatement. He was beyond amazing. "It was… unbelievable." I sighed dreamily as I flopped back on the bed. "He made me feel things I've never felt before, and gave me the best orgasm of my life. There just aren't words."

Nori giggled. "Wow, that's awesome, Ky. I'm really happy for you."

"Can you believe what he said to me after, though?" Thinking about it still hurt, and it was hard to push the thoughts away when they were so fresh.

"He's a guy. They aren't good with rejection. He thought you were blowing him off after literally just having sex with him—total ego killer. Obviously, he didn't mean what he said or else he wouldn't have gone to the club looking for you, and he definitely wouldn't have saved you from that asshole. Actions speak louder than words, girl."

I picked at the ends of my hair as I released a sigh. "True. Words still hurt though."

"I can't believe you told him about Kaleb." Her voice was filled with disbelief.

"Me neither. I mean, I didn't tell him everything."

"Why did you tell him?"

That had surprised even me—I hadn't told anyone anything involving Kaleb except Kamden and Nori.

"When he saved me, I felt like I at least owed him some of the truth for my actions. And, even after what he said to me, I trusted him. Like you said, actions speak louder than words."

"Yeah, he seems like a great guy that just has some issues. If anyone should be able to understand that, it should be you."

I snorted. "Yeah, I'm sure his issues are nowhere even close to being as fucked up as mine."

"You never know, Ky. Maybe you should ask him about them."

"I don't like being asked about mine. He'll tell me when he's ready."

"Just like you will?" she countered.

Will I? "I don't know if I'll ever tell him—I don't want him to look at me differently."

"If he cares about you, he won't. Then, you'll know whether he's worth it or not."

"I'm not ready for that yet." I blew out a deep breath. "I don't think either one of us are. We just agreed to start dating. Baby steps, Nori, baby steps."

"You've made a lot of progress. I'm really proud of you, Ky. Seriously."

I smiled from her words. "Thank you. It's hard, but I'm trying. Oh, I almost forgot! Monday is our appointment at the hospital."

"I know. I thought that's why you were acting all crazy yesterday."

"Oh. No, I totally forgot. Kamden just reminded me." My smile began to fade as I thought about the appointment, my chest tightening in anxiety. I rubbed my hand over it, trying to ease some of the tenseness.

"I'm planning to come over to your apartment that morning and we can all ride together."

We talked a little more about Monday before we hung up. Heading to the bathroom, I searched for some aspirin since my cheek and head were still pulsing with pain.

I didn't realize how exhausted I was until I lay back down on my bed. Sleep found me within seconds.

I was extremely wound up at class on Sunday because of my impending visit to the hospital the next day. I was so not prepared to be in the same building as Kaleb. It also didn't help that I was unsure of how to act around Ryker in front of the other students and instructors. It was probably against policy or something for him to be with me, so I didn't want to get him into any trouble.

Ryker approached me as I was hitting my bag. "Everything okay?" he asked as he eyed me warily. *How could he always tell when something was bothering me?*

"Yeah, just a little stressed." *A lot stressed, actually.*

"Anything I can help with?"

"No—I'll be okay. Hitting the bag helps." I forced a smile.

Those warm eyes told me he knew better, but he didn't question me further. "Just don't overdo it, Warrior," he said as his lips curved up slightly.

After class ended, I waited for Ryker to close up before we left together. He walked me to my car, then crushed his lips against mine, stealing my breath as he passionately kissed me. *Holy crap.*

Pulling back slightly, we both gasped for air.

"I've been wanting to do that all night, that and so much more," he said, holding my face in his hands.

Our mouths reconnected in a frenzy as Ryker's hands roamed over my body. He hooked my legs around him, pushing me against the car as his erection pressed into my core. I might have moaned, I wasn't really sure since I couldn't process anything but the feel of Ryker all over me.

"Come home with me," he murmured against my lips.

Oh, how I wanted to—so badly. It probably wasn't the best idea given what I had to do tomorrow, but then again, it might be good for me to lose myself in Ryker before I had to deal with Kaleb.

"Okay."

Even though I answered him, Ryker didn't release me. He kept relentlessly devouring me right there in the parking lot. I couldn't have even told anyone my name once we finally stopped—that was how amazing that man kissed.

"My warrior finally gave in," he teased when we finally stopped. "You can follow me there."

As I drove behind him, I started to reconsider what I was doing. *I'm going to have to explain my rules do I really want to go into that right now? What if he laughs in my face? Shit, why did I agree to this? Maybe I should just turn around and go home... no, I can't do that to him. I'll just have to tell him something came up and leave—that'll work.*

Once we were up in his apartment, I tried to give Ryker the excuse I came up with, but his mouth silenced mine, capturing my lips as soon as he locked the door. *Shit I can't lie to him—I'm just going to have to tell him the truth.*

Pushing him away, I disconnected our lips and locked our eyes. "We need to talk."

Chapter Fourteen

Ryker

"We need to talk."

No man wanted to hear those words, especially when first starting out, but Kaiya was standing right in front of me saying them. The last time I'd heard those words, things didn't end well for me.

"About?" I questioned as I searched her face. I rubbed my hand on the back of my neck anxiously. I had no idea what Kaiya was going to tell me—with her, it could be anything.

Sighing, she led me to the couch, and we sat down. "Before we have sex again, you need to know my rules," she advised me matter of factly.

Some tension lifted off me. I expected worse. *Rules? This is going to be interesting.* "Go on."

She exhaled a heavy breath. "One, I don't do foreplay—strictly sex."

Raising an eyebrow, I caught her gaze. "No foreplay?" *We'll see about that.*

"No foreplay. Two, my throat is off limits. I don't like having it touched."

Her hand had gone instinctively to her throat, covering her small scar. She still refused to tell me what had happened. I wondered if it had anything to do with the scar I'd seen across Kamden's chest when he worked out.

"Three, I have to control when I... when I go." she stammered nervously.

"Go? Go where?" I teased, trying to lighten the mood and pry out the words she was having such a hard time saying.

"You know what I mean, Ryker." She blushed as she avoided looking at me, staring down at her hands in her lap. She was so innocently sexy when she was embarrassed.

I sat back and shrugged, playing dumb. "No, I don't. You're going to have to elaborate."

Sighing with exasperation, she flung her hands out. "Come, okay? I have to control when I come."

Interesting. "You didn't seem to have a problem with that before." I smirked.

She glared at me and pressed her lips in a tight line. "Well, I have a problem now. If you can't accept my rules, then maybe we shouldn't do this."

Raising my hands in surrender, I apologized, "I'm sorry. Any more rules?"

"Just one more—I don't spend the night."

Leaning forward, I propped my elbows on my knees and rubbed my hands together. "Okay—anything else?"

"No. Are you okay with them—with this?" she asked as she gestured between us.

I considered her question, thinking about her rules. I knew all these stipulations for sex had to do with her abuse when she was younger. On one hand, I didn't want to push her away by disregarding her rules, but on the other, rules were made to be broken. And I wanted to break hers.

"For now." I grinned mischievously. We silently stared at each other for a few seconds. "But one day, I will break each of those rules—one... by... one. And you're going to love every second of it when I do."

"I wouldn't be so sure about that," she weakly challenged as she broke away from my gaze.

Suddenly pulling her into my lap, I grasped her hips, pushing her down against my cock. She gasped as I grazed my lips against hers. I gruffly murmured, "I'm going to let you have your way now, Warrior. But trust me when I say that those rules will be broken—soon. I guarantee it."

I claimed her lips with mine, smothering any response or argument. The only sounds I wanted to hear were the moans and whimpers she was already making as my tongue entered her mouth and twined with hers. I'd been waiting all night to feel her, to taste her, to just lose myself in her—class had been torture since I couldn't touch and kiss her like I wanted to, and I was going to make up for it the rest of the night.

My hands rubbed along the curves of her ass before I gripped it and rose from the couch. Carrying Kaiya to my bedroom, I kicked open the door and walked to the bed, laying her down. I reluctantly separated our lips, tugging my shirt over my head before doing the same with hers, eager to feel her bare skin against mine.

Once the rest of our clothing was removed, my mouth easily found hers as I pressed against her on the bed, covering her flesh with mine. My hands ran up and down the curves of her naked body, enjoying the feel of her silken skin as I savored her sweetness.

I rubbed my dick against her pussy, causing her to writhe under me. "You're so wet for me already," I growled against her lips while I rocked against her.

She whimpered as I bit her bottom lip before sucking it into my mouth. Nudging against her entrance, I barely pushed the tip of my cock inside her before dragging it out again. Kaiya's moans became deeper and louder as I teased her, gripping her hips and readying to thrust inside her.

Slowly, I sank myself into her, enjoying the feel of how she stretched to accommodate me. Her body arched into me as I spread her thighs, pushing myself deeper into her warmth.

Once Kaiya was completely full of me, I pulled out before pounding back in again, causing her to cry out as she dug her nails into my forearms. Pumping in and out of her pussy, I increased my strokes, building up the pleasure within both of us.

Kaiya wrapped her legs around my waist before squirming under me, attempting to turn us over. As I told her I would, I let her flip me and have control. *This time.* I wasn't going to complain about having a hot woman riding me.

Her hair curtained around my face as she rocked against my cock, caressing it with her soft flesh. Biting her lip, she closed her eyes in pleasure as she rode me, driving my cock further inside her. *Fuck, she feels so good.*

Her fingers dug into my chest as her pace increased, her walls tightening around my dick as she neared climax. Throwing her head back, she cried out my name and her body shuddered in ecstasy, pulsing around me as she went limp.

Flipping her over, I repeatedly slammed into her, seeking my own release. Her pussy was freshly moist from her orgasm, making it easier for my cock to slide in and out of her.

The combination of her wetness and snug walls clenching around me finally sent me over the edge. I groaned as I pulled out, coming on the inside of her thigh as I buried my face in her neck. *So fucking good.*

We both lay there for a few minutes, catching our breath before I got up to grab Kaiya a towel. When I walked back towards her, she averted her gaze from my naked body and the flush on her face deepened.

As she took the towel from my hand, she commented, "We need to start using protection."

"Why? It feels so much better without it." I gave her a crooked grin.

She gave me a look, like the one a mom gives her child when she's trying to be mad at them, but couldn't.

"Besides, we've already done it without one." I shrugged.

She shook her head as she fought a smile, propping herself up on her elbows. "You better not have given me any STDs."

"I don't have any STDs. I've always used a condom."

"Yeah, I'm sure you use that line with all your women." Her expression and tone were full of disbelief.

Laying back next to her, I brushed some hair out of her face. "Seriously. I've always used a condom before you." *And her.*

She stared at me, searching my eyes for a sign that I was lying. She opened her mouth to say something, but changed her mind and closed it before getting up and picking her clothes up off of the floor.

"What's wrong?" I sat up on the edge of the bed while she moved around.

"Nothing," she brusquely replied, avoiding looking at me.

"Bullshit." I stood and walked over to her. Turning her around, I softly demanded, "Tell me."

After several seconds of silence, she sighed, looking down at the clothes in her hands. "I'm afraid that I'll be just one of the many women you've been with and that you'll just toss me to the side when you get bored with me."

Her words were like a jab to the gut. I didn't make it a secret that I went through women like a college frat boy, but Kaiya had to know things were different between us, that she wasn't just a hook-up. Hadn't I told her that? By the sad look on her face, she had no clue how I felt about her, that I didn't plan on using her like I did the others.

Taking her face in my hands, I lifted it until she looked at me. "I'm not gonna do that to you. You're not like the others, Ky."

"How do I know you're not just saying that?"

"Because I'm standing here telling you that I'm not. I'm a lot of things, but I'm not a liar. If I wanted just a one-time thing, I wouldn't have bothered with you after Thursday night, especially after the fight we had. I wouldn't be here with you right now—I would be with someone else."

Once again she searched my gaze with hers, looking for the truth in my words. Doubt and apprehension still resided within her eyes, which I expected given her past. I knew it would take more than just my words to make her believe me, so I showed her how I felt with the only way I could think of.

Leaning down, I softly pressed my lips to hers, hoping I could chip away at some of her walls. The clothes fell from her hands and her arms slowly glided up around my neck as she reciprocated my kiss, pushing her body against mine.

I grabbed the undersides of her thighs and picked her up, wrapping her legs around me as I took her back to the bed. As soon as we met the mattress, I entered her in one, swift thrust, rooting myself deep within her.

I wanted to take my time with her, show her that I meant what I had said, but that was so fucking hard with the way her body fit mine, perfectly molding to me as we tangled in sexual ecstasy.

Kaiya lifted her hips, making me sink deeper within her. I groaned against her lips before tracing over the bottom one with my tongue ring. She moaned, then sucked my tongue back in her mouth, eagerly consuming me while I fucked her.

My hands tangled in her hair as I devoured her, loving the taste of her hot mouth. Pulling on the soft strands, I caused her to gasp against my lips while I thrust slowly inside her, bringing us both closer to climax again.

I wanted to make her come, especially since she told me she needed to control it—that made me want to do it even more. I lowered my hands, slowly caressing each curve of her soft body, intensifying my strokes. "I want to make you come, baby."

She weakly protested, shaking her head, but she continued to kiss me. Fuck, I wanted to break her rules so bad, demolish every boundary between us, but I knew I couldn't do it all at once. We'd already broken this rule before, so it was a good place to start. "Please, baby, let me make you come."

After a few seconds, she whimpered in my mouth, "Yes."

I nibbled her bottom lip, then sat up. Her half-lidded gaze found mine as I hooked my arms around her thighs, gripping the delicate flesh in my hands as I began to pummel her.

"Fuck, baby, you're so tight around me. I love the way your pussy hugs my dick," I growled.

Kaiya's eyes rolled back before she closed her eyes in bliss, fisting the sheets while I pounded into her. She was so close to coming; I could feel her tightening around me as she repeatedly moaned my name.

Then, her thighs began to tremble in my hands as she orgasmed. Tremors of pleasure racked her body as her walls throbbed around my cock, sending me into euphoria with her. I barely pulled out before I started coming, streaming my release all over her stomach.

Reaching over the side of the bed, I picked up the towel I had brought for her earlier before wiping my cum off her skin.

Once I was finished, I pulled her body to mine, wrapping my arms around her and pressing a kiss to the top of her head. "I know you don't completely trust me, but it's different between us. I'm not going to use you."

She kissed my chest, then looked up at me. I loved the flush I put on her skin from just having sex with her. "Prove it." Her voice was strong, but those beautiful eyes looked vulnerable.

My eyes playfully narrowed. "Is that a challenge, Warrior?"

"Yep. And I think it will be your biggest one yet."

Leaning down, I grazed my lips over hers. "Accepted."

When we finally broke apart, Kaiya rose off the bed, grabbing her clothes once again from the floor.

Once she finished getting dressed, I slipped on some shorts and walked her out to her car. "See you tomorrow?"

"Maybe." she smiled. When I raised my eyebrow at her, she giggled. "If you're lucky."

I scoffed as she got in her car. I watched her drive away before I went back up to my apartment. That night, I slept the best I had since Thursday.

Chapter Fifteen

Kaiya

Fear burrowed in my body, making every muscle and joint uncomfortably stiff as I sat waiting for the hospital administrator with Kamden and Nori. I hadn't been this close to Kaleb since the *incident*, and that was eight years ago. Nausea assaulted my insides as my leg bounced frantically, my hands gripping the armrests of the chair to keep myself from bolting out of the door.

Reaching over, Kamden placed his large hand over mine. "Everything's going to be okay, *sorella,*" he assured with a comforting smile.

Giving a tight, forced smile of my own, I nodded. I didn't want to speak, afraid my voice would crack if I did. *I can't do this. I can't do this. He's going to come out here and find me. He'll finish what he started. I have to get out of here.*

As I was about to make a run for the exit, Nori silently linked our fingers before squeezing my hand gently. "You got this, girl."

Squeezing back, I released a deep breath. *You can do this. Don't let him win. You can't let him get released. He'll hurt more people. He'll hurt you.*

Just then, the door opened, causing my head to whip around—an older man with glasses in a white coat walked in with a bunch of thick files in his hands. His gaze perused over us as he rounded the desk in front of us to stand on the opposite side.

Setting the files down, he introduced himself, "Good morning. My name is Dr. Samuel Owens, and I oversee things here at the Massachusetts Treatment Center."

The Massachusetts Treatment Center was a division of the Bridgewater Correctional Complex for sexually dangerous persons. Kaleb had been diagnosed with a combination of different mental disorders, including schizophrenia and narcissism, before he was committed for his long-term sexual abuse of me.

Kamden stood to shake the doctor's hand before introducing Nori and me.

The doctor spoke, his tone authoritative and clinical. "So, you're here concerning your brother's release?"

Kamden replied, "Yes, we wanted to see if there was an appeal process—we want to prevent it."

Dr. Owens looked perplexed as he responded, "I'm sorry, but his release is determined by his doctors and other hospital personnel."

Kamden's jaw ticked. "You don't take into account his victim's testimony?"

"We do—we review his whole file, including the progress he's made since being here. You do realize that it's been eight years since he was committed? People change." His tone was defensive and condescending. *Asshole.*

Kamden started to speak again, but I interrupted as fury took hold of me. My chair toppled over behind me as I angrily stood. "Do *you* realize what he did to me? What I had to go through for all those years?" Hot, angry tears began to stream down my face as my voice increased in volume. "Do you know what the aftermath is following something that traumatizing? Do you know what I've had to deal with for the past eight years? How afraid I am of other people? All because of him!" I screamed as my tears blurred my vision.

Kamden wrapped his arm around me, trying to comfort me as he pulled me into him. I clutched his shirt as I glared at the doctor.

His eyes softened some as he addressed me, "I'm sorry for what happened to you, but I can assure you that Kaleb is much different than he used to be. We wouldn't be considering his release otherwise. The treatment and therapy have done wonders for him, and his current medication has proven to be successful in controlling his behaviors."

I didn't respond—Dr. Owens would never understand. He had looked at everything logically, only taking into account what his research had dictated, not my feelings or opinions. Kamden, however, was a different story. He wasn't having any of the doctor's bullshit.

His grip on me tightened as he seethed, "Monsters like that don't change. They just find a way to adapt to their surroundings, to fool everyone into believing they're something that they're not." His voice cracked, and he took a deep breath to calm himself down. "Kaleb had me fooled for our entire lives. I… I never knew what he'd been doing to our own sister for all those years, and we lived under the same roof."

As I slumped into Kamden's seat, tears slid down my face. I began to zone out, the heated discussion between Kamden and Dr. Owens sounding garbled and distant. All of this talk about Kaleb and the fact that he was somewhere in the building started clawing at me. I clutched my head as images of him and memories of all the times he had violated me played in my head like a deranged slideshow made specifically to torment me. *I need to get away from him, need to get out of here.*

Shooting out of the chair, I bolted for the door, ignoring everyone's calls as I ran. All I could think about was getting out of there, of getting as far away from Kaleb as possible, especially since his release seemed more eminent based on what Dr. Owens had said. My legs pumped harder as I headed for the exit doors, and I almost collapsed in relief once I passed through them. Bracing my hands on my knees, I sucked in heavy breaths of air as I tried to compose myself.

Nori came through the doors shortly after I did. She wrapped her arms around me and held me until Kamden exited about ten minutes later. His hardened eyes and tight frown told me that the meeting didn't end as we had hoped.

The whole ride home was silent. Kamden tensely clutched the steering wheel with a white-knuckled grip as he drove. Nori held my hand the entire way, stabilizing my frenetic emotions, keeping me from coming completely unglued.

Once we got home, I headed straight for my room and shut the door. I could hear footsteps in the hallway directly outside, but no one knocked or entered.

Nori's muffled voice sounded through the door. "I'm worried

about her, Kam."

"You think I'm not?" He sounded frustrated, and I could practically see him running his hand over his buzzed head.

"Well, what are we going to do?"

"I don't know," he sighed.

"Maybe you should call Ryker—have him come see her."

"No," Kamden raised his voice angrily. "He is not a part of this. He doesn't need to be involved."

Shutting my eyes, I blocked out the rest of their conversation. I wanted to see Ryker, but things were different now. Kaleb was going to be released, and then he would hurt Ryker because of me. My heart clenched, my stomach turning at the thought of Kaleb causing any kind of harm to Ryker.

I had to protect him. I couldn't let Kaleb hurt him. I'd never forgive myself if anything happened to him. Even if Kaleb wasn't involved, my unstable emotions would destroy both of us eventually, and I didn't want that for Ryker. He deserved a normal woman free of issues that could love him completely, that could give him more than I ever would be able to.

Tears surfaced as I thought about what I had to do. *Don't be selfish. Do what's best for him. He'll hate you, but at least he'll be safe.* I knew I never should've gotten involved with him. I just prayed that it wasn't too late to save him.

Chapter Sixteen

Ryker

Kaiya had been avoiding me for weeks, including missing class. I'd called and texted her several times with no response, so I was done. At least I was trying to tell myself that, but who was I kidding? I couldn't get her off of my mind, no matter how hard I'd tried.

I didn't understand what had happened—the last time I saw her, everything was fine. Well, except for that small argument, but I fixed that—at least, I thought I had. I could never tell exactly what she was thinking, so there was no way for me to know why she had started avoiding me.

Occasionally, I'd seen Kamden in the gym, but he avoided me like I had some contagious disease. I was getting fed up with him, almost reaching the point where I didn't mind causing a scene to get information about Kaiya.

I stalked toward him in the weight room as he executed leg presses. Hovering next to the machine, I looked down at him. "We need to talk."

He abruptly stopped and got off the bench. As if I was invisible and hadn't said a word, he walked away from me. *Fuck this, I'm getting some answers.* Determined, I followed after him and grabbed him by the arm.

His muscle tensed under my grip as he stopped. "Let me go," he seethed.

"Not until you tell me what's going on with Kaiya," I growled.

Turning his head towards me, he narrowed his eyes and snarled, "That's none of your fucking business."

Fuck, I'm not going to get anywhere this way. Maybe hostility wasn't the best approach. I softened my tone as I let go of his arm. "I just want to know if she's okay."

His hardened expression eased slightly. "She's fine," he replied, shaking his head. "Just forget about her."

Not possible. I squared my shoulders. "That's not going to happen."

"Why? There are tons of other girls out there."

I clenched my fists, trying to control the anger gripping me. "I don't want any other girls—I want her," I snapped.

"Well, she doesn't want you," he countered, shifting uneasily, avoiding my eyes as he swallowed hard.

"You're a terrible liar," I said before walking away across the gym to my office. I knew Kaiya wanted me, but something had happened to freak her out. I just didn't know if it was something I had done, or if another factor was in play.

"Fuck!" I cursed once I shut the door to my office. I couldn't figure out what was wrong if she refused to see me or talk to me. *How can I fix this when I don't know the damn problem?*

I picked up my phone to text her but changed my mind. *Maybe I should just forget about her and save myself all this trouble. She obviously doesn't care, so why should I?*

Exhaling a frustrated breath, I tossed my phone onto my desk. *Quit being a pussy and move on. Kamden is right. There are plenty of other women out there.*

Picking up my phone again, I typed a text to Drew:

Me: Bar tonight?

Drew: U know I'm always down

We planned to meet at the bar at midnight. It was one of our regular spots, and we always found girls to take home when we went

I found myself driving to her house, but I changed course when I realized what I was doing. I'd done the same thing many times since we stopped talking, but I could never bring myself to go through with it. *She'd probably just slam the door in my face.*

I drove home, where I showered the smell and feel of the woman off me before collapsing into bed. *What the fuck am I going to do?*

Chapter Seventeen

Kaiya

I'd spent weeks avoiding Ryker, and they were definitely taking their toll on me. Every part of me missed him, especially my neglected body, which craved his touch. I hadn't had sex since the night before the meeting with Kaleb.

I'd been ignoring him and Bryce. I hadn't returned any of their phone calls or texts, and I'd been skipping class. Before Ryker, I had hooked up with Bryce at least once every two weeks, if not more often. We hadn't had sex in over a month, and he had definitely noticed. He called and texted me multiple times daily.

I was waiting for one of them to show up at my door since I wouldn't return any of their calls or messages, but neither had. I guess both of them respected my privacy, but that selfish part of me wished that Ryker would come searching for me.

Avoiding Ryker meant I had to stop going to self-defense class, and that was definitely affecting me. My body harbored so much pent up energy and anxiety from not releasing it that I thought I was going to come out of my skin.

Knowing that Ryker didn't usually go to work on most days until the afternoon, I decided to go to the gym early one Saturday morning with Kamden. I had to get out of the house, had to release some of the frustration and nerves eating away at me.

As we parked in the lot of the gym, he asked, "Are you sure you want to do this?"

Looking among the cars, I searched for Ryker's truck, but I didn't see it. A combined sense of disappointment and relief washed over me, and I scolded myself for being selfish and wanting to see him. *You can't be with him. He'll only get hurt.*

Once we entered, Kamden wanted to stay with me while I exercised, just in case Ryker showed up. Rolling my eyes, I walked away from him to get on the elliptical. He didn't follow me, so I assumed that he went to the weight room.

After I finished, my muscles felt strained, sore from lack of use. I decided to use the sauna to help relax the tight tension, so I headed to the locker room to swap my clothes for a towel.

After I had the towel securely wrapped around me, I padded to the steam room, hoping that since it was so early no one would be in there. I'd been wanting to use it since we started coming to this gym. But the sauna was always filled with people, and I could never bring myself to go in, afraid of being alone with strangers with only a towel on.

Peeking in, I smiled—no one was inside. *Hopefully, no one will come in.* I went in and sat on the bench, already starting to perspire from the humidity within the room.

Closing my eyes, I leaned my head back and let out a breath as my body began to relax. A couple of minutes passed when the door abruptly opened, causing me to stand and grip my towel. When I focused on the person in the doorway, I blinked several times to make sure I wasn't dreaming.

"Why are you avoiding me?" Ryker angrily spat, closing the door to the sauna. His eyes ran over me as he crossed his arms over his broad chest. Clad only in a pair of gym shorts and no shirt, his skin gleamed with a sheen of sweet. He looked like he'd just finished working out. *Fuck me.*

"Are you really going to do this in here?" I snapped back as I clutched my towel to me.

His voice was gruff and matter of fact. "I have no other choice— you've missed class for almost three weeks now, and you won't answer my calls."

"I've been busy," I lied.

The truth was that I'd been sulking around my apartment trying not to think of Ryker, which was almost impossible. He dominated every thought, much like his presence did in real life.

Eyes narrowing in determination, he advanced toward me, causing me to back up into the tile wall. Surprisingly, I wasn't scared—Ryker never caused that kind of fear in me. What he made me feel was more of an exhilarating kind of fear, the kind you get when you're about to do something like bungee jump or skydive, the kind that excites your soul.

Caging me between his arms, my already fevered skin heated more from his proximity as he pressed against me with his body. I hadn't realized just how much I missed his touch until his skin reunited with mine, making me feel as though a piece of me had been lost since we'd last been together.

Ryker's eyes met mine, and there was no denying the desire and longing in them. "Always fighting me, Warrior," he softly spoke as he caressed my cheek with the back of his knuckles. Leaning in, he grazed my neck with his lips. The combination of heat from the steam and his mouth began to blanket me in a heady fog, evaporating all thought and replacing it with lust.

"I've missed you," Ryker murmured against my skin before tracing the curve of my jaw with his tongue. My breath escaped in a low moan as he pulled my body closer to him, leaving no space between us while he continued to taste me.

My hands tangled in his hair, leaving my loose towel barely clinging to my sweaty skin. When he brought his lips to mine, I let go of everything, losing myself in him and how he made me feel.

He groaned in my mouth as our tongues met, tangling together seamlessly as he lifted me. My legs automatically wrapped around him as he pressed me up against the wall, his hardened erection pushing against my already heated core.

Ryker nipped at my lips as he ripped the towel from my body, tossing it to the floor as his callused hands reacquainted themselves with my skin. *God, I missed him. I don't think I'll ever be the same without his touch.* Finding my breasts, Ryker's talented fingers massaged my stiff nipples before his mouth claimed them. The blissful combination of his soft, wet mouth and hard, smooth tongue ring against my sensitive flesh caused a moan to escape from my throat.

Leaning my head back against the wall, I let Ryker consume me. He eagerly suckled my breasts, pulling each nipple with his teeth before caressing it with that amazing piercing again. *I love how he makes me feel— so alive… almost whole.*

"Ryker," I breathlessly moaned as I reached for his shorts. Slipping my hand inside, I found his cock and pulled it out, needing him to fill me.

He didn't hesitate—he never did. Gripping my hips, he thrust himself inside my slick sex as his mouth reclaimed mine. Sweat beaded on our skin as he roughly pummeled me against the tile, taking me closer to heaven with each stroke.

Ryker's thick shaft stretched my walls, the pleasurable pain spreading throughout every inch of my limbs. I reveled in how he made me forget everything else, immersing me in us and the beauty of how our bodies perfectly connected. He unraveled and completed me all at the same time.

"Fuck, I missed you, baby, missed the taste of your sweet skin," Ryker groaned against my lips.

I love it when he talks to me like that.

I forced him deeper inside me with my legs, tightening my hold around his hips. He growled his approval, increasing the pace and intensity of his thrusts as his cock blissfully ravaged me.

Ryker's lips left mine as he nuzzled his face into my neck and placed soft kisses along my skin. "I haven't been able to get you off my mind. I've been going crazy thinking about you, baby."

"Me too. I've missed you so much," I whimpered as I guided his mouth back to mine.

His strength amazed me, unwavering as he supported my weight while simultaneously using his body to fuck me senseless. Ryker continuously pumped into me, creating a sensual rhythm just for us as our bodies molded together in harmony.

Ryker pulled back and grasped my face in his inked hands. "Never again, Warrior." His voice was gruff and deep, laced with emotion. "Can't go through that again."

"Never, baby, never," I whispered.

His mouth crashed on mine again. Every press of Ryker's lips, every caress from his hands, and every stroke of his amazing cock pushed me closer to ecstasy. My body ached for it, needing release after craving Ryker for so long.

As if sensing how close I was, Ryker pounded harder into me, creating the perfect combination of pain and pleasure within my body. My nails raked across his back as I cried out in euphoria, my climax sending tremors of sensation throughout my limbs. My thighs trembled against his hips as his strokes intensified in both speed and strength, seeking his own release. Seconds later, he withdrew his throbbing cock from my sex before shooting his cum up between my breasts.

The sticky heat of the room was stifling, making it more difficult to breathe as we disentangled ourselves. Picking up my towel, Ryker gently wiped his release from my skin, snapping me out the sensual fog we'd created. Immediately, I felt self-conscious, causing panic to root within me. Anxiety began to tighten in my body, trying to seize every muscle in its grasp as it attempted to take hold.

Ryker's hand cupped my cheek. "What's wrong?"

My eyes snapped to his, trying to focus on him to pull myself out of my downward spiral. My chest heaved as it struggled to breathe, causing Ryker's eyes to crease in worry. "Breathe, baby, breathe. It's okay, everything is okay."

Breathe. In, out, in, out. The pressure began to relinquish as I concentrated on Ryker's face. Both of his hands clasped my face. "You with me, baby?"

I gave him a tight nod. My chest was still somewhat constricted, and my muscles were stiff, but the tension was slowly easing away.

"I'm sorry—I have to go," I stammered as I snatched the towel from Ryker's hand. I darted around him toward the exit while trying to wrap the cloth around me.

"You don't have to run from me, Warrior," he called out after me.

Ryker's words stopped me, only a few feet from the door. I felt him behind me as his arms wrapped around my waist, pulling my body against his. Pressing a soft kiss to my shoulder, he murmured, "Talk to me, baby."

My mouth dried up, the words stuck in my throat. I blinked rapidly, willing back tears. Ryker slowly turned me to face him and pressed our foreheads together as he released a breath.

"I know you've been hurt before, experienced things that no one should ever have to. Just know that I'd never do that to you. Ever. I know you're probably not ready to talk about it yet, but when you are, I'll be here."

And with those words, Ryker smashed a small hole in the barrier surrounding the broken pieces of my heart. My eyes watered as I looked away. "My demons are torturing me a lot lately. I'm having trouble dealing with them."

"You know I'm here for you, Warrior. You don't have to fight alone," he said as he caressed my cheeks with his thumbs. My eyes closed from the blissful sensation, wishing I could just stay like that with him forever.

Opening my eyes, my gaze locked with Ryker's. My voice cracked, sounding weak and small as I spoke, "You know how I told you that someone abused me when I was little?"

"Yes," he growled angrily.

"Well, that person was institutionalized, but he's being considered for release." I sighed deeply and looked away as the reality overtook me. "Kamden and I went to protest it. The whole thing overwhelmed me." My hands wrapped around my body, keeping the towel in place and the shiver coursing through my body at bay. "I… I hadn't been that close to him in years, and I didn't deal with it well."

Ryker enveloped me in a hug. "Why didn't you tell me? You shouldn't have dealt with that by yourself."

Laying my head against his chest, I confessed, "I didn't want to bring you into it. You shouldn't have to deal with my issues." *With my psychotic brother.*

Ryker pulled back, gripping me softly by the shoulders and leaning down to look in my eyes. "Don't start this shit again, Ky. If I didn't want to deal with your issues, I wouldn't be here right now."

"I don't want you to get hurt," I choked.

"Hurt? Why would I get hurt?" His eyebrows furrowed in confusion and his forehead creased as his eyes ran over my face, looking for an answer.

I swallowed the lump in my throat. "If my… he gets out, he'll come after me. He'll hurt you just for being with me."

He laughed—actually laughed. "Baby, you don't have to worry about me. I can take care of myself." He paused before his eyes steeled, his voice deepening angrily. "And if he lays one finger, one fucking finger on you, he won't be breathing for long."

My eyes searched his, looking to see if he was joking—he wasn't. This had to be the most serious I'd ever seen him. My heart swelled at his protectiveness, and my resolve to stay away from him crumbled.

Melting against him, I wrapped my arms around his waist, pressing my cheek to his muscular chest. "I'm not good for you," I whispered.

His body rumbled beneath me with a soft chuckle. "Oh, yeah? Why not?"

"I'm just not." I'd already divulged too much, and I didn't want to reveal anymore, afraid he'd leave if he learned the whole truth about me. *That might be best for him.*

Tilting my chin up, he stared deep in my eyes. "You are." His voice was firm, leaving no room for argument.

Then, he leaned down and pressed his lips to mine, evaporating all my fears and doubts and replacing them with hope. He made me feel as if one day, I could be complete, not the fucked-up, fractured version of a person that I was.

The door opened, causing me to jerk away from Ryker and tightly grip my towel around me. An older man walked in, giving Ryker and me a suspicious look as we darted around him and exited.

A laugh burst from Ryker as soon as the door closed. My heart beat fast as adrenaline rushed through me from almost being caught. I couldn't fight my own laughter when Ryker's was so contagious.

Draping his arm over my shoulder, he led me toward the locker rooms. We both were still laughing as he said, "That was a close one."

"Yeah, and whose fault is that? You're such a bad influence," I joked.

"Me?" His eyebrows rose incredulously as a playful grin tipped up his lips. "You're the one who makes me crazy. I can't control myself when it comes to you. Especially when I haven't seen you in weeks."

My stomach and chest bunched tightly from his words. I felt so terrible for avoiding him, especially when I considered how I just stopped talking to him with no explanation or reason. Who knows what was going through his mind that whole time; he probably thought he'd done something wrong, and it was really me and my madness.

"I'm sorry," I looked up at him as we walked. "I was only trying to protect you."

"I don't need you to protect me, Warrior. I just need you."

Need? Needing someone was way different than just wanting someone—did he really need me? I wasn't ready to go into that, and I doubted he was either, but I couldn't ignore the joy that fluttered within me at the thought.

We had reached the locker rooms, and Ryker stopped and faced me. "Are you going to stop fighting me now, Warrior? Or do I have to keep chasing you?"

I held his gaze with mine. "I don't want to keep running, but it's hard to let go of my ways. If we do this, it's not going to be easy."

"Easy is boring—you know I like a challenge."

My lips curved up in a smile. "Well, good luck because I'm definitely a challenge. I'll probably try to run again—will you keep chasing me?"

"Until you don't let me catch you anymore," he softly grinned, sending a tingle through my body.

I wasn't really afraid of Ryker hurting me any longer—I didn't think anything could hurt me as much as Kaleb had. I was more scared of myself, of what my emotions could do to him if I let him in. I might not have been ready to let him in completely, but I wanted to try to make things between us work.

"You'll stop chasing me before that happens," I teased, placing my hand on his chest as I dipped my face to hide the blush that touched my cheeks..

His finger tilted my chin up. "I don't think I'd be able to stop chasing you—you're like an addiction."

"That's really what I want to be compared to, thanks," I replied sarcastically as I moved away from him.

He pulled me back to him, not letting me get away. "That was a compliment." I raised an eyebrow and pursed my lips in doubt. He cocked his head to the side and tightened his arms around me. "Addictions give you a high unlike anything else, make you crave whatever it is you're addicted to. And, Warrior, I crave you."

His lips found mine, fueling the flames his words had started

148

inside me. The kiss was greedy and hungry, filled with passion and longing. It spoke volumes without needing words. It was the kind that made your stomach knot while igniting your soul.

When we finally broke apart, I was breathless and flushed. The feelings that kiss evoked within me confirmed that it would be almost impossible for me to walk away from Ryker. I'd never be the same after him, and I wasn't sure if that was a good or a bad thing yet.

Chapter Eighteen

Ryker

After finally fixing things with Kaiya, I felt like a huge weight had been lifted off my shoulders, and I was the happiest I'd been in weeks. It kind of fucked with my head how much she got to me, but she made me feel things I hadn't felt in a long time. The thought of being with her didn't give me the urge to run like it had with every other chick since that stupid bitch.

After working on the bags at Sunday's class, I decided to have the students work on techniques for what to do if they fell down during an attack.

"Today, we're going to work on ground defense. You can easily fall during an attack, whether it's because you were knocked down or because you tripped. What you don't want is for your attacker to get on top of you if that happens. The moves we are going to show you will prevent the attack from escalating, and can also disable your attacker if executed correctly."

Kaiya and I found a spot on the mat as everyone broke into their pairs. She smiled at me shyly when we locked eyes, and her face started to flush.

"Still nervous around me, baby?"

"No, things are just different now that we... that we're you know," she softly stammered.

"Having sex?" I blurted.

Her eyes looked around then glared at me. "Yes! We probably shouldn't be hooking up since I'm your student."

"It's frowned upon, but it's not forbidden. Don't worry about it, okay?"

"What if the other students find out?"

"Who cares?" I shrugged. "It's none of their business."

Her lips twitched as she fought a smile, but it broke through after a few seconds. "So, what's the first technique?" she asked, changing the subject.

I laid down on the mat. "If you ever get knocked down, the first thing that you need to do is turn on your side and pick your leg up to defend yourself. Most attackers will try to pin you from here." I shifted my body demonstrating what I was doing. "Your only concern is to avoid him from climbing on top of you and getting knocked out." I made sure to keep my eyes on hers. "Come toward me."

I stopped her when she got about a foot away from my legs. A few strands from her ponytail fell across her face and she quickly tucked them behind her ear. "Once your attacker is this close, you can kick them in the stomach or the groin. Hook your bottom foot here." I moved my foot to the back of her ankle. "Use all your force to kick them in the knee with your top leg."

We continued the technique until she got it. I'd go over it again and again just to make sure that nobody would ever hurt her again. Now that we were together or dating or whatever it was we were doing, I felt more protective over her. I didn't even want to think about the possibility of her being attacked, and just the thought of it laced my veins with rage. I wished she'd known how to defend herself when she was a little girl. *What kind of sick motherfucker would hurt her?* I shook away those thoughts and focused on her face.

Once class was finished, I closed up the gym and walked Kaiya to her car. "You wanna come back to my place?" I asked as I framed her against the driver's side door.

"I wish I could," she answered, her voice full of disappointment.

"Mondays are hell for me. I have to wake up earlier." She placed her hands on my chest and traced over the tattoos showing with her fingertips. "If I go home with you, I won't get any sleep."

"Are you sure?" I leaned closer before trailing soft kisses along her jaw line.

She lightly moaned but still resisted. "I can't, baby. I've been slacking at work the past few weeks, and I really need to catch up."

"Okay." I nuzzled my face in her neck, getting as close to her as I could as I slid my hands in hers. Pulling back, I said, "Hey, don't make any plans for Friday night. I have a surprise for you."

"Oh, yeah? Will I like it?" she smiled coyly at me.

I pressed a kiss to her lips, then another to each side of her neck. "I don't know. I hope so."

When I pulled away, her eyes were closed as she wore a look of contentment. They slowly fluttered open as she smiled at me. "I can't wait."

Me neither. If everything went according to plan, I'd be breaking one of Kaiya's rules that night, getting closer to her in the process. "See you tomorrow?"

"Yes. Do you want to meet for dinner after I get off of work? I'll tell Kam that he's on his own."

"Sure, baby. I'll talk to you tomorrow," I replied as I opened the door for her.

As she drove away, my mind was racing in preparation for Friday. *Everything needs to be perfect.*

I picked up the earlier shift at work on Friday so I could get off with enough time to get everything ready for my date with Kaiya. As I was leaving, one of the receptionists stopped me. "Hey, Ryker, someone left a message for you."

No one usually calls me at work. "Who was it?"

"Um, I'm not sure." She rifled through some papers at the desk. "Some guy—he said something about it being important and for you to call him as soon as possible." She snatched a small paper from the mess and read the name aloud, "Ethan Campbell."

All my muscles tensed as anger gripped every limb, just the sound of that name infuriating me. I clenched my fists as I gritted, "If he calls back, tell him to never contact me again."

Storming out of the entrance, I didn't wait to hear a response from her. *Why the fuck would Ethan be calling me? He knows that I want nothing to do with him.*

Brushing the thoughts away, I focused on getting everything ready for my night with Kaiya. I sent her a text telling her to be at my place at seven. Just seeing her reply put a smile on face and wiped away most of the anger that lingered from hearing about Ethan.

I found out from Nori that Kaiya loved gnocchi from a little Italian bistro two towns over. She didn't get to go very often because it was out of the way and never had time to make the trip. So I made arrangements to pick it up for our date.

My palms were sweaty as I set up everything, which was strange for me—women never made me nervous. But Kaiya had me feeling like I was some high school kid about to take the hottest girl to prom.

When the doorbell rang, my heart rate kicked up as my stomach tightened in anxiety. *Chill out, it's just Kaiya.* Walking over to the door, I opened it and took Kaiya in. She was wearing a light blue strapless dress, almost the same shade as her eyes, and her hair was loosely curled.

"Hi," she smiled, her cheeks flushing as her gaze settled on mine. I didn't need words for her to know what was going through my mind at that moment, my eyes said it all.

"Hey," was about all I could manage before I had to clear my throat. *Smooth. How does she do this to me?* "You look beautiful." I leaned down to kiss her cheek before I brought her inside and closed the door.

Her eyes widened and an astonished smile spread over her face as she looked around my apartment. Candles and rose petals were scattered along every surface, including the table, which I had set with my best dinnerware, but that wasn't really saying much. Bachelors didn't have fine china.

Kaiya looked up at me, her eyes lighting up her whole face. "Ryker, you didn't have to do all this for me."

Leading her to the table, I pulled out her chair. "I wanted to."

I picked up her plate before taking it to the kitchen and serving the gnocchi on it. I returned and gently placed the plate before her. "It's not

gnocchi on it. I returned and gently placed the plate before her. "It's not homemade or anything, but Nori said that this was your favorite."

She stared at it for several seconds, then darted her gaze to mine. "Is this from Luciano's?"

Grinning, I answered, "Yeah. I picked it up before you came."

Another wide smile spread over those beautiful lips. "Thank you."

I bent down to kiss her. "You're welcome."

I'd also bought a bottle of her favorite wine, the house Moscato from the restaurant. I poured us both a glass and sat down to eat.

Throughout dinner we talked about everything, from favorite movies to hobbies. Kaiya loved to read, and I, of course, was a workout junkie. I found out that she hated scary movies, loved the water and animals, except snakes, which she was deathly afraid of, and her favorite color was pink.

After we finished dinner, I cleared the table while Kaiya finished her third glass of wine. I could tell she was already a little tipsy by the flush on her face and her glassy eyes, which she had locked on mine as I walked toward her on the couch.

Setting her glass on the coffee table, she pulled me down next to her before leaning in and kissing my lips. "Thank you for dinner. Everything was amazing."

"No problem, baby. I rented some movies for us—which one do you want to watch first," I asked as I held them out for her to see.

Her lips bunched to one side as she looked over the DVDs. She decided on an action flick, which surprised me, but she surprised me on a regular basis. I never knew what to expect with her, and I loved that.

Kaiya cuddled into my side after I started the movie. About ten minutes in, she started trailing her fingers under my shirt, lightly tracing the ridges of my abs. Just that small touch was causing my dick to harden. She ventured lower, making my breathing slightly erratic as her delicate fingers played under the waist of my jeans.

"What are you doing, baby?" My hand skimmed under the hem of her dress, rubbing the delicate skin of her inner thigh.

"Nothing," she replied sweetly as she peered up at me, giving me a flirty smile.

"Oh, yeah?" Shifting her on to my lap, I rubbed my hands along the curves of her hips to her ass, squeezing the soft flesh lightly as I pressed her against me.

Her breath caught right before our lips met. Wrapping my arms around her, I pulled her tighter against me as I parted her lips with my tongue, letting her sweetness flood my mouth. I doubted I could ever get enough of her taste. She really was my addiction, making me want more and more.

Rising off the couch, I took us to my bedroom. My plan was in full swing as I set Kaiya on the bed. This wasn't just about breaking her rules—this was about getting her to open up to me, to connect with her on a deeper level. I wanted her to trust me with her body, let me show her how it was meant to be touched.

I pulled down her dress as she simultaneously tugged my shirt over my head. Laying her back on the bed, I trailed light kisses down her body, hoping to ease her into letting go, into losing herself in pleasure. I wanted to erase the memories constantly tormenting her, to replace her pain with happiness.

She squirmed under my lips as I ventured down, hooking my thumbs under her lacy thong as I pressed more kisses on her lower abdomen. Looking up at her, locking our eyes, I slid her panties off as I traced her skin with my tongue.

Once she was completely naked in front of me, I admired her bare form. *Fuck, she's gorgeous.* She had no idea how beautiful she was, how she caused an eruption of desire within me that was unmatched by anyone else. I wanted to show her exactly how she made me feel.

"Can I taste you, baby?" I pressed a soft kiss to her inner thigh.

Holding her gaze, I placed another kiss on the inside of her other thigh. She looked uncertain, unsure about giving me trust over her body. I wanted to shatter that doubt, reassure her that I only wanted to cherish her, not hurt her. "I won't hurt you, baby."

Using my lips to caress her skin, I traveled back up until I reached her mouth. Hovering over her, snug between her thighs, I darted my tongue out to trace her soft, lush lips before slipping my tongue inside.

A moan escaped her, vibrating the inside of my mouth as our tongues laced together. I pressed my erection against her bare, wet pussy, eliciting another sound of pleasure from her as she arched against me. I had to resist the urge to unbutton my jeans and sink into her right then, but I was on a mission, one that would hopefully bring us closer together.

Breaking the kiss to nibble her bottom lip, I gruffly spoke, "Fuck, you taste so good. I bet your pussy tastes even better. Lemme taste you, baby."

Whimpering, she writhed beneath me, shaking her head 'no' as I dragged my tongue along her jawline before sucking her earlobe into my mouth.

Shifting down, I moved my lips over her collarbone, pressing soft kisses as I continued lower. Reaching her breasts, I sucked one of her nipples into my mouth and played with it with my barbell. She jerked underneath me, fisting the sheets as I sucked her tits.

I moved to the other nipple before teasing it with my tongue. More moans escaped her as I repeated, "Let me taste you, Warrior. Let me show you how good I can make you feel."

After a few seconds, she finally groaned, "Yes, yes, yes."

Yes. I trailed my mouth back down, back between her thighs. I wanted to take things slow, wanted to savor Kaiya while crushing her fears and doubts.

Slowly, I traced my tongue along the outside of her delicate center before flicking her clit with it. Sucking the sensitive skin into my mouth, I slowly sank two of my fingers inside her tight opening. Her hands tugged my hair as she arched against my fingers, pulling them deeper within her.

After several seconds, I swapped my fingers for my tongue, thrusting it inside her snug entrance.

Her hands tightened in my hair as she pushed at me, crying softly, "Stop. Please, stop."

The pain in her voice immediately halted my actions. I sat up on my knees to look at her, and saw that tears were trickling down her face. I felt like a bucket of ice water had been dumped on me. *Fuck, I didn't want this to happen.* "Baby, what's wrong?" I asked as I moved from between her legs to by her side.

Sitting up, she brought her legs to her chest and wrapped her arms tightly around them. "I'm sorry," she sobbed as she buried her face in her knees.

I rubbed her back in gentle circles. "Ky, look at me. Talk to me, baby."

Peeking at me, she inhaled deeply before saying, "He... he used to do that to me. I… I can't."

Running a hand through my hair, I blew out a breath. I didn't want her to think about him, about what he did to her. All I wanted was to take away her memories of him, replace them with better ones, make it so she never hurt again.

"Ky, I know this is hard for you. I know that he hurt you, that he mistreated your body. I don't want to do that, baby. I want to erase what he did by showing you that your body was made to be cherished, not abused."

She propped her head on her arms as she stared at me, sniffling before she replied, "Some scars can never be erased."

"Lemme try, Warrior," I urged.

Exhaling, she replied, "I don't know, Ryker. I-"

"We'll take it slow—if you feel overwhelmed at any point, just tell me, and I'll stop. I stopped when you asked me a few minutes ago, right?"

"You promise?" she softly asked, locking our eyes again. I knew this was huge for her, to be able to trust someone not to hurt her. I wanted to kill that fucking bastard for doing whatever he did to her, making my warrior afraid of being intimate with someone.

I looked into those beautiful, blue eyes. "I promise, Ky."

Leaning in, I gently pressed my lips to hers as I cradled her face in my hands. Laying her down on the bed, I separated our mouths to feather kisses over her face and neck, leaving no area untouched by the soft touch of my lips.

Using the tips of my fingers, I lightly caressed her skin as my mouth followed. I ventured down over her tits and stomach before kissing her hips and thighs, avoiding her pussy.

Descending down her body, I enjoyed the taste and feel of her supple flesh. I stopped to massage her legs as I placed kisses on the inside of her ankle before switching to the other. Retreating back up, I ran my hands along her skin, causing her to writhe under my touch.

I spread more kisses along the sensitive area of her inner thighs, eliciting moans of pleasure from Kaiya. Nearing closer to her pussy, I dragged my tongue along the tender skin before stopping at the juncture between her thighs. "Do you want me to stop, baby?" I murmured huskily. I sure as hell didn't want to, but I didn't want her to feel forced. I'd never force a woman to do anything she didn't want to.

She only moaned incomprehensibly, lost in passion. I softly kissed her clit a couple of times before repeating my question. "Do you want me to stop?"

"No," she cried out, her voice thick with desire.

Yes.

My lips curved as my tongue darted out to taste her again. Her body jerked slightly as her hands found my head and brought me into her pussy. Kneading her thighs, I began to slowly devour her, my tongue dancing inside her.

My fingers found her clit, deftly massaging the bundle of nerves as my tongue played with it and sucked it in my mouth. A high-pitched moan escaped Kaiya as her body jolted in pleasure again. Her hands tightened in my hair as she pushed me closer against her, her body squirming as she neared climax.

My hands moved around to her ass, gripping the voluptuous flesh and bringing her closer to me as I delved back inside her. The more I had of her, the more I wanted, the taste of her sweet pussy feeding my addiction, intensifying my desire for her.

Her thighs tensed and trembled along with the rest of her body as she moaned in orgasm. I eagerly consumed her sweetness as it flooded my mouth, savoring the evidence of the pleasure I gave her.

Trailing kisses back up her slender torso, my hands caressed the curves of her body before I finally stilled, hovering over her. Lidded with desire, her eyes met mine as she seductively smiled, raking her hands down my abs before stopping at my jeans.

I held her gaze as I ground my erection against her. "Did you like that, baby?

Her hands began to fumble with my jeans as she bit her lip and nodded. Voice throaty with arousal, she answered, "Yes. I want you inside me, now."

I wanted to plunge my dick deep inside her, fill her until she repeatedly cried out my name, but I loved teasing her, loved unraveling her until she was overcome with desire.

"Oh yeah, baby? How bad do you want me?" I asked before grazing her nipple with my teeth.

Her hand slipped inside my jeans before grabbing my cock. "So bad," she moaned.

"You want me to fuck you, baby?" I murmured against her tit

before sucking it into my mouth. *Fuck, she tastes so good.*

"Yes," she moaned, arching against me. I nipped at her breasts as she pulled my dick out and slid my pants down with her feet.

Guiding me with her hand, she pressed my cock against her slick opening.

"You're so wet for me," I growled as I rocked against her.

When she wrapped her legs around me, pulling me to her, urging me to enter her, I couldn't contain myself anymore. Gripping her hips, I thrust inside her, sinking my cock deep within her pussy as I captured her mouth with mine.

Kaiya's nails dug into my back as I pounded in and out of her. Moving my hands to her ass, I lifted her upwards. Her pussy clenched tighter around my dick from the slight movement. Her moans increased with each of my strokes. Finding orgasm, her body shuddered as she cried out my name, waves of pleasure finally overtaking her.

As she throbbed around me, I could feel my release approaching. I moved my hands around to spread her thighs, burying myself further inside her.

Pulling out, I shot my cum on Kaiya's breasts and stomach, loving how it looked on her flawless skin. I rolled off next to her before catching my breath and getting up to grab a towel for her.

As I stood at the edge of the bed, her gaze had traveled to my dick, and the lustful look in her eyes caused me to get hard again. "You want more, baby?"

She bit her bottom lip as she nodded. I was on her within seconds, and I spent the rest of the night showing her how her body was meant to be worshiped.

Chapter Nineteen

Kaiya

I left Ryker's at around three in the morning. He wanted me to stay, but I'd already broken one of my rules for him, and that was enough for me for one night. It scared me how easy it was for me to break them for him, but I was happy for once in my life, and I wanted to focus on that and all the other wonderful things Ryker made me feel.

My whole body felt amazing, like I had a full body massage that released all the stress and tension plaguing me. Ryker was definitely gifted, and he spent so many hours showing me exactly how talented he was. The way his rough hands were able to caress me so softly, how he used that delicious mouth to please me so expertly, and how every movement was used to show me how my body should've been treated all along blew my mind.

I slept late Saturday, exhausted from my amazing night with Ryker. When I checked my phone, I had several text messages from both Ryker and Bryce. I opened up Ryker's first, a smile involuntarily spreading over my face as I thought about him.

Ryker: Good morning beautiful

Me: Good morning

About a minute passed before he replied:

Ryker: You free today?

My fingers started typing my reply automatically:

Me: Yes :)

Ryker: Pick you up in an hour?

Me: Ok :)

Before I got out of bed, I looked at Bryce's message:

Bryce: Haven't heard from you in a while everything ok?

Me: Yeah I'm good

Bryce: When can I see you again?

Shit. I needed to tell him that I couldn't hook up with him anymore, but I felt terrible about it. He'd been there for me when I needed him, understanding when most guys would've blown me off. I hesitantly typed the text, but my thumb hovered over the send button. After several seconds, I finally pressed it.

Me: I can't see you like that anymore but I still want to be friends

My phone started ringing as Bryce's number popped up on my screen. I swiped the reject key and left my phone on the bed to get ready before Ryker arrived. I heard the phone ringing again as I hopped in the shower, but I ignored it. *Hopefully, he'll understand.*

Once I finished getting ready, I put on a pair of jeans and an off-the-shoulder tee before putting on some light make-up. I'd always been okay with using a small compact mirror because I didn't see every feature at once, so I didn't see *him.* Otherwise, who knew what I would go outside looking like.

As I went downstairs to meet Ryker, I looked at my phone and noticed that I had more missed calls and text messages from Bryce. I'd have to figure out how to deal with that later before it blew up in my face, but I was too excited about going out with Ryker that I pushed my worries aside.

He was waiting for me at the bottom of the stairs again, wearing a snug, white Henley shirt that looked ridiculously amazing on him, but he looked good in everything. Ryker would look hot even in a garbage bag.

Once I reached him, he picked me up in a hug. Slowly, he let me slide down his body before kissing me deeply. I was beginning to understand what Ryker meant about addiction, because he was becoming my own personal drug, especially when he kissed me like that, to where I felt it all the way in my toes.

"Ready to go?" he asked after he pulled away from me.

"Yes. Where are we going?"

"I thought we'd get some lunch in Boston before my surprise."

"Another surprise?" I questioned as a smile curved over my lips. *A girl could get used to this.*

He smiled as he helped me into his truck before wordlessly closing the door. When he got in on his side, he was still grinning from ear to ear. *What is he up to?*

"What are we doing?" I asked.

"I can't tell you, or it'd ruin the surprise. But, trust me, you'll like it."

He started the truck and started driving toward Boston. We grabbed a quick lunch at a local eatery before we drove toward the Boston Wharf. Excitement started to fill me as we neared—I loved the water, envied how it was so fluid and free, something that had always been an unattainable feeling for me.

When we headed toward the Central Wharf, I had a good idea of where we were going. "Are you taking me to the New England Aquarium?" I practically squealed in delight.

He didn't answer, but his smile told me my answer. I clapped happily and actually squealed in glee that time. Ryker began to laugh as the aquarium came into view and I couldn't wait to get there. I'd visited a couple of times when I was little, but I'd never been back.

Once we parked in the garage directly across from the aquarium, I basically jumped out of the truck and bounced up and down in excitement as I waited for Ryker. I had told him last night how much I loved the water and animals, especially ocean animals—he was definitely gaining some serious points with me.

After we got out of the elevator, he linked our hands together as we walked toward the entrance. My chest and stomach tightened happily from the gesture, and I felt all tingly inside. Ryker caused me to feel so many things that I'd never felt before, and I briefly contemplated whether any of the new feelings could be love.

The idea should've scared me, would've scared me before I met Ryker. Love was dangerous because it meant trust, and trust meant vulnerability. Vulnerability meant that I would be opening myself up to be hurt, and I couldn't afford to be hurt by anyone else; I'd never survive it. I always avoided commitment and attachment for that reason, but Ryker was starting to change my mind. He was showing me that trust could be earned, and that love might not be such a bad thing after all. It might be just what I needed to heal.

After Ryker bought our tickets, we started with the first area on the floor level, which housed harbor seals, penguins, and the Shark and Ray Touch Tank exhibits. The seals were outside, so we started there and worked our way in, spending extra time playing with the sharks and rays.

We made our way towards the back, going through the penguin and tropical fish exhibits. While we were looking at the fish, I noticed Ryker was texting on his phone. A smile tipped his lips as he typed, and I couldn't help but wonder if he was texting another girl. My happiness began to fade, and I hated the ugly twisting in my gut.

I almost pulled away when he grabbed my hand, but I didn't want to overreact and jump to any conclusions. I knew the gnawing feeling I had would eventually eat at me until I said something, but I wanted to try and hold it in until we got back to his truck.

Ryker guided me to the back of the first level, which housed more seals and sea lions. "We already saw seals," I said, irritated, my mood beginning to sour.

We stopped right outside the doors that led outside to the exhibit. His phone chimed with a new text message and he took it out to look at it, causing irrational anger to take over me.

"I'm right here, you know. You could at least wait until I go to the bathroom or something to text one of your other girls," I spat before storming off.

His hand lightly gripped my arm and pulled me back to him.

"What are you talking about, Ky?"

I snatched my arm from his grasp and accused, "You know what I'm talking about. I saw how you looked when you were texting—you were talking to some other girl."

"No, I wasn't—I told you there are no other girls, baby."

I scoffed. "Then, who were you texting?"

Just then, a guy in a diver's suit walked inside from a side door. He saw Ryker and greeted, "Hey, ready?"

I looked between them, perplexed about how they knew each other and what the man was referring to. Ryker then spoke, "Kaiya, this is Mike, a client of mine from the gym. He's arranged for us to have a personal encounter with the seals. That's who I was texting."

"Oh," I replied, my face heating from embarrassment. *Way to overreact.*

I was about to apologize when Mike interrupted, "Let's go—we're not even supposed to be doing this right now, so we have to do it quick."

Mike turned around and sped back through the door he came in, which had an "Employees Only" sign on it. I looked up at Ryker. "I'm sorry," I meekly apologized.

"It's okay. I kinda like that you were jealous," he teased with a smirk.

I rolled my eyes and followed after Mike. Ryker came up next to me before holding the door open and ushering me in. Mike waved us over to a desk before saying, "I've lost almost a hundred pounds thanks to Ryker. I would've never been able to do it without his training, so I owe him big time. This was the least I could do."

"I really appreciate this, Mike. Thanks," Ryker replied.

"No, thank you. I wouldn't have reached my goal without your help."

Ryker smiled proudly as Mike led us into an adjoining room. "Put these on and meet me back in the waiting area when you're finished."

He handed Ryker and me a pair of the pants that fisherman wear over their clothes when they walk in shallow areas of water to fish. They reminded me of rubber overalls as I slipped into them. Excitement began to fill me again, and I felt terrible for accusing Ryker of something he didn't do when he was planning something special for me. I locked eyes with him as I apologized again, "I'm really sorry. Thank you for this."

He wrapped me in a hug, "Don't worry about it, Warrior. Let's have some fun."

Draping an arm over my shoulder, he led me back into the waiting area. Mike then took us through the doors outside to the pool where the seals were.

There were five seals swimming in the water, along with another employee in a scuba suit. Mike got in before us, then Ryker followed and helped me in. Mike then introduced us to the other trainer, Sarah, before giving us more information about what we were going to be doing.

"During your interaction, you can feed and touch the seals. You'll probably get wet, but this is definitely an experience you'll never forget so have some fun with it."

Some of the seals had started swimming around us in circles, while the others jumped in and out of the water a short distance away. Reaching out to the one that was closest to me, I placed my hand on it as it glided by. I laughed as it turned around and stuck its flipper out of the water and waved as it came back toward me.

"It wants to shake your hand," Sarah commented.

I looked at Ryker, who nodded. Focusing back on the seal, I tentatively stretched my hand toward its flipper and grasped it. It wiggled in my hold as I shook it and giggled. When I pulled away, it sat up in the water and swam to me before kissing me on the cheek and diving back under the water.

"Did you see that?" I exclaimed with a huge smile as I turned toward Ryker.

He laughed, "Yeah. I think he likes you. Should I be jealous?"

"I don't know, he was pretty cute," I joked.

"Maybe I need to show him that you're my girl," he replied before moving toward me and kissing me deeply. "Think he gets the picture?"

"I don't know, I think you need to show him again," I teased before smiling up at him.

Ryker pressed his lips against mine again as he pulled me into him, framing my face in his hands. As usual, his kiss left me slightly breathless when we broke apart, and I hoped that never changed.

We spent another twenty minutes playing with the seals before we fed them and exited the tank. Before we left, Mike stopped us and said,

"We took some pictures of your interaction. Would you like to see them?"

"Sure," I replied enthusiastically. I definitely wanted some mementos to remind me of our experience, even though I knew that I'd never forget it.

Mike led us to a computer before pulling up our photos on the screen. I wasn't great with photos, but I was able to deal with them better than mirrors. There were some great candid shots, but the one that caught my eye was of when Ryker kissed me.

The shot was of right before our lips met. Ryker's hands cupped my face and my arms were wrapped around his waist. Both of our eyes were closed as we anticipated the kiss, and the look on our faces... well, it reminded me of two people in love. I was no expert, but I'd seen couples in love before. They had that stupid, enamored look that I'd always envied because I thought I'd never have it. And there I was, on that screen, with it plastered all over my face. And so was Ryker.

There was a sign on the wall behind the desk where the computer was that listed the prices of the photos. I pulled my wallet out of my purse as I told Mike, "I want to buy some, please."

"I'll get them, baby," Ryker offered.

"It's okay, I can pay for them—you've spent enough today."

Ryker scoffed and firmly stated, "You're not paying."

As I was about to argue more, Mike interrupted, "Write down the numbers of the ones you want and I'll get them processed while you two figure out the payment."

"I'm paying," Ryker repeated as I started to write down the numbers of the ones I wanted. I wanted them all, but it would've cost way too much, so I chose the five that I liked best before sliding the paper to Ryker. He wrote down only three, including the one of us right before we kissed.

He handed the sheet to Mike, who began typing on the keyboard. Once he finished, he stood and said, "I'll be right back with your pictures."

When he returned, he held two photo envelopes and a disc. "These are on the house."

"No, Mike, you've done enough today. I—"

Mike interrupted Ryker's statement, "I insist. It's the least I can do after everything."

"I was just doing my job—you really don't have to do this."

Mike looked at me. "Is he always this persistent?"

"You mean stubborn?" I replied, laughing.

Ryker glared at me as Mike insisted, "Seriously, man, it's on me."

"Thank you," Ryker conceded, shaking Mike's hand. "I'll give you some free training sessions for all this."

"I can't say no to that. I'll text you to set them up, okay? I have to get back to work."

We said our goodbyes and thanked Mike again, then went back into the main aquarium. We toured the rest of the floors before heading back to Ryker's truck.

When we got in, my phone started ringing. The screen showed that Bryce was calling me again. I declined it and stuffed the phone back in my purse.

"Who was that?" Ryker asked as he started the truck.

"Bryce."

"Bryce? You still talk to him?" Ryker questioned defensively, his tone becoming harsh as his face hardened slightly.

"I've been ignoring him, but I finally told him that I couldn't see him anymore, but that I still wanted to be friends. He's called me a few times after I sent the message, but I haven't answered."

His features relaxed some, but I could tell he was still pissed off. "Maybe he needs to be talked to personally."

I shook my head. "I don't think seeing him will help—he'll probably try to convince me to change my mind."

"I meant me," he replied gruffly.

That wouldn't end well. "You don't have to do that—I'm sure he'll get the picture."

"He better," he grumbled.

His irrational jealousy caused a smile to take over my lips. I tried to hide it, but it was almost impossible when he looked so adorable scowling over the whole thing when he had nothing to be worried about. "There's no reason for you to be mad, baby."

"I'm not mad at you. I'm just pissed that he wants what's mine, and doesn't seem to be taking the hint."

"I didn't know I had become property all of a sudden," I replied, slightly offended, even though Ryker referring to me as his caused a little spark of pride within me. Not to mention lust.

"You know what I mean, Ky."

"No, I don't. I don't even know what to call this," I gestured back and forth between us.

"It doesn't matter what this," he mimicked my movement, "is called—together, dating, whatever. All that matters is that you're mine, and I'm yours."

We had locked eyes during the exchange, and his softened once he finished speaking. "I just don't want him to think he has any chance with you when he doesn't. He doesn't, right?"

In that moment, Ryker looked… vulnerable. I'd never seen him look that way—he was always so confident and cocky. "No, he doesn't," I smiled reassuringly.

The left corner of Ryker's lip curved into his trademark grin that I loved so much. "Ready to go home?"

"Yours or mine?"

His smile morphed to a devious, lustful smirk. "Mine."

Chapter Twenty

Ryker

Everything had been going so well with Kaiya over the past few weeks that I was afraid something bad was going to happen to balance it all out. Things just couldn't possibly stay this good; they never did.

We had been spending every other Saturday working on self-defense routines one-on-one. Kaiya had been wanting more practice ever since she started coming back to class after her hiatus. The meeting she had about her abuser had really shaken her up, but at the same time, it had made her more determined. She had begun to ask more questions and wanted to try new techniques to improve her form and skills, in addition to wanting the extra classes.

One Saturday morning, Kaiya and I were working on rear hold escape techniques when *he* walked in. At first, I thought I was dreaming, possibly hallucinating, because there was no fucking way that he would really be there. The last time we spoke, I threatened to bash his face in if I ever saw him again.

Stepping away from Kaiya, I clenched my fists in anger. "What the fuck are you doing here, Ethan?" I growled.

Ethan held his chin up confidently, but I could see the apprehension in his eyes. His Adam's apple bobbed as he swallowed nervously. "Good to see you, too, Ryker. Tristan's birthday is coming up. I thou—"

"You thought what? That I'd forget what you and that whore did to me?" I seethed.

A muscle in Ethan's jaw ticked as he gritted, "She's not a whore. She's my wife and the mother of my child—your nephew."

"I don't have a brother, so how can I have a nephew?" I asked condescendingly as I crossed my arms over my chest.

"I don't know why I thought you would've changed. Everyone told me you wouldn't have, but I hoped that you would've matured after this long," he spat.

"This has nothing to do with maturity. This," I emphasized as I gestured between us, "is because my own brother betrayed me. I don't know if you forgot, but I told you that I never wanted to see you again. So, get the fuck out!" I roared angrily.

Ethan's furious expression faded somewhat as sadness took over his features. *Good—I hope he hurts as bad as he hurt me.* Wordlessly, he turned and exited the room, glancing back only once before he walked out of my sight.

I don't know how long I stood there before Kaiya tenderly placed her hand on my bicep. "You okay?"

I was far from okay—seeing him had ripped open my scars and threw acid in the open wounds. But I lied, not wanting to burden her with my issues since she had enough to deal with on her own. "I'm fine, baby."

She gave me a knowing look as she moved in front of me. "You can tell me, Ryker. I'm here for you." She linked our hands together.

Kaiya's words thawed some of the ice that had started to freeze within my chest from seeing Ethan. She smiled warmly at me when I looked down at her. She'd already trusted me with so much, opened up to me more than she had with anyone else besides Kamden and Nori. I owed it to her to open up, as well. Sighing, I replied, "That was my brother, Ethan. We haven't spoken in over four years."

"Why?"

"Right after high school, I met this girl, Molly. We dated through college, and she ended up getting pregnant during our senior year. At first, I was scared, shocked actually, but then I was so happy. I loved her and was excited to be starting a family together. I proposed to her a few months after we found out, and she said yes."

"What happened?" Her eyes held a look of concern as they searched my face.

I released another heavy breath. "When Molly was around eight months pregnant, she told me that the baby wasn't mine—it was Ethan's."

Kaiya's hand flew to her mouth as her eyes watered. "Oh my God! Ryker, I'm so sorry!"

"Don't be—it's not your fault. I blamed myself for the longest time, wondering what I did wrong." *Wow, I'm really opening myself up here.*

"You did nothing wrong! They're the ones who were wrong! I can't believe that your own broth—" She abruptly stopped, her eyes widening as if she realized something.

"What?" I asked as she shook her head and hugged herself.

"Nothing," she quickly responded. Avoiding my gaze, she began to tense up. Most people wouldn't have even noticed it, but I did. I had learned so much about her over the past few months that I knew that she was holding something in.

Pulling her to me, I wrapped her in my arms. Even though she probably thought I was only trying to comfort her, in reality, I also needed to hold her, to feel her against me. Seeing Ethan had resurfaced so many bad feelings that I wanted her to wash away, like she always was able to do. I pressed a kiss to the top of her head. "You can trust me, Warrior."

She buried her face in my chest. "I know, it's just hard for me to talk about." Her voice was muffled against my shirt. "I… I don't want you to be disgusted by me."

Framing her face in my hands, I forced her to look up at me, "I could never be disgusted by you. Ever."

Her lips trembled as tears began to rain down her cheeks. "I… I have another brother. His name is Kaleb. He… he was the one who abused me when I was little."

Holy shit. I had no clue what to say, what to do to make it better, but I wanted to do anything to take the pain from her. "Oh, baby, no wonder you fight so much. I'm so sorry."

"I didn't fight hard enough—I should have made him stop, but I was too weak. I'm still weak," she sobbed, burying her face in my chest again.

I tilted her chin up to look at me again. "Hey, you're not weak. You know how strong you are to survive something like that?"

"I survived, but I'm… damaged—completely damaged. Everything he did to me slowly broke me, leaving nothing but fragments for me to try and put back together."

Looking deep into her eyes, I caressed her cheeks with my thumbs. "I'll help you pick up the pieces if you let me, Warrior. I want to be the one to make you whole again."

More tears flowed freely down her rosy cheeks as she clasped my face in her hands, bringing my mouth to hers. Her lips claimed mine with desperation as she pressed our bodies together, showing me how much my words meant to her. So much was said in that kiss, more than we could have expressed in words at that point—it spoke of hope, faith, and trust, helping both of us in the right direction to becoming whole again.

My arms had wrapped around her waist, lifting her to where her toes barely touched the ground. My hands began to roam lower, and I knew if we didn't stop that I was going to end up taking her right there on the mat like our first time. The problem was that there were still people in the gym, unlike before when we were the only two there.

Breaking away, I set my forehead against hers. "If we don't stop, I'm going to take you right here, right now."

Reconnecting our lips, she whimpered with desire. "I need you."

Fuck me. There was no way I could say no to that. Picking her up, her legs wrapped around my waist as our mouths collided. I walked to the door before fumbling with the handle and locking it, then headed to the closet.

Once inside, I kicked the door closed. I maneuvered around most of the boxes and equipment before positioning us against one of the bags that lined the walls. No one should find us, unless one of the other employees happened to come in for some reason, but I really didn't give a fuck at the moment—I had to have her.

As I moved her shorts and panties to the side, she grabbed my cock and pulled it out, eager for me to enter her. Guiding me to her, her hands placed my tip at her opening, which was already wet.

Slowly, I pushed myself inside her, gradually filling her until her pussy surrounded my length. We groaned in unison as I began to pound her against the bag, grasping her hips for deeper penetration.

My mouth found Kaiya's neck as she continuously moaned, her cries of pleasure becoming louder and louder with each of my thrusts. Savoring her skin, I began to push her shirt up, needing to feel her flesh against mine. Kaiya maneuvered to help me take off her top before removing her sports bra, letting it fall to floor.

My shirt was added to the pile as Kaiya eagerly pulled it off. Her hands roamed over my shoulders and arms as my mouth claimed her breast, my tongue ring flicking over her hardened nipple. She arched against me as I moved to her other tit, sucking it deep into my mouth.

Wrapping her legs tighter around me, she forced my dick deeper inside her sex. Growling my approval, I thrust harder as her nails dug into my biceps and her head tipped back against the bag.

"Ryker?" a voice called out from outside the door. *Shit.*

I stilled, my cock still inside Kaiya. Her eyes widened as she looked from me to the door and back again. Putting my finger to my lips, I gently set her down and slid myself out of her. I motioned for her to hide behind the bag as I put my dick back in my shorts and went toward the door.

Glancing over my shoulder, I made sure Kaiya was hidden from view then turned back around and exited.

One of the other trainers was in the middle of the studio, searching for me. "You need something?" I asked as I shut the door.

He turned around. "Where were you?" he asked suspiciously, looking over my shoulder.

"Doing inventory in the supply closet. What's up?"

"I just wanted to tell you that Mark can't make it to class tomorrow night, so he asked me to fill in for him. Is that cool?"

Really, you came in here and interrupted my sex session for that? "Yeah, that's fine. Be here at seven."

"All right, see you tomorrow," he replied as he walked to the door.

Once he left, I waited a minute or so before going back into the supply room. "The coast is clear," I called out.

Kaiya peeked her head out from behind the bag before coming out of her hiding spot. Her face reddened in embarrassment. "That was a close one," she said, straightening her sports bra and brushing her hair behind her ears with her fingers.

Chuckling, I made my way to her. "Yeah, it was. You want to pick up where we left off?"

"Ryker, we almost got caught," she chided, even though a smile lined her lips.

"So?" I teased, but she gave me a disapproving look. "Fine, but we're finishing this tonight."

Grinning seductively at me, she agreed, "Deal."

We spent another hour or so working on more techniques before I had a personal training session with another one of my clients. Kaiya planned to come over to my place after my shift ended, and I was looking forward to finishing what we had started.

When Kaiya arrived at my place, I had already set another plan into motion. I had been working on breaking another one of her rules, the one about staying over. I routinely broke the other two rules, almost nightly, so I was determined to break them all. *Two down, two to go.*

Whenever she came over, I always asked her to spend the night, but she resisted me. I hadn't stayed the night with a girl after that whore and I broke up, and I'd never wanted to until Kaiya. Everything was different with her, from the way she was able to make me smile so easily to the way she set a fire inside me with just one look. I loved every minute I spent with her.

We were hanging out on the couch watching T.V. when Kaiya mentioned, "I feel like dancing."

I played with her hair, twirling it around my fingers. "Yeah?" I replied in surprise. We hadn't been out to a club since the night that she'd been attacked.

"Can we go tonight?" She asked hopefully as she looked up at me.

I didn't really see the point in going to a club when the main reason that I had gone to them before was to pick up girls. I didn't need to do that anymore now that we were together. But I knew that Kaiya loved to dance, so I gave in. "Sure, baby. Where?"

"How about that new one that just opened up? I think it's called," she paused, looking up to the side and pursing her lips as she thought. "Tunnel."

"Yeah, I've heard of it. We can go if you want."

"Yay!" She hopped up off the couch excitedly. "I'll call Nori. Maybe you should text Drew to meet us—they seemed to have fun together the last time." She giggled as she tromped toward my bedroom.

I loved seeing her laugh—her smiles and laughs had become regular occurrences, replacing the scowls and sorrow that I had thought were permanently etched on her face. Some of the sadness still lingered at times when she thought I wasn't looking, but I was able to chase it away for a while. My goal was to totally eradicate it one day. That would be my biggest challenge yet.

I got off the couch to get my phone from the counter. I sent a text to Drew, who was down with the idea since he had fun with Nori the last time. He hadn't been able to close the deal with her, so I knew he'd be planning to tonight. If she was anything like Kaiya, he'd need all the luck he could get.

Kaiya came back into the room before grabbing her purse. A smile lit up her face. "Nori's in. I need to go home and get ready, then we'll meet you there, okay?"

"Yeah. Text me when you're on your way."

She stood on her toes to kiss me. "Okay, baby. See you later."

Once she left, I decided to head over to Drew's to wait until they were ready. We drank some beers to pass the time and when Kaiya finally text me, it was quarter till midnight. I didn't know what took women so long to get ready, but the end result was usually worth it.

This time was no exception. When Kaiya walked up to us outside the club, my pulse raced as the blood rushed to my cock.

She was wearing a tight, black one-shoulder dress that stopped right above her mid-thigh. She bit her lip as our eyes locked, her cheeks flooding with color as I admired her. I doubted I would ever get tired of looking at her; everything else paled in comparison to her stunning beauty.

Peering up at me with those captivating eyes, she smiled shyly. "Hey."

I leaned down to kiss her. "Can I just take you home now? I don't think I can wait with you looking like that."

Her grin spread as she laughed. "Then, all my hard work to look this way would be wasted."

"Oh, it won't go to waste. I'll make sure of it."

She rolled her eyes playfully then slid her hand into mine. As we walked to the entrance, Drew draped his arm around Nori, who was already giggling flirtatiously. *Yeah, he should be getting some tonight.*

We had to wait a few minutes in line before we were let into the club—the place was packed wall to wall, and the heavy bass of the music vibrated the air as we squeezed through the throng of people to get to the bar.

Decorated in various shades of gray with splashes of reds, the club was long and narrow, like its namesake. Rows of lights ran overhead, and they pulsed to the music as the colors fluctuated, taking on every hue of the rainbow. Couches lined the walls of the VIP area, but there was only standing room everywhere else, so we chose a spot close to the dance floor after taking a shot and ordering our drinks.

Kaiya sipped her cocktail as her eyes scanned through the crowd before settling on mine. A shy, yet seductive smile came over her lips as she glanced away.

Nori started pulling Drew towards the dance floor, but he resisted. "I'm not drunk enough for that yet." He chuckled.

Nori pouted. "Please. I promise I'll make it up to you later."

Drew conceded, letting Nori pull him out to the floor. They soon were lost in the sea of bodies as I directed my attention back to Kaiya. "You wanna dance, baby?"

Eagerly nodding, she threaded her free hand with mine and pulled me into the dancing crowd. Swaying to the beat, Kaiya pressed her ass into my cock, and my hands automatically went to her lithe hips as she moved against me.

Leaning into me, her body undulated rhythmically against mine, making me want to take her home early even more. My dick began to stiffen from her sensual movements as my mouth found her neck. Tilting it, she allowed me better access to taste her as my tongue traced along the slender flesh.

Pushing my erection against her, I caused her to bite back a moan as she turned her head to connect her lips with mine. Our tongues tangled along with our bodies, the sensual movements making our skin heat from a combination of body heat and arousal. I was on the verge of hiking up that dress and slipping inside her right in the middle of everyone—that's how crazy she made me, making me want her unlike anything before.

"Kaiya?" someone shouted over the music, interrupting us.

Kaiya broke away from me, her fair skin flushed and those full lips slightly swollen. My head followed hers as it turned in the direction of the voice, and anger began to simmer under my skin once I saw the source—Bryce.

Kaiya stiffened nervously as she uncomfortably said, "Hey, Bryce."

He stepped towards us, causing me to instinctively move in front of Kaiya. His eyes hardened as they met mine, and I knew he was pissed about her being with me. *Too fucking bad. She's mine.*

He looked around me, focusing back on Kaiya. His eyes softened some as he spoke to her, "You haven't returned my calls—I wanted to talk about what you said. I—"

"She obviously doesn't want to talk to you about it, or she would have answered your calls. Why don't you take a hint and leave her alone?"

Bryce moved toward me, coming right up in my face. *Brave, but stupid.* "I don't remember asking your opinion."

Clenching my fists, I snarled, "Back the fuck off before you get hurt."

"Guys, stop," Kaiya pleaded as she squeezed between us, pushing Bryce away from me. She put her back against me as she faced Bryce, keeping her hands on his chest. I growled low as I put my arms around her waist and pulled her away from him.

Kaiya gave me a look over her shoulder, but didn't say anything until she redirected her attention to Bryce. "Look, Bryce, I'm... Ryker and I... we're together now. Like I said in the text, I can't see you like that anymore, but I still want to be friends."

Glaring between me and her, he patronizingly remarked, "Really? After everything we've been through, you're just going to drop me for some... some... meathead that you just met?"

Meathead? Did he really just call me a meathead? What are we, in middle school? "This meathead will beat your ass if—"

"Stop!" Kaiya yelled, gaining both of our attentions, as well as some of the people's around us. "Look, Bryce, I'm sorry, but I can't help the way I feel. Ryker and I just connected, and—"

"Save it, Ky. I'm glad to finally see where I stand," Bryce spat before pivoting and disappearing into the crowd.

Shoulders slumping, Kaiya gazed sadly in the direction he went and sighed. "I didn't mean to hurt him."

"I know, Warrior. Try not to worry about it," I said as I rubbed my hands up and down her arms, hoping to comfort her. I knew from some of our talks about him that Bryce had provided stability for her when she needed it, and that she cared for him. I could tell that Bryce felt the same for Kaiya, too, maybe even loved her. How could he not? I was falling hard for her myself, and there was nothing I could do to stop it, even if I wanted to. I should've wanted to, should've been more concerned with protecting myself from being hurt again, but Kaiya had found a way to slip past my defenses, making me let my guard down.

Turning around, she wrapped her arms around me, hugging me tightly. I returned her embrace, enjoying the warmth it stirred in my stomach. I'd only felt this way once before, but it was already becoming stronger than it was back then. *Holy shit, I think I love her.*

Being the coward that I was, I pushed the thoughts away. Neither of us was ready for that, and I couldn't bring myself to say the words yet. I wasn't prepared for the repercussions of speaking them, especially if Kaiya didn't feel the same way, even though I was pretty sure she did. When she thought I wasn't looking, I caught the way she stared at me sometimes, that look of love—the one that was so evident on both of our faces in that picture we took at the aquarium.

Even still, I couldn't voice my feelings, too afraid of her rejection. I didn't want to push her away, unsure of how I would deal with not being with her anymore. The idea twisted my stomach uncomfortably, and I quickly pushed it away and focused on something else.

"Ready to go, baby?"

"Yeah." She scanned the dance floor. "Where's Nori and Drew?"

Looking around the club, I searched for them, finding them making out on the dance floor. Pointing them out to Kaiya, I joked, "I don't think they're ready to leave yet."

"I need to tell her we're leaving—she gets pissed when I leave without telling her," she replied before walking toward them.

When she came back, I linked our hands and led her through the crowd to get to the exit. The fresh breeze that hit us once we stepped outside was a welcome change from the hot air inside the club.

Once we got to my apartment, I was on Kaiya as soon as we

walked through the door. Our mouths collided as I lifted her, my hands gripping her exposed thighs as she hooked her legs around me. I slipped her dress up further as I headed for the couch, unable to wait any longer. I had been waiting all day to have her, and now that we were finally alone, I was taking full advantage.

Kaiya straddled me once I sat down. Her hands immediately found my jeans and she hastily unbuttoned them, as eager as I was for me to sink inside her.

As she pulled my cock out, I moved her panties to the side, and then she was lowering herself down on me. Filling her inch by inch, I groaned as she cried out in pleasure until she took all of me.

Slowly, she moved her hips into me as I removed her dress. Pulling her flush against me, my mouth found her tits as she continued to ride me. I teased her nipple with my tongue before nipping and sucking it lightly, causing her to moan over and over again.

Kaiya's pace increased as my hands caressed her silken skin and my mouth consumed her. I traced my teeth and tongue along her collarbone to her neck, then brought her lips to meet mine, needing to taste her sweetness. Our tongues threaded together as her hands knotted in my hair and pulled tightly as she rocked harder on my dick, bringing us both closer to ecstasy.

Grasping Kaiya's ass, I began to thrust upward, meeting her movements stroke for stroke. I could feel myself nearing release, so I broke my mouth away from Kaiya's, breathing heavily as I spoke against her lips, "I'm gonna come."

She didn't stop as she replied, her voice full of desire, "Come inside me."

Fuck me. "Are you sure?" I asked before biting her bottom lip.

"Yes," she moaned. "I'm on the shot."

I didn't know what that was, but I figured it was some form of birth control. I didn't really care, plus I was sure that Kaiya wouldn't let me come inside her if she wasn't on some type of contraceptive.

Rolling her hips, Kaiya's snug walls continued to perfectly caress my cock. I pounded up into her, jetting my cum inside her after only a few more strokes. Her pussy pulsated around my dick as her body shuddered her orgasm against me.

We stayed like that until our breathing evened. Then, Kaiya

reluctantly sighed, "I better get going home. It's late."

I brushed her hair out of her face, then caressed her cheek with my thumb as our gazes met. *Here goes nothing.* "Stay with me."

Her eyes searched mine. Framing her face with my hands, I pulled her to me, pressing a tender kiss on her lips before softly saying, "Please."

Silently, she lay her forehead against mine as she exhaled a deep breath. She remained quiet, and the longer time passed, the more I was sure she would say no. My pulse pounded as I waited for her response, and after what seemed like hours, she finally whispered, "Okay."

Abruptly pulling back, I looked at her in surprise. "You'll stay?"

She smiled softly at me. "I'll stay."

Grinning back, I stood and carried her to the bedroom. After getting ready for bed, I slid under the covers as Kaiya stood nervously on the other side. "This is the part where you get in with me," I teased with a grin.

Toying with the hem of the shirt I let her borrow to sleep in, she bit her bottom lip nervously as she looked at me. "I've never spent the night with a guy before."

"Never?"

"Never," she repeated.

Sitting up, I scooted to the edge of the bed where she stood, framing her between my legs. I linked both of my hands with hers as I pressed a kiss to her stomach, then tilted my head up to look at her. "Are you afraid of me, Warrior?"

Her brows furrowed as she firmly responded, "No."

"Do you trust me?" That was the million dollar question.

We stared at one another as she contemplated her answer. My heart pounded in my chest waiting for her response, wanting so badly for her to trust me, needing her to. "Yes," she finally replied, barely above a whisper.

The tension in my chest faded away from her answer. I moved back on the bed, pulling her with me as I lay down. Facing each other, I brought her into me as I covered us with the blanket. Pushing some hair behind her ear, I gently kissed her lips, then her forehead before wrapping my arms around her. "Goodnight, Warrior."

Sighing, she rested her head on my bicep as her arms draped over my bare side. Her stiff body relaxed as I rubbed her back, and she snuggled closer to me. Burying my face in her neck, I inhaled deeply, enjoying my smell still lingering on her skin. Closing my eyes, I loved the feel of her warm, delicate frame against my much larger one. Even though our bodies were so different, hers was perfect for mine in every way.

Tangled with the girl of my dreams, it didn't take long for me to surrender to sleep.

Chapter Twenty-One

Kaiya

My eyes fluttered open to Ryker's sleeping face. Once the fog of sleep lifted, realization sank in. *Holy shit, I spent the night.* Anxiety attempted to trap me in its clutches, my heartbeat and breathing starting to speed up as panic tried to set in.

Focusing on Ryker's handsome face, I took deep breaths as I studied his features. *You're with Ryker. You're safe. He won't hurt you.* That warm, fuzzy feeling that he gave me so often began to set in as I stared at him, melting away the anxiousness building inside me.

My eyes moved down, scanning over the beautiful artwork inked on his chest and arms. I wanted to trace over them with my fingers, commit them to memory, but I didn't want to wake him when he was so peaceful.

After several minutes, he began to stir before stretching lazily like a cat as he opened his eyes. When they met mine, a sleepy smile spread over that sexy mouth. "Good morning, beautiful," he said, his voice still thick with sleep.

"Morning," I murmured back.

He leaned forward, eyes on my lips, but I pulled away. He gave me a questioning look, to which I replied, "I haven't brushed my teeth."

Laughing, he threaded his fingers through my hair as he said, "I don't care about your breath, baby. Before I do anything else, the first thing I want to do is kiss my girl."

Damn, he just gets better and better. I smiled before conceding, "Okay, but closed lips until I brush my teeth."

He chuckled again, the sound vibrant and full of life. "Whatever you say, Warrior."

Leaning toward me again, he pressed his lips to mine. Even just that small kiss sent tingles throughout my body.

When he pulled away, he rubbed my back. "How'd you sleep?"

"Surprisingly well."

"You didn't think you would?"

"Honestly no. I have nightmares, and I don't sleep well, even at home. I definitely didn't think that I'd get any here, but that was the best sleep I've had in a while."

"Maybe you should stay over more often," He raised his eyebrows suggestively.

"Maybe I will," I replied teasingly. "If you're lucky."

Ryker gave me a playful grin before he pounced on me. Pinning my body beneath his, I squealed as he tickled me. Our laughter filled the room as I squirmed under him, trying to free myself from his grasp.

"I'm going to pee if you don't stop," I warned, still laughing.

Relenting, he propped himself on his elbows, framing my face between his arms as he gazed down at me. His lips parted to say something, but he closed them and stayed silent as he brushed some hair back that had fallen across my face and kissed me again. *I wonder what he was going to say.*

My internal thought was forgotten as the kiss deepened, the feel of his almost naked body atop mine so alluring that I didn't care whether I brushed my teeth or not. When his tongue parted my lips, I eagerly reciprocated, twining mine with his as he pressed his morning erection into me.

Ryker's hands pushed the shirt I was wearing up until it came off. I slipped down his boxer-briefs as he moved my panties to the side, just like last night. His hard shaft pressed against my slick entrance, slowly pushing in as he stretched me. His mouth captured a moan that escaped me as he cupped my face in his hands, passionately kissing me.

Ryker slowly pumped his hips into me, gently thrusting in and out of my sex. The delicate way he was touching and fucking me was so different from the way we normally had sex, but it was just as amazing. The emotion he was creating within me was unlike anything I'd ever felt before, connecting us in a way I'd never experienced with anyone else. In that moment, I knew no one would ever compare to Ryker—my body was made for his, and his for mine. He completed me in every sense of the word.

Pleasure swarmed every nerve from his touch, filling me with molten fire. Electricity began to build in my core, radiating through my body as my orgasm approached. *How does he do this to me?*

My hands knotted in his hair as he continued to rock into me, possessing all of me with his sinful mouth, inked hands, and divine cock.

Arching against him, he sank further inside me, my walls molding to him as he caressed them.

"Fuck, baby, I love your pussy," Ryker growled against my lips before slipping his tongue back in my mouth. *Fuck, so good.*

I could only moan in response, my mind already lost in oblivion from Ryker pleasuring my every cell. *Almost there, almost there.*

Pushing deeper each time, Ryker repeatedly thrust into me. After a few more strokes, my orgasm found me, trickling through every limb and drowning me in bliss. One hand tangled in my hair, softly pulling the long tresses as the other stroked every curve of my body. He stilled above me as warmth coated my core and his cock throbbed inside me.

Panting breathlessly, Ryker hovered over me as he stared down at me. Sweat glinted over his golden skin and dampened his messy hair as he smirked at me. *I could get used to this every morning.*

He gave me one last kiss before we disentangled ourselves. As I made my way to the bathroom, my phone rang. I went back to grab it, and saw Kamden's face and number on the screen. *Shit.*

I answered the phone to hear Kamden's enraged voice, "Where the fuck are you, Ky?"

"Good morning to you, too, Kamden," I greeted sarcastically.

"Morning? It's almost one in the afternoon, Kaiya. Where are you?" he gritted through the phone.

"I'm at Ryker's," I snapped back, immediately regretting it. *Fuck, I shouldn't have told him that.*

"What? You stayed the night at Ryker's?" he exclaimed angrily.

"Yeah, I did. I'm a grown woman for fuck's sake."

"You could've at least called me—I've been worried sick." His voice was strained, but it was more with concern than anger. He was still upset, but I could tell that he was relieved that he was hearing from me.

I sighed, feeling like shit. "I'm sorry. I didn't mean to worry you. I'll be home soon, okay?" I said, softening my tone, as well. I should have been more considerate—I'd only spent the night at Nori's before, and I called him beforehand to let him know. I felt like such a jerk for worrying him over something that could have easily been avoided.

After we said our goodbyes, I hung up the phone and turned around to go to the bathroom.

Ryker stood against the door, looking concerned as he asked, "Everything okay?"

"Yeah. Kamden was just upset that I didn't let him know I was staying here."

"He's protective over you," Ryker commented.

"He's been like that since the whole thing with Kaleb." I still couldn't believe that I had told him that Kaleb was my brother the day before.

"I would be, too if something like that happened to my sister."

Reaching him in the doorway, he blocked my path before tugging me in his arms. He must have sensed my unease about talking about Kaleb because he stated, "He's never going to hurt you again, Ky. I'll kill him if he tries."

Our eyes had locked as he spoke, and the warmth normally present when he looked at me was gone—he was completely serious. I knew without a doubt that he meant what he said, and that both comforted and scared me. If Kaleb ever did get released, he'd come after me. And that meant Ryker would protect me, and possibly get hurt. Kaleb always hurt people I got involved with, and I didn't want that for Ryker.

I didn't know how he found me—I hadn't told anyone at home about the party. They all thought I was spending the night at Nori's house.

One of the varsity football players, Liam, and I were upstairs. It was his best friend's party, so he let us use his bedroom to hook up.

We were both pretty drunk, and had been all over each other the whole night. By the time we made it to the bed, lust had gripped us in full force, and most of our clothes were off.

Liam ripped a condom open with his teeth and fumbled to slip it on. I needed him to be faster, wanted him to rid me of Kaleb's touch and replace it with his; anything to make me forget, at least for a little while.

Finally, he entered me, flushing out my thoughts and filling me with sensation. I couldn't focus on anything else except the intimate tangling of our bodies, and that was exactly what I wanted; to lose myself, if only for a short time.

Noise filled my ears, like a door slamming, but it didn't completely register, my mind lost in sexual oblivion as it closed off the outside world.

Only when I felt the loss of Liam against me did I start to comprehend what was happening. Kaleb was atop Liam on the floor, repeatedly punching him. Shit.

"Kaleb, stop!" I screamed as I pulled the blanket to cover my naked body.

Hand raised in the air, ready to throw another punch, he stilled before turning to look at me. He had that look in his eyes, the one that I had come to fear, the one that there was no reasoning with. Fuck.

I clutched the comforter tighter to me as he approached. Sitting next to me on the bed, he pried the covers from my hands and pulled them away, exposing my bare flesh to him. I cringed as he began to trace his fingers down my skin, trembling in fear for what he might do to me, how he would punish me.

"Kaleb, don't," I whimpered.

His fingers dug into my thigh as he snarled, "So, he can touch you, but I can't?"

Flinching, I cried out, "You're not supposed to touch me like that, Kaleb. You're my brother!"

His other hand came up to roughly grab my jaw, squeezing it painfully. "Yes, and that means that you're mine! No one else's! You let him fuck you, gave him what was mine," he accused angrily.

There has to be something wrong with him. He shouldn't be this way with me. Or maybe there's something wrong with me. Maybe I'm crazy. No one else makes their brother act this way.

"Look at me, Kaiya!" he yelled as he gripped my jaw harder.

My eyes snapped open to meet his, which were identical to mine. Same unique shade of blue, but I hated them. Tears trickled down my cheeks as he let go of me and roamed his hands over my breasts down to my sex.

I pushed his hands away and prepared for the backlash, clenching my eyes shut. Noise of footsteps and talking from outside the door caused them to snap back open. Kaleb stood up and backed away. Thank God.

Kaleb made his way for the door, glancing over his shoulder as he said, "This isn't over. I will take back what's mine."

I zoned out after that, pretending that I didn't hear his words, and wishing that my life was different.

"Ky? You with me, baby?" Ryker asked, cupping my cheek, bringing me back to the present. His eyes were brimmed with concern as he searched my face.

"Yeah, I'm fine. I get lost in my head sometimes." I smiled weakly. *Too much.*

"Don't get too lost up there. I want to be able to find you," he said as he grazed his thumb softly over my skin.

I couldn't stop myself from speaking what I felt in my heart. I'd always been strangely drawn to Ryker, like iron to a magnet, unable to stay away from him, even from the beginning. There was no way I'd be able to now. "I'll always find my way back to you."

Ryker brought my body into his as our lips joined in a tender, passion-filled kiss that made my knees feel like quicksand. When we finally separated, I wavered a little as I braced myself against him. He grinned cockily as he steadied me before smacking me lightly on the butt and letting me pass him to go into the bathroom.

After I finished getting ready, Ryker drove me home. He walked me up to the door, but I didn't want him to come in, afraid that he and Kamden would get into a fight because of last night. I really couldn't deal with that right now. I was trying to hold myself together after my flashback of Kaleb.

"See you at class tonight?" I asked as I tiptoed to kiss him, kissing him always chased away the darkness that threatened to swallow me.

Wrapping his arms around my waist, he placed his hands on my lower back, deepening the kiss before pulling away seconds later, way too soon. My lips tingled and I immediately missed the warmth of his mouth on mine. "Yeah. See you later, Warrior."

His smirk tightened my stomach, making me think about the morning and night before. My hand clumsily fumbled for the doorknob, and I slipped slightly as I missed it. Blushing profusely, I gave him an embarrassed smile as I found the handle and turned it. "Bye."

"Bye, baby," he replied, still wearing that grin. Turning, I entered my apartment and shut the door before leaning against it and letting out a breath. *The things he does to me.*

"Have fun?" Kamden questioned, notes of anger still lingering in his voice from earlier.

Really? Is he still mad? I thought we worked things out over the phone.

I pushed off the door. "I did, actually. Thanks for asking," I replied as I walked past him down the hallway.

"Kaiya, we need to talk."

"About what?" I asked as I stopped.

He approached me with his arms folded over his chest. "You and Ryker. Since you didn't take my advice and stay away from him, we need to talk about things."

"What things? Our relationship is none of your business, Kamden." I didn't understand why I was being so abrasive—I knew he was only concerned about me, but I hated that he was so adamant that Ryker and I not be together.

"Why are you acting like this? I'm just worried about you."

Sighing, I replied, "I know, but I'm not a kid anymore. I don't need you to protect me."

Kamden looked pained as he responded, "I didn't protect you when you needed me. It eats at me every day, Ky. Every. Single. Day. I just don't want you to get hurt again."

My eyes watered. I hated that he felt responsible when it wasn't his fault. If anything, it was our parents' fault for not paying more attention to their children. I set my hand over his crossed arms. "It wasn't your fault, Kam. We were just kids."

His mouth set in a hard frown as he inhaled deeply and shook his head. "You're my baby sister—I was supposed to protect you from anything like that ever happening."

I'd never be able to convince him otherwise, no matter what I said. We were both stubborn in that way. Once we got something in our head, there was no changing our minds. "You've more than made up for it by taking care of me and supporting me. I would've never made it without you," I replied sincerely.

He gave me a weak smile. "Yes, you would've. You're stronger than you know."

I rolled my eyes—I was the weakest person I knew. Having breakdowns and being afraid of your own reflection didn't equate to being a strong person in my book.

"Look, I know you're just worried about me, but don't. I haven't been this happy since… well, ever. Ryker may seem like an asshole, but he's… he's amazing. If anything, you should worry about me hurting him. My kind of crazy isn't good for people," I joked, or at least attempted to.

Kamden didn't laugh, but his smile broadened a tiny bit.

"You're not crazy, *sorella.*"

"Whatever you say. Seriously, don't worry about me. Ryker treats me very well." *Huge understatement.*

"If that changes—"

"You'll be the first to know," I interrupted, finishing his sentence.

Continuing my way down the hall, I headed to my room and stripped off my clothes before jumping in the shower. Once I emerged, fully refreshed, I made my way to my office, wanting to check my calendar to see the upcoming projects for the next few weeks and possibly get some work done on them. Ryker occupied a lot of my time, so I tried to squeeze in work whenever possible so I wouldn't get behind.

After I scanned over my desk calendar for the rest of August, I flipped up the page to look at September, my eyes zeroing in on a date circled in red. My body stiffened as fear began to root itself in my stomach, the darkness attempting to creep back in. *Kaleb's release. Holy shit, it's only a month away. Fuck, fuck, fuck.*

My leg bounced nervously as I stared at the date, unable to tear my gaze away from it. My pulse pounded in my ears as a thin sheen of sweat started to cling to my skin, making me uncomfortably hot. The blackness began to suffocate me, trying to blanket it me with its poison and send me spiraling into a breakdown. *Fight it, fight it. Focus on something else.*

I knew exactly what the perfect something was—Ryker. He always saved me, and breaking me from the tainted darkness was no exception. His face came into my mind, chasing away the inky mass threatening to crush me.

I broke free of the trance I was in as I threw the calendar, sending it flying off my desk. Pens and other office supplies joined it as they scattered over the floor. *Breathe, breathe, breathe.* Needing to escape, I rushed to my room as I repeated the phrase over and over in my head. Grabbing my phone, I immediately dialed Ryker, but it went to his voicemail. *Fuck, he's probably already at work.*

I paced nervously back and forth in my room, gnawing on my bottom lip. *Calm down. You're safe. Ryker and Kamden will protect you. Breathe, breathe, breathe.*

My hands shook with nerves as I sat on my bed. Pulling my knees up, I wrapped my arms around them and began to softly rock back and worth, attempting to soothe myself. Wet warmth coated my cheeks, my fight to contain my tears lost. *So weak.*

My phone rang, startling me. Glancing down at it next to me, Ryker's face filled the screen. I instantly grabbed it and answered. "Hello?" My voice was strained, thick with emotion.

He must've heard the panicked sadness in my voice because his response was quick and full of concern. "What's wrong, baby?"

I thought about lying, but I couldn't lie to Ryker. I was so good at it with everyone else but not him. Taking a deep breath, I tried to steady my voice. "Kaleb's release is a little over a month away. I just saw it on my calendar."

"Are you okay? Do I need to come over?"

My knight in shining armor. My lips curved up slightly from the gesture, warmth filling my body and ridding me of the cold that the darkness left snaking through my veins. I wiped my cheeks, which were tight from my dried tears. "No, I'm okay. I just wanted to hear your voice."

"Are you sure, Ky? I can leave work if you need me."

He didn't even understand how much I needed him. He had become the glue that held me together, the stitches that were slowly repairing the scars on my heart.

"No, I'm fine. I'll see you at class in a little bit."

"Call me if you need me, okay? I'll keep my phone on me." His voice was still edged with worry.

"Okay."

"Bye, baby."

"Bye."

When we hung up, I exhaled another breath before getting off the bed. Grabbing my laptop, I decided to do some work on it instead of facing the mess that I left in the office. Anything to keep my mind occupied.

I thought about going to Kamden, but I had been selfish with him our entire lives. I needed to learn to cope on my own, no matter how difficult it was. And now I had Ryker to help me through until I could handle everything on my own. Kamden deserved a break.

By the time I made it to the gym, I was like a balloon that was inflated to the point of bursting. I needed to see Ryker, to have him calm me down like only he could.

I arrived thirty minutes early so I could talk to him before the other students showed up. If not, I'd probably lose it and have a meltdown during class.

When I walked into our training room, Ryker immediately came over to me. His eyes searched mine. "Are you okay?"

"Yeah. Better now that I'm with you," I said as I forced a smile. It wasn't a lie, but I was still being plagued by the impending date looming over me, overshadowing the happiness Ryker brought me.

Slowly rubbing both of my arms up and down, the concern in his voice increased, "Maybe you should skip class tonight."

My brows furrowed as I frowned. "No. If anything, I need to get this out. Bottling it in only makes it worse—trust me, I know."

His mouth set in a tight line. He knew he wouldn't win this argument. "Fine, just take it easy."

Yeah, right. Me, take things easy? Nothing is ever easy when it comes to me. "I'll try. I really need to kick the shit out of something, though."

Ryker's lips quirked up to one side in a lopsided grin. "Always fighting."

Before I could respond, another student came in with David and an unfamiliar employee, not the normal instructor Mark. Ryker followed my gaze and said, "Mark couldn't make it tonight. Another one of the staff is filling in for him—I need to go brief him on class."

"Go ahead, I'll get my gear on."

Ryker walked away as I dropped my stuff by the bag I always used. I wrapped my hands with athletic tape, which I started using upon Ryker's insistence since I bruised so easily, then slipped on my gloves.

When class finally started, my pent-up frustration and stress still coursed through my body, making my muscles ache from the tension. I couldn't completely push the thought of Kaleb being released from my head, probably because of how soon it was. If I didn't expel everything soon, I was going to spontaneously combust. *What better way to release it all than to take it out on the bag?*

I began with simple jabs and punches, but after my fists connected with the vinyl, my moves intensified as fury took over my body. The bag morphed into Kaleb, and I completely lost it. Control was no longer mine as I cascaded into that abyss inside me, the source where all my demons lay.

My arms and legs flew as I pummeled Kaleb with elbows, kicks, and punches, making him hurt as he had hurt me all those years. Sweat drenched my face as I continued, unable to stop; if I stopped, he would only hurt me back, punish me for fighting him.

My chest burned as I struggled to breath, but I couldn't stop. I had to keep going, had to protect myself. Dizziness settled over my body like a heavy weight as my vision blurred, and I felt my knees meet the ground. *No.*

Ringing filled my ears from the piercing scream of someone, and I covered them to drown out all the noise. I clenched my eyes shut as I folded into myself, wanting to conceal as much of my body as possible from Kaleb's backlash.

Rough hands gripped my shoulders, causing me to strike outward. The hit was weak, but I still connected before slumping forward in exhaustion. I heard a familiar voice, but it didn't sound like it normally did; it was frantic and laced with fear. "Look at me, Ky! Come back to me, baby."

Trying to concentrate on the sound, I lifted my head slightly, but it caused everything to spin around me so I put it back down. My heart thudded as the voice urged, "Breathe, baby, breathe."

Closing my eyes again, I focused on taking deep breaths, trying to claw my way out of the dark chasm I was buried in. That voice kept talking to me, saying soothing things that helped bring me back towards reality, helped me regain some control.

Some of the pressure constricting me lifted, enough so that I opened my eyes to try and focus on my surroundings. The first thing I saw was a pair of warm, brown eyes that were creased in worry. *Ryker.*

Some of the tension eased from his strained face as he forced a smile. "There's my Warrior. I knew you'd fight your way back."

I blinked a few times to combat my blurred vision and dispel the rest of the disequilibrium clinging to me.

Ryker pushed my sweaty hair out of my face before handing me an open water bottle. "Drink."

Sipping the cool liquid, what had happened started to sink in. Embarrassment heated my already fevered face as tears stung my eyes. I glanced around the room, expecting to find a bunch of scared faces staring back at me, but there were none. The room was empty except for Ryker and me.

I gave him a confused look, and he answered my unspoken question. "I made everyone leave."

Completely humiliated didn't even come close to how I felt. I doubted that I'd be able to come to class ever again; Ryker would have to give me private lessons. If he still wanted to be with me.

"I'm sorry," I whispered as a tear rolled down my cheek..

"Sorry? For what?" His eyes held a look of confusion.

"That I flipped out and totally lost it, that you had to stop class because of me, that I embarrassed you," I bitterly replied as I looked down, angry for my lack of control.

Ryker gripped my chin and tilted my face to look at him. "I'm not embarrassed by you. Concerned, yes, but not embarrassed. And I don't give a fuck about stopping class—you are all I care about."

There's that amazing feeling stirring. "Thank you. I think I'm okay now."

"What happened?" He brushed his knuckles down the side of my face as his eyes met mine.

"I'm not exactly sure. I was trying to let my anger over Kaleb out on the bag, but I lost control. All I could see was him, and then I got lightheaded and disoriented. I can't really remember too much after that."

"You went crazy on the bag. You probably felt that way because you were holding your breath. When you fell, you scared the shit out of me—you were screaming so loud, and I had no idea what was wrong."

I was the one screaming? This just gets better and better. "I'm sorry. That happens sometimes. I thought I had better control over it now, but getting closer to his possible release is starting to get to me."

"That's understandable, baby. Don't stress yourself out about it." He rubbed his hands up and down my arms before threading our fingers together. "You know you're not alone in this—you have me. You don't have to fight by yourself, Warrior."

There was that feeling in my chest again—that one that made my heart beat faster and wrapped me in happiness. He was borderline perfect, knew exactly what I needed and the right words to say. I had no clue what the hell he saw in me—I was a hot mess.

"It's not easy to talk about. It's bad enough that I can't escape him since I see him whenever I look in the mirror."

"You look a lot alike? You and Kamden don't," Ryker commented.

Shit. I really didn't want to go there, but Ryker had become my rock, my anchor when I needed security and strength. I'd already realized if things didn't work out between us, there'd never be anyone that could take his place. He was it for me. If anyone deserved my trust, it was him. "He... he's my twin."

Ryker's face hardened, his beautiful mouth being dragged down in an angry frown as he seethed, "What?"

I didn't say anything. His rage was palpable, and even though I knew he wasn't angry at me, I didn't want to set him off. He abruptly stood before slamming his fist into the punching bag a few feet away from me. Roaring angrily, he threw it like it weighed almost nothing towards the center of the room.

His outburst didn't scare me. In fact, it made me feel good; it showed me that he truly cared. Never trusting anyone besides Kamden and Nori made it hard for me to judge whether someone's intentions or feelings were genuine, but there was no denying Ryker's. There was no doubt that he cared about me, maybe even loved me. *Could he possibly love me?* The thought was almost laughable since I was certain that I was completely crazy. Even if I wasn't, Ryker was still too good for me. Girls like me didn't get guys that looked like models. Not to mention that Ryker had such a good heart. *Yeah, he's way too good for me.*

Pacing the room, he cursed furiously. His face was painted red with anger as he looked toward me, locking his eyes with mine.

"He's your twin?" he asked again in disbelief.

"Yeah. We look identical, which makes it harder for me. I see him staring back at me all the time when I look in the mirror, so I avoid them as much as possible."

He looked utterly confused, almost at a loss for words. "How? Why?" he stammered, seeking answers that I'd been searching for years, answers I still didn't really have.

My eyes glistened as my chest tightened, but not in the same way Ryker caused. The tightening I was experiencing was from pain, anger, and sadness because of everything my own twin did to me.

"I never really got an answer to that. Kaleb always said that I was made for him. I was his. The psychiatrists and doctors said he had several mental conditions that caused him to be the way that he was, that it wasn't his fault," I bitterly replied. Even though I knew it was true, that his disorders contaminated him, controlled him, I couldn't forgive him for everything he did to me, for scarring me so deeply.

"Fucking bullshit," he muttered angrily. Approaching me, he sat beside me on the floor before cradling me in his lap. The position made me feel vulnerable and safe at the same time. Ryker tucked some hair behind my ear, releasing a sigh before promising, "He'll never get his hands on you again. No one will *ever* mistreat you again."

His statement broke the dam holding my tears. "I don't know what I did to deserve what he did to me," I choked through the sorrow clenching my throat.

Ryker clasped my face in his hands, forcing me to look at him. "You didn't deserve *any* of what he did. You hear me, Ky? None of it. What you deserve… what you deserve is to have everything you ever wished for. You deserve happiness, not sadness, love, not pain. You deserve more than I could ever give you, but I'm damn well going to try to give you everything you deserve."

I wanted to tell him that he was everything I ever wanted, more than I deserved, but there was still that small part of me that cowered in fear, afraid to give myself completely to Ryker. So I didn't say anything, like the coward I'd always been.

His thumbs wiped away the tears on my face before he kissed me, ever so gently. "Let's get you home."

Ryker drove me home, despite my protesting that I was okay to drive. I usually took the underground transit to work so I wouldn't have to pay ridiculous amounts for parking. Kamden could take me to pick up my car the next day when we went to work out, so it wasn't a big deal.

When we got to my apartment, I asked Ryker to come up. I was still fighting the feelings brought on by the events of the day and really needed him. Enough so that I was willing to deal with whatever Kamden had to say about it.

I walked up to the door, worried that Kamden would be on the other side and give me a hard time about Ryker. But as I opened it and stepped in, our apartment was dark except for a small light shining from the kitchen.

"Kam, I'm home," I called out, but there was no response. Ryker followed behind me to the kitchen and laid down the bag from the Chinese takeout we had picked up. When I went to the refrigerator to get plates and drinks, I found the note Kamden left, letting me know he had gone out with some friends. *Good for him.*

Ryker's arms wrapped around my waist and I leaned back against him. "He's not here. Went out with friends," I said, feeling a sense of relief. Kamden spent so much time taking care of me that he seldom did anything for himself.

"That's great. I get you all to myself," he whispered in my hair before pressing a kiss to my temple.

I brought my hands over his, smiling. "That sounds really nice." I took in another deep breath, inhaling his masculine scent before I pulled out of his hold. "We better eat."

Grabbing some dishes, Ryker helped me set the table. I glanced up at him periodically as we fell into a comfortable domestic routine, and I couldn't keep the smile off my face, thinking about how normal we seemed.

After finishing dinner, I started cleaning up the to-go boxes and plates when Ryker disappeared from the kitchen. I was slightly irritated that he wasn't helping me, but I wasn't going to say anything about it, not wanting to cause any tension between us. I'd had enough drama for one day.

As I was putting the last of everything in the trash, Ryker called from down the hall, "Hey, babe, can you come here for a second?"

I wiped my hands on a dish towel and threw it on the counter. I went to my room, but when I entered, he wasn't in there. *What is he up to?*

"In here," Ryker said, his voice coming from my bathroom. *What's he doing in there?* The door was slightly ajar, so I slowly pushed it open before stepping into the room. My eyes widened in surprise as a smile spread over my lips.

The room was dimly lit by candles that I had along the rim of my garden tub. Bubbles crested the top of the bath water that Ryker must have drawn for me while I cleaned up our dinner.

"I thought you needed to relax after today, so I got a bath ready for you. I hope you don't mind."

Walking over to him, I slipped my arms around his neck. "No, I don't mind. This is just what I needed. Thank you so much, baby."

"I'll let you relax," Ryker said as he leaned down. He pressed a kiss to my lips, then grinned and stepped around me and out of the bathroom.

The bath was exactly what I had needed, and I felt so much better after getting out. My muscles felt relaxed and most of the negativity still plaguing me had washed down the drain with the bathwater.

Wrapping my towel around me, I walked into my bedroom, ready to thank Ryker again for being so considerate. As I opened my mouth to speak, I immediately closed it when my gaze landed on him. He was sleeping on top of the comforter of my bed.

My heart warmed at the sight of him sleeping so peacefully. He had said earlier that I deserved more than him, but he was wrong. He was perfect for me; if anything, I didn't deserve him.

Not wanting to wake him, I quietly grabbed clothes to change into for bed and went back in the bathroom. He was still asleep when I came out, and I gnawed on my bottom lip as my thoughts attempted to ruin everything. *I've never had a guy spend the night in my bed before. I don't know if I can do this. Sleeping over at his house was one thing, but at mine is another. This is more personal, more intimate.*

Sitting cautiously on my bed, careful not to wake Ryker, I studied him as my mind warred. *Ryker won't hurt you. Look at everything he's done for you. You already broke your rule anyway.*

My decision made, I slipped under the covers. The movement caused Ryker's eyes to open. He blinked several times before his gaze met mine. "I didn't realize how tired I was," he yawned. "I better get going."

"You wanna stay?" My tone was hopeful, yet nervous.

"Isn't that against the rules?" he asked with a teasing grin.

Rolling my eyes, I smiled. "You're right. I guess you should go, then." I started pushing him off the bed for emphasis.

Grabbing my arms, he pulled me into him. "You know I like breaking rules, especially yours. I'll stay."

Letting go of me, he stood and kicked off his shoes. I was entranced by the rippling of his muscles as he removed his shirt and stripped his shorts off, leaving him in only his boxer-briefs. *Dear lord, thank you for this man.*

Joining me under the covers, he wrapped me in his embrace, spooning me. I felt his hot breath on my neck right before he placed a kiss there and whispered, "Night, Warrior."

Laying my arms over his, I snuggled back into him. The smile was still on my face as I drifted into sleep.

Chapter Twenty-Two

Ryker

Kaiya's screams woke me in the middle of the night. Gasping for air, she sat up and clutched her throat as tears ran down her face. I tried to rub her back once I sat up, but she jerked away as soon as I touched her.

"Hey, it's just me, Warrior. You're safe," I murmured softly, trying to soothe her.

Her eyes were wide with fear as she looked at me, examining every inch of my face, making sure it was really me. Finally, she leaned into my body and sighed before starting to sob again. *Fuck, I hate when she cries.* Pulling her into my lap, I attempted to comfort her, just like earlier that day. "Shh, baby. Don't cry. I'm not going to let him hurt you ever again."

Heavy footsteps pounded outside the door, getting louder with every step. Bursting into the room, Kamden flipped on the light, and his eyes darted from Kaiya in my arms to my face. "What did you do to her?" he seethed, his teeth gritted and fists clenched as he approached the bed.

"Nothing—she had a nightmare," I defended. Kaiya had her face buried in my chest. Her tears dripped down my skin as she continued to cry uncontrollably.

"Let me have her," he demanded, motioning with his hands for me to hand her to him.

I felt like I was having deja vu from the night she was attacked. I shook my head. "Nah, I'm good. I've got her."

Kamden's nostrils flared as we stared each other. "You and me," he gestured stiffly, the anger evident in his tone and body. "We need to have a talk."

"Not right now we don't," I countered, not backing down.

He stuck his jaw out defiantly. "In the morning."

"Fine," I clipped. *Leave already.*

He angrily stalked out of the room without another word, leaving me alone with Kaiya. *Finally.* Softly stroking her hair, I whispered words of comfort and rocked her gently. I didn't know how long we sat there like that, but I didn't care. She needed me, and I was going to do everything I could to be there for her.

Once she finally pulled away, her face was splotchy and her eyes were red. Moisture streaked her cheeks as she gazed up at me, still loosely holding her throat.

"Wanna talk about it, baby?"

She scanned over my face again as she bit her bottom lip, deciding whether or not to tell me. I expected her to say no, but she shocked me by nodding and letting out a heavy breath.

"We were seventeen. Kaleb had been more aggressive than normal for a few weeks, so I'd been avoiding him as much as possible, staying late at school, hanging out at Nori's, partying, going anywhere but home. That really pissed him off, and..." She paused as a sob broke through. I rubbed her back while she took some deep breaths to calm herself. Her voice was still shaky when she spoke again. "He... he took it out on me one afternoon when no one else was home. He took off my clothes, and started touching me, which I was used to already, but then... then he started taking off his clothes, too," she softly cried, choking back another sob.

My body was a volcano ready to erupt with rage. *How could her brother, her twin no less, do that to her?*

"He'd never done that before, and I put two and two together, knowing what he planned to do. Usually he just took my clothes off, but he'd caught me having sex with a guy from our school, found out that

I'd given something away that was supposedly his, so he wanted to take it back. I mean, it wasn't the first time that I'd had sex, but it was the first time Kaleb had found out about it."

One hand squeezed mine as the other fingered the scar on her throat. "I fought against him, but then he pulled a knife to my throat. He touched me more before stopping to take off his shirt. I tried to get away then, but he caught me before I got to the door. He pinned me and pressed the knife into my neck." She took a deep breath, and her lip quivered as a few more tears trickled down her face. She composed herself some before continuing, barely above a whisper, "Kamden came home early and busted through my door. He pulled Kaleb off me, but I ended up getting cut in the process. Kamden beat Kaleb unconscious, and then called 911."

Wow. "What happened after that?"

"I had to tell the police everything, which was so much. Things had been going on for as long as I could remember, even when we were really young. I didn't know it at the time, but he was overly affectionate and touched me inappropriately. It progressed over time, and he started becoming aggressive and possessive, touching me regularly when we started middle school. Everyone questioned me, asking me why I didn't say anything sooner, but it was all I ever knew. I thought it was normal until high school, but even then, I was too scared of him. He always said he'd kill me if I told anyone, and I believed him. I didn't think anyone would believe me anyway. I mean, Kaleb was my twin. Who would think that my own—" she sobbed, unable to speak anymore.

"I'm so sorry, Warrior," I murmured as I placed a soft kiss on her forehead.

Tilting her head, she looked up at me as I cradled her in my arms, her hand covering her throat. Gazing down at the beautiful, broken woman in my arms, all I could think about was how I could save her from her darkness, the darkness created by someone who should have never been the cause of it.

Reaching my hand up, I lay it on top of hers. I wanted her to feel less self-conscious about her scar, to let go of the fear and negativity associated with it. Slowly pulling her hand away, I kept our eyes locked. She slightly stiffened but didn't pull away or object to my actions.

I ran my fingers through her hair as I gently tipped her head back.

Bringing her closer to me, I leaned down to her neck and pressed light kisses along the scar on her throat. Her body trembled as she cried beneath my lips before she grasped my face in her hands.

Moving my head away from her neck, she brought my mouth up to meet hers. Connecting our lips, she wrapped her arms around my neck and molded against me. I felt her tears on my face before she pulled away and brought our foreheads together. "Thank you," she whispered.

I wiped the tears from her cheeks before laying us back down. Positioning our bodies together, I enveloped her in my arms as my body fit to hers. Kissing the back of her neck, I murmured, "Go back to sleep, baby. I got you."

Moving closer to me, she relaxed in my embrace. A short while later, her breathing deepened as sleep found her again, and I hoped that I could keep her nightmares away.

The blaring of Kaiya's alarm clock woke us. She withdrew from my arms and slid to the edge of the bed to turn the stupid thing off.

"Come back to bed. It's still dark out," I grumbled as I reached for her.

"I have to go to work," she replied as she rubbed her face, her voice heavy with sleep.

"Call in sick or something. We can play doctor," I said as I raised my eyebrows suggestively with my eyes barely open. She laughed, but still rose up off the bed.

"I'd like that, but Mondays are busy for me at the office. There's no way I could miss."

Throwing the sheets off me, I sat up before stretching and yawning. "I'll drive you."

"It's okay, you can sleep. I'll take the T," she called from her closet.

I scoffed. Like I'd really let her take the transit. "You're not taking the T. I'll drop you off."

We went back and forth a few times before she finally conceded. I got dressed before Kaiya made Kamden and me breakfast. Then, she went back to her room to finish getting ready, leaving us alone.

"So, about that talk," Kamden started as he stirred his coffee.

It's too early for this shit.

"Yeah?" My voice was gruff and irritated. I was so not in the mood to talk to him.

He turned in his seat to face me, crossing his arms over his chest. "What are your intentions with my sister?"

I laughed dryly, "None of your business."

"Kaiya is my business!" he roared as he slammed a fist on the counter. He craned his neck to look down the hall toward Kaiya's room before directing his attention back to me. He lowered his voice, but the anger in it was still obvious, "If you hurt her, I swear to God, I will-"

"Look, I lo-" I paused for a split second, catching myself, "care about Kaiya. I'm not going to hurt her."

We glared daggers at each other until Kaiya walked back into the room. Tension radiated from both of us as she looked from Kamden to me. "Everything okay?" she asked.

"Everything's fine, *sorella*," Kamden answered with a forced smile, his voice still strained with lingering anger.

Kaiya met my eyes, seeking my agreement with her brother's statement. "Yeah, everything's great, baby."

I could tell by the wary look on her face that she didn't completely believe us, but she didn't press the issue further. "Ready to go?" she asked as she came up to me.

Nodding, I followed her to the front door. She said goodbye to Kamden before we walked out. As we went down the stairs, she questioned, "What was that all about?"

"Just Kamden being protective, that's all. Don't worry about it." I shrugged nonchalantly.

Rolling her eyes, she responded in irritation, "He acts like I'm a child."

Chuckling, I replied, "He's just worried about you—he loves you."

"I know," she sighed as a small smile took over her face. "He can be a little much sometimes, but he really is a great big brother."

"Great for you; me, not so much," I joked.

"Yeah, I'd hate to be in your shoes. He doesn't like you very much," she admitted with a light laugh.

"His opinion doesn't matter to me—only yours does."

We reached my truck, and I walked Kaiya to the passenger side. She turned to face me, placing her back against the door. "I guess you're lucky that I like you," she teased with a playful grin.

Tugging on one of her curls, I twisted it around my finger and leaned in to kiss her. As I pulled away, I looked into her eyes, letting go of her hair as I ran my knuckles down her cheek. "Yeah, I'm pretty lucky."

Kaiya's cheeks flushed as I opened the door. I helped her step into the raised cab before getting in on my side and starting the engine.

Kaiya rested her hand on my knee the whole drive to her work. She leaned over to kiss me when we reached her office and groaned when we broke apart. "I really don't want to go to work."

Pulling her back to me, I gave her another kiss. "I told you to call in sick, but you insisted that you had to come."

She glanced up at the tall building before looking back at me. "Fine," she moaned. Gripping the handle of the door, she cracked the door open. "See you later?"

"Yeah, baby. Have a good day."

She smiled as she hopped out of my truck and shut the door. Blowing me a kiss goodbye, she waved and walked toward the building.

After I dropped her off, I went back to my house to sleep before I had to go to work. I had a busy schedule filled with training sessions and classes to look forward to, so I needed to have as much energy as possible to get me through the day. I couldn't imagine having to get up early every morning like Kaiya did to go to work.

I woke up a little before lunch time, and I didn't have to go in until a couple hours later. I decided to see if Kaiya had gone on her lunch break yet.

Me: Have you had lunch yet

Warrior: No

Me: Can I pick you up

Warrior: Sure :) my break is in twenty

Me: See you soon

Kaiya met me outside her office building twenty minutes later, and we decided to go to a deli around the corner to save time. After we were seated, I asked, "How's your day been?"

She groaned unhappily, "Grueling. Mondays are the worst. We have so many meetings. How about you?"

"Good. I went home and slept for a couple of hours."

"Must be nice," she replied sarcastically.

"Eh, it was okay." I shrugged. "I'd much rather have stayed in bed with you." I wiggled my eyebrows suggestively.

"Me too, but I don't have the luxury of working after lunch time like some people." She gave me a playful glare.

The waitress, a cute blonde with a heavy Boston accent, came to take our drink order. Once she left, we talked about one of Kaiya's meetings until the server brought us our waters and wrote down our meals.

When she walked away, Kaiya asked, "Do you have a busy day today?"

"I have a few classes and personal training sessions. They should keep me busy."

Kaiya swallowed nervously before saying, "Speaking of classes, I don't know if I should go to self-defense anymore."

"What? Why?" My face scrunched in confusion.

Sighing, she looked away at the wall. "I totally embarrassed myself last night. How am I going to be able to look those people in the eye after they saw me freak out like that?"

"Hey, look at me." I grabbed her hand across the table and rubbed it until she met my eyes. "No one will judge you. Hell, some of them have been in abusive relationships, and probably can relate to feeling out of control. Don't worry about what everyone else will think."

She exhaled a breath. "Can't you just give me private lessons?"

"Although I would love to," I paused, smirking as I thought about all the things we could do if I gave her private lessons. I put the thoughts to the side, saving them to act out later. "I'm not going to. I know you can do this, Ky."

Pouting, she reluctantly gave in. "Fine. I'll keep going."

"That's my girl," I stated proudly as I squeezed her hand. She was used to running when things made her scared or uncomfortable, but she had become much stronger than she was when we first met, even if she didn't believe it. I knew she could do anything she set her mind to as long as she fought her fear.

After we finished our lunch, I took Kaiya back to her office, then went back to my apartment to get ready for work.

As I drove to the gym, I thought about the conversation Kaiya and I had at lunch, about how much Kaiya and I had changed since that first day we met. I was glad I had decided to go after her, even though she fought me and made me work to finally have her. She was so worth it, and I couldn't imagine my life without her now. *Things would be so different.*

I headed straight for my office when I entered the gym, needing to look over my schedule one more time to make sure I was prepared for all my sessions and classes.

The day went by pretty quickly, and it seemed like only a couple of hours had passed when Kaiya and Kamden arrived at their usual time. Both of their faces were lit up in smiles when they walked in. *I wonder what's going on.*

I had to wait until I finished with a client before I was able to talk to Kaiya. Dragging me into my office, she shut the door, threw herself into my arms, and kissed me.

"Well, hello to you, too," I mumbled against her lips.

"I have great news. Kaleb's release was denied!" she exclaimed excitedly after pulling back from me.

"That's amazing, baby!" I hugged her and gave her another kiss.

"I feel like a huge weight has been lifted off me. I still can't believe it." Her eyes were bright with happiness and a huge smile spread from ear to ear.

I loved seeing her so happy. Maybe she would be able to get rid of all the negativity dragging her down since Kaleb wasn't getting out now.

"We need to celebrate. Anything you want to do this weekend, consider it done."

Squealing giddily, she bounced up and down. "I can't wait. Thank you for being so wonderful throughout this whole mess. Most guys would have turned and run once they got a glimpse at my issues."

I wouldn't have been able to stay away from her—I had tried and failed miserably. Kaiya had captivated me from the very beginning, and although we had some rough times, she brought so much good into my life, changing me for the better.

"I'm not most guys. You know I like the challenges you give me," I said with a playful wink. Pausing, I debated saying more, wary of going deeper into how I felt about her. I wasn't ready to tell her everything, but I wanted her to know that she meant something to me. "My life wouldn't have been the same without you, Ky."

Giving me a sweet smile, she laughed lightly. "I know that I wouldn't be the same if I didn't have you, but I doubt it goes both ways."

"Oh, it does, Warrior. I definitely wouldn't be this... alive if you didn't come fighting into my life," I replied sincerely as I cupped her cheek, grazing over it with my thumb.

Standing on her tiptoes, Kaiya pressed her lips to mine and slipped her tongue in my mouth.

Suppressing a groan, I snaked my hand around to the back of her head, cradling it as I deepened the kiss, my fingers tangling in her soft hair. Her hands traveled up my chest to around my neck as she pulled herself against me, moaning softly in my mouth. *Fuck, I don't think anyone will ever taste as good as she does.*

Pushing her back against my desk, I propped her up on it as her legs wrapped around my waist. Our hands roamed over each other's bodies, eagerly exploring as they sought more.

A knock on the door jarred us apart, leaving us both panting for air. Kaiya slid off the desk, keeping her distance from me as she stared at the door.

I cleared my throat from the lust clogging it. "Come in."

One of the other trainers walked in, holding a stack of papers in his hands. "Oh, I'm sorry, I didn't know you were with a client. Can you come to my office when you're finished?"

"Sure thing," I replied, irritated at the interruption. We shouldn't have been doing anything in the first place, but that wasn't the point. I wanted as much of Kaiya as I could get. It didn't matter where we were, even my work.

Once he left, my eyes ran over her, appraising her hungrily. "Now, where were we?"

Chapter Twenty-Three

Kaiya

There was no word to describe the elation I felt when I heard that Kaleb wasn't going to be released. Joy, relief, and excitement all combined within me to form some amazing emotion I hoped I felt more of in the future. Everything was finally falling into place for me, and I was ready to move on with my life without Kaleb looming over me.

I was really nervous about going back to class on Tuesday following my meltdown, even after my talk with Ryker. Although I was afraid of facing everyone, I didn't want to be ruled by my fear anymore. There was nothing I feared more than Kaleb, and now that he was out of the picture, I wanted to try and face any challenge presented to me.

Sitting in my car outside the gym, I took some deep breaths before getting out. The entire walk to the kickboxing room, I silently chanted, *you can do this, you can do this.* The whole situation might not have been a big deal to anyone else, but it made me so self-conscious that other people had a glimpse at my personal demons. I worked so hard to keep them private, and now everyone in class knew there was something wrong with me.

Stopping outside the door, I reached for the handle, but stilled before grabbing it. I noticed that my hand was shaking. I balled it into a fist to stop the trembling. *What if they make fun of me?* I laughed at myself. *What am I in high school? Who cares if they make fun of me? It's not like their opinions matter. Suck it up and quit being afraid.* I took another deep breath, repeated my mantra again, and opened the door.

Avoiding eye contact, I searched for Ryker, needing his support if I was going to make it through class. If he wasn't the instructor, I doubted I would have come back at all.

Our eyes met from across the room. His sexy smile sent warm tingles through my body, and my stomach flip-flopped, making me forget my apprehension about class.

He wore that grin as he approached me, wrapping his arms around me once he reached where I stood. Placing a kiss below my ear, he murmured in that deep, husky voice that I loved, "I missed you."

Ryker hadn't been hiding his affections for me for the past few weeks at class, so most of the students, if not all, knew that we had something going on. That was another reason I worried about returning—I didn't want them to judge Ryker because of my actions. I was sure they already questioned why he was with me in the first place; hell, I asked myself that question daily. After witnessing my breakdown, they probably thought he was just as crazy to be with me.

"I missed you, too," I softly replied, feeling my cheeks heat. Ryker still affected me the same way after almost six months, and I prayed that it never changed.

When he pulled away, I could feel the stares on us. I'd always hated that feeling, the one that made the hair stand up on the back of my neck. But with the way Ryker was looking at me, I didn't care about what anyone was thinking as they watched us. All that mattered was that look in his eyes, the one I first saw in the picture we took at the aquarium, the one I'd glimpsed on several occasions since; the one I was sure was evident on my face every single day.

I'd never been in love before, but I was never more certain of anything in my life than I was at that moment. I loved Ryker. But was I going to tell him? No. I was scared. My number one fear had gone from Kaleb being released to losing Ryker.

Telling him I loved him might chase him away. I knew that many guys ran when a girl said those three words, and that was the last thing I wanted to do. Not willing to chance it, I decided to wait until he said it first. If he ever did. *I hope he does.*

Another student had started talking to Ryker, so I headed for my bag to get ready for class to start. I avoided making eye contact with anyone as I stretched out and slipped on my gloves.

As soon as my fists and legs hit the bag when we started the first combo, I was happy that Ryker convinced me to come back. I didn't know why I thought I could give it up—kickboxing had become a part of me, just like Ryker had. Both made me feel stronger, more empowered… capable of anything. Even though I started taking the class to protect myself for when Kaleb was released, I couldn't see myself giving it up now that he wasn't.

Ryker came over as I was working on the second combo that he demonstrated. Those full lips of his tipped up playfully as he teased, "And you didn't want to come back."

Stopping, I rolled my eyes. "You were right. Thank you for making me come back."

"I couldn't let you give it up. Plus, I'd miss watching you work that amazing body of yours." His voice had deepened, taking on the tone that meant he was getting turned on.

I let out a laugh before I pushed him away. "Stop distracting me."

Backing up, he gave me a sexy pout, then headed to another student. I fought the butterflies he caused in my lower abdomen as I focused back on the bag.

Once the first part of class was over, we gathered as a group like always. When Ryker asked if anyone had requests for the next portion of class, I surprised everyone, including myself, when I raised my hand. Ryker gave me an inquisitive look, his eyebrows raising in surprise as he called on me. "Kaiya?"

I lowered my hand. "Can we learn how to defend against knife attacks?"

He smiled proudly at me, causing more butterflies to somersault in my stomach. "We can. Knives are easier for criminals to get their hands on than a gun, so many attacks involve a knife. Get with your partners."

As Ryker walked toward me, he had a look of admiration on his face.

"What?" I asked with a shy smile as our eyes met.

"Just proud of you," he grinned widely. "Are you sure you want to do this?"

"I'm sure. I want to know what to do if it happens again. I might not be so lucky the next time around."

Ryker's eyes hardened, and his jaw tensed as his lips set in a frown. "There won't be a next time, that's for damn sure," he practically growled.

I waited for his expression to soften, but it didn't. He was actually upset at the thought.

"Hey, it's just a precaution, right? No reason to get upset," I said calmly as I placed my hand on his bicep.

His stiff body relaxed some as he gave me a small smile. "Yeah, you're right. I just don't like the thought of you getting hurt."

His words warmed my insides like coffee on a cold day. *He really cares about me, doesn't he?*

He walked over to one of his supply tubs and brought out a prop knife. Stiffening slightly from the reminder of my attack, my hand instinctively went for my throat. Ryker noticed my apprehension as he came back to me. "We don't have to do this if you're not ready, Ky. Kaleb isn't getting released anymore."

Our eyes met again, and I remembered how his loving touch the other night had made me realize that I couldn't let my attack have the kind of power it had over me; I couldn't let Kaleb have that kind of power over me anymore. I was done being afraid.

"No, I'm ready." I said after taking a deep breath.

Ryker paused, searching my face briefly. "Okay. First, I'm going to show you what to do if someone is coming at you with a knife. Then, we can work on defense from behind."

Ryker took up his fighting stance, holding the knife in his right hand. "Typically, an attacker is going to try to stab you in the stomach, thrusting directly forward like this," he demonstrated, slowly moving the knife towards the center of my abdomen. "And, most will repeatedly stab you, so you need to disable them, not just block their initial attack because they'll come at you again."

Handing me the knife, he instructed, "Pretend that you're going to stab me." When I did as he said, he shifted his hips back, moving his torso out of the way as he threw his arms out to trap mine. The back of his right arm was on top of mine while the back of his left sat under, sandwiching it in place. "When they thrust at you, you need to block their arm, prevent it from getting near you while moving your body back. Your dominant hand needs to be on top, right above their elbow, and your opposite arm needs to be under their forearm. So, for you, your right arm will be on top. I basically made my arms into an X, trapping yours in between and securing it from going further."

Nodding, I asked, "Then what?"

"Then, you're going to turn your top hand over, gripping the bottom of the tricep. Once you have a secure grip, move your other hand to their elbow and pull their arm into your chest, trapping it there. Act like you're sawing their tricep with your right hand until your wrist is digging into it and then clasp your hands together. Now, you have them in a simple arm bar."

He had executed the moves as he spoke, so I was bent over with my arm pulled back and trapped between his two, huge, muscular ones. For me, I wasn't in any pain, just uncomfortable, because I was pretty flexible, but Ryker could easily snap my arm from the position I was in.

"Now, you're going to want to take a step back to protect yourself from getting hit. Most people will reflexively put their other hand down on the ground to stabilize themselves. If they do, you can stomp on their fingers, which will almost guarantee breakage. Or you could just do some knees to the face, which will knock them out after a few solid hits."

Ryker loosened his hold on me, then helped me stand upright. He rubbed my arm. "You okay?"

"I'm fine. You know I'm flexible." I gave him a playful smile.

"That I do." He winked, and his dark, seductive eyes gleamed with mischief. "Let's go through it again."

We repeated the maneuver twice more before we switched roles. Ryker had to talk me through the moves as I completed them at a snail's pace the first two times, but they were becoming more fluid after my third try. By the fifth time, I had a pretty good grasp on the concept, but I knew I would need to practice again to really get it. Something to do at our next Saturday session.

"Now, I want to practice if someone comes up behind you and puts a knife to your throat. You think you can handle that?"

My stomach contorted uncomfortably at the thought. *It's not a real knife and it's only Ryker. You can do this. You wanted this.* Swallowing the knot of fear in my throat, I nodded. "I can do it."

Ryker didn't look convinced as his eyes perused my face. "If it gets too much for you at any point, just tell me and we'll stop, okay?"

"Okay," I meekly replied, my voice sounded frail and gauzy as I tried to hide my nerves and push down the fear trying to take over.

"Baby, I don't like seeing you like this. Maybe this isn't a good idea." His eyes filled with concern, and his voice was heavy with doubt.

I was about to take the easy way out and agree, to tell him that I couldn't do it, but I wanted to be stronger, wanted to make him proud. "I'm okay. I can do this," I replied, hoping I sounded stronger than I felt.

Ryker didn't say anything for a few seconds before he conceded, sighing. "Fine. I'll talk you through the whole thing."

As usual, Ryker had me act as the attacker first, walking me through the steps of how to defend. That was the easy part. After demonstrating several times, he asked, "Ready to try?"

I nodded, afraid to speak and betray the fact that I was borderline terrified of having that thing pressed against my throat, scared that it would cause another panic attack in the middle of class.

Ryker's familiar body pressed up against my back. Leaning into him, I reveled in the feel of his large body and strong frame, needing it to get me through the maneuver. *You can do this. Conquer your fears. Overcome your weakness.*

Closing my eyes, I waited for the pressure of the knife against my scar. Instead, Ryker's hands grazed my bare arms, trailing down until he linked our fingers together. I felt the warmth of his breath on the side of my neck before his lips met my skin. His mouth lingered there several seconds, causing a shiver to run up my spine as he whispered, "You can do this, Warrior. You're one of the strongest people I've ever met. I believe in you."

My heart stuttered in my chest, my breath catching at the tenderness of his words. *What would I do without him?*

His hands left mine, but he continued to talk to me. "I'm going to put the prop to your throat now. Remember, it's not real, and I would never hurt you."

One of his hands came up to grip my shoulder as he brought the fake knife to my neck. Stiffening as I felt it push against my scar, my heart started to beat erratically. *It's not real. Don't freak out over nothing.*

"It's just me, baby. Relax. You can do this."

I eased against him, focusing on his words.

"Good, now grab my arm with both hands, one hand on the outside, one on the inside, pulling it away as you throw your head back."

Doing as he instructed, I fit my hands around his bulky, inked forearm, near his wrist, and threw my head back. Ryker angled to the side so that he wouldn't get hit, expecting my move.

"Good, now after you connect, step to the side opposite of the knife, lean forward, and push that sweet ass into me."

A laugh burst from deep in my belly because of his words. Feeling the tension leaving me over the whole situation, I followed his directions, rubbing my ass against his growing erection as I leaned over. A low, strangled groan came from him as he buried his head in the middle of my back.

"You okay back there?" I asked in a teasing tone, loving the reaction I had caused.

"Great," he replied before clearing his throat. "Now, use your left hand to throw a hammer-fist to my groin. If I were using my other hand to hold the knife, you would use your right hand instead. After you connect, use that same arm to elbow me in the stomach and or face."

I performed all the moves lightly, so that I wouldn't hurt him. Ryker continued his instructions, moving on to the next step, "Keep your hands securely around my wrist as you rotate your body outward, away from me, twisting my arm around. You should end up facing me with my arm upside down in front of you, between us. From here, kick the groin and then keep twisting my arm in the opposite way from its natural bend until I fall."

Believe it or not, I made Ryker fall flat on his ass when I did that, but he probably fell for my benefit.

"Now, you can either kick me in the ribs a few times, pry the knife from me and run, or both; your choice. I would do both just to be safe because you don't want them to chase after you, especially if they still have the weapon."

Opting to do both like he suggested, I completed the maneuver. Ryker stood and came over to me, wrapping me in his arms and praising in my ear, "You did it, baby. You did it."

Squeezing him back, I held back the tears that were trying to escape. They were happy tears, but I still didn't want to cry in the middle of class again. *I did it, I really did it.*

Ryker pulled back, smiling proudly at me. "You wanna practice it again?"

"Yeah. Let's do it again." I smiled back.

"That's my girl. I knew you had it in you, Warrior."

As we continued to practice the routine, I couldn't keep the smile off my face.

The following Saturday morning, loud banging on my front door woke Ryker and me. The sun was barely creeping in my window, so I could tell that it was still early.

"Who the fuck is that?" Ryker muttered groggily.

I started to get out of bed, but Ryker pulled me back into him, wrapping his arms around me and burying his face in my messy hair. "Let Kamden get it."

Kamden's footsteps sounded a few seconds later, so I snuggled into Ryker and closed my eyes to go back to sleep. The sound of yelling caused them to snap back open again moments later. *I know that voice.*

Outraged and shocked, I threw the covers off me and flung open my door. I could hear Ryker calling after to me, but I stormed down the hallway towards Kamden and the person he was arguing with. My mother.

When she saw me, her face reddened in anger as every feature tightened. Pointing her finger at me, she screamed, "You! This is all your fault."

My fault? Is she fucking serious? "None of this is my fault. Kaleb did this to himself!" I shouted.

"Mom, you need to leave," Kamden replied stiffly.

Our mother ignored him, and instead of doing as he requested, she lunged for me. Ryker stepped in front of me as Kamden grabbed our mom around the waist and pulled her out the front door.

"No! This is all her fault. My baby is stuck in there because of her! He's devastated!" she wailed before Kamden slammed the door.

I could still hear them arguing outside the apartment as my face burned with a combination of rage and sadness. *How can my own mother blame me for what Kaleb did to me? How is it my fault?*

Hot tears ran down my cheeks as a small sob burst through my throat. Ryker turned around, abandoning his defensive stance to cradle me to his chest. "Don't cry, baby. She doesn't know what the fuck she's talking about."

The feel of his smooth, bare skin against me was soothing, helping calm my ragged emotions. My mom and I were never that close. Kaleb had always been her favorite, but her words still stung regardless.

"She hates me," I cried into his chest.

"She doesn't hate you. And if she does, then it's her loss." He rubbed my back softly. "For her to choose that monster over you is ridiculous. You're a beautiful, amazing woman."

Hearing the door open and shut, I peeked under Ryker's arm to see Kamden walking towards us. I pulled back and wiped my face when he reached us.

"You okay?" he asked with concern.

I sniffled as I nodded. "Yeah, hurt and confused, but I'll be fine."

Ryker continued to rub my back as Kamden said, "I'm not condoning her actions or anything, but she's just having a hard time dealing with all this. I don't know how I'd cope if my son had molested his twin sister for most of their lives, especially when I hadn't known."

"But it's not Kaiya's fault. There's no reason for your mom to blame her, especially after everything Ky's been through," Ryker defended with a scowl.

Kamden gave him a death glare before focusing his attention back to me. "I'm not trying to justify her actions, I'm just trying to help you understand why she's acting the way she is."

"I know," I sighed. I couldn't help but feel a little pang of pain in my chest because it did seem like he was defending her. I knew it must have been difficult for her to deal with the issues within our family. My dad had left after Kaleb was committed, making it worse, but there was no reason for her to start pointing fingers, especially when they were being directed at the wrong person. It was too early for me to try to make sense of what had just happened, so I opted for escape. "I'm going back to sleep."

Ryker followed me back to my room, where we cocooned back in the warmth of my bed. Facing him, I placed a kiss on his collarbone as his arms came around me. His lips pressed against my forehead as he draped my leg over his thigh, fitting the lower half of our bodies together. He pulled the blanket over us, and as we lay there, entangled in my bed, I never felt safer.

Chapter Twenty-Four

Ryker

After Kaiya's confrontation with her bitch of a mom, she stayed in bed, pretending to sleep, long after I knew she was awake. I lay there with her, faking sleep, too, until I figured out a plan I thought would cheer her up. Then, I got out of bed and headed for the kitchen.

Kamden was sitting at the breakfast bar drinking coffee when I walked in. Remaining silent, I walked to the refrigerator and opened it, pulling out a few items and setting them on the counter.

"How is she?" Kamden asked. I could feel his eyes on my back as I began making Kaiya breakfast.

I didn't turn around. "Not good. She's laying in bed, pretending to sleep."

"I'm going to go talk to her," he stated. The sound of his chair pushing against the tile followed his words, and then I heard his footsteps leaving the room.

Kaiya loved French toast. Luckily, it was one of my favorites too, especially since it was a cheat day only meal, so I knew how to make it.

After I fixed a plate for Kaiya, I poured her a small glass of milk, grabbed the syrup, and put it all on a tray before carrying it down the hall toward her room. Kamden exited, leaving the door slightly cracked.

He didn't say anything as he walked past me, but I caught the smile that crept over his face when he saw the tray in my hands.

I gently kicked the door open and walked in. Kaiya was still in bed, facing the window. When I rounded the bed, her puffy, red eyes locked on mine, and I wanted to punch something because of the pain in them. I never wanted her to feel pain again now that her bastard of a brother wasn't getting released.

Her gaze traveled down to the tray in my hands. Those pretty lips curved slightly as I sat down beside her, placing the tray over her lap. "I made you breakfast," I said, hoping the gesture would brighten her mood.

As she focused on the plate, her smile widened and her eyes lightened as she looked back at me. "Baby, you didn't have to do this."

Leaning toward her, I kissed her temple. "I wanted to cheer you up. I know how much you love French toast."

"I do. Thank you," she replied genuinely, her voice losing most of the sadness present earlier. Picking up the fork and knife, she started cutting the bread into small squares before pouring syrup on top.

As she ate, I stole bites from her plate, getting my fingers sticky with syrup. After I took my fifth piece, Kaiya smacked my hand and playfully scolded, "Stop taking my food. Get your own."

Chuckling, I slowly sucked the syrup from my fingers, making sure she was watching me. Those beautiful blue eyes heated with desire as she focused on my mouth, her lips parting slightly as she swallowed deeply. *Fuck me.*

As I moved toward her, I heard her breath stutter right before our lips met. Her mouth was slightly sticky and sweet from the syrup as my tongue parted her lips, meeting hers and tangling languidly.

I nibbled on her bottom lip before pulling away. Her cheeks were flushed as she peeked up at me from beneath her dark lashes. I loved when she looked at me that way, so innocent and seductive at the same time.

"French toast is definitely my favorite," I joked as I licked my lips.

Kaiya burst into a laugh from my words. "Mine too."

After Kaiya finished eating, she seemed to be in a much better mood. Her face was no longer weighed down with sorrow as a smile replaced the frown from earlier. Her eyes returned to their normal, vibrant hue instead of being tainted with redness and tears, but I could still see a trace of unhappiness in them, no doubt from her mother's harsh words. I hoped she'd be able to get over it soon—there was no reason for her to be upset over her mom or Kaleb ever again.

We took the dirty dishes back to the kitchen, where Kaiya insisted she make me my own plate of French toast.

I sat at the breakfast bar as she cooked, inhaling the smell of cinnamon and vanilla as it wafted through the kitchen. "You excited about tonight?" I asked as I watched her.

She nodded as she flipped a piece of bread in the pan. "I can't wait! I've never been to the opening of a club before."

A new club was opening in downtown Boston, and I planned to take Kaiya out to a late dinner at an upscale restaurant before heading there. I hadn't told her where we were going, and the anticipation was eating her up.

"Why don't you just tell me where you're taking me for dinner?"

"Nope. That would ruin the surprise."

Letting out a frustrated groan, she flipped the bread again. A few minutes later, she brought my plate, and pressed a kiss to my cheek. I couldn't help but smile, thinking about how I could get used to being this way with her. Sleeping in before making breakfast together on the weekends. Waking up to that gorgeous face every morning. Going to bed with her wrapped in my arms each night.

"What?" Kaiya asked as she sat next to me.

I wanted to tell her how I felt, but the words were stuck, caught in my throat. Clearing it, I replied, "Nothing, babe. Thank you." *Pussy.*

She smiled sweetly back at me, kicking my heart rate up. Just her smiles made me crazy. "You're welcome."

After I ate, I helped Kaiya clean up the kitchen. Then, I got dressed, and went back to my apartment to get ready for work. I planned to pick Kaiya up after my shift ended, and the day passed by sluggishly since I was excited about our date, thoughts playing in my head of what I wanted to do to her once we were alone afterward.

When she opened the door to greet me, I knew I wasn't going to be able to wait until after the date. The dress she was wearing—fuck, it was so hot on her, but the only thing I wanted to do was rip it off, revealing that creamy, soft skin underneath. I needed her right there and then.

Her expression told me that she felt the same. Nibbling that full, bottom lip, it basically looked like she was fucking me with her eyes as they traveled down my body.

"You want to come in?" she asked seductively. "Kamden's not home. He should be gone for a while."

Fuck yes. "Yeah," I answered, my voice already thick with lust as my eyes greedily devoured her body, taking all of her in.

When she turned around, leading me into her apartment, my eyes focused on that sweet ass swaying back and forth as she walked. I wanted to bend her over the bed, lift that dress up and sink into her from behind. And that's exactly what I planned to do.

"Like what you see?" Kaiya asked, interrupting my thoughts, a sinful gleam in her eyes as she glanced over her shoulder at me.

Reaching her bedroom, I smirked. *Hell yeah I do.* "Yeah, baby, just wait till I show you how much."

Then, I was on her. Our hands were everywhere as our mouths crashed together, nipping and sucking as we consumed each other.

Backing her up toward the bed, I turned her around when I felt her legs hit the mattress. Bending her over, I roughly pressed my dick against her ass, causing her to moan.

Kaiya pushed against me, rubbing that perfect ass on my cock, which was straining through my jeans.

"Yeah, baby, lift that sweet ass for me."

My hands slowly inched the bottom of her dress up over her hips, revealing her lacy thong. Unbuttoning my jeans, I pulled my dick out before rubbing it over the soft skin of her ass.

Reaching between her thighs, I moved her panties to the side as my fingers found her pussy, which was soaked. "Fuck, baby, you're so wet for me. So fucking wet."

I continued to play with her clit as my cock neared her entrance. Teasing her, I rubbed it back and forth along her pussy, causing strangled cries of pleasure to sound from her.

"You like that, baby? You want my dick inside you?"

"God, yes," she groaned.

In one, hard thrust, I sank myself into her until she was completely full of me. Her pussy clenched me tighter from our position as I gripped her hips, pumping in and out of her.

Our skin slapped together as I pounded into her. She fisted the sheets in her hands, moaning loudly as I fucked her. My pace increased as I felt her pulsing around me, knowing that she was close to coming. One of my hands reached around, my fingers finding her drenched clit before rapidly stroking it, causing her to tremble beneath me.

Seconds later, Kaiya came, her pussy throbbing around my cock as she gutturally cried out my name. I loved how it sounded coming from her lips, loved that I made her as out of control as she made me.

Gripping her hips tighter, I thrust roughly into her, shooting my cum inside her. Fuck, I loved coming inside her, claiming her pussy as mine. And she was mine—my drug, my addiction, my high. Kaiya was my everything.

Rolling to the side, I pulled her with me, keeping my dick inside her. I nuzzled her neck before kissing her, murmuring against her skin, "You like that, baby?"

"Mmm, hmm," she mumbled in pleasure as she lazily traced her fingertips along my arm.

Pulling out, I got off the bed to grab a towel. Once we were all cleaned up, Kaiya straightened her dress before fixing her hair and make-up.

"Ready to go?" she asked when she came out of the bathroom.

I couldn't help but notice the rosy flush on her cheeks from our sex. Smirking, I nodded and grazed my knuckles over one of her cheekbones before taking her hand in mine and walking down the hall.

I had made reservations at a fondue restaurant. Neither of us had ever been to one, but I had heard that the experience and the food were one of a kind.

When we entered, the room was dimly lit, each table had a trio of candles, and soft, romantic music played in the background. Kaiya smiled widely as she took in the environment, squeezing my hand in excitement.

Once we were seated, a waiter came to take our drink order. We decided to get a bottle of wine for the special occasion, and after our server left, Kaiya was beaming with happiness. I loved seeing her like that, especially when I was the cause.

"You excited, baby?" I asked as I rubbed her thigh softly.

"Yes! I've heard amazing things about this place. I can't wait!" Her voice came out as a squeal as she smiled giddily.

When the waiter came back with our wine, he poured both of us a glass before asking, "Have you ever dined with us before?"

"No, this is our first time," I answered.

"Okay, well thank you for choosing us to spend your evening with. Let me explain your options. If you want the full experience, I suggest all four courses, which is cheese, salad, entree, and dessert." His tone was formal and polite as he continued to discuss our choices. Once he finished, he questioned, "Which option would you like go with?

I glanced at Kaiya, who still had a huge smile on her face. "I think we'll go for the four courses so we can get the full experience."

"Excellent choice, sir."

After we made our selections for cheese and salad, the server left to put our order in. When he returned, he had the ingredients to make our first course and prepared it tableside. Kaiya watch with enthusiasm, her eyes wide and the same huge smile still overtaking her whole face, as the waiter crafted our cheese fondue. Just the sight of her so happy made everything right in the world.

Once dessert came, we were both already getting full, even though the portions in each course were small. We had chosen a white chocolate Crème Brulee, and it came with sliced strawberries, bananas, cheesecake squares, marshmallows and other small cake and dessert bites. The spread looked too good to pass up.

When Kaiya dipped a strawberry in the melted chocolate, I suddenly wished we were at home. Grabbing the elongated fondue fork from her, I guided it to her mouth before feeding her.

Our eyes met as it slipped into her mouth. Some of the chocolate dribbled on her lip, and I used my thumb to wipe it before bringing it to my mouth. She licked her lips when I pulled the utensil away, keeping our gazes locked.

"I wish we had this at home. I know so many places I would love to lick chocolate off of, all of them on your body," I said huskily.

Kaiya flushed, pinker than the Moscato in her glass. "Then, we'll have to buy one. Like tomorrow."

She giggled as she mimicked my action, feeding me a piece of banana dipped in chocolate.

The rest of the course continued that way, with us taking turns feeding each other, giving seductive glances, and basically fucking with our eyes.

After the waiter cleared the table of everything but the wine that we had left, I reached in my pocket and grabbed the small box I had brought with me. "I have something for you."

Kaiya's lips curved and her face lit up. "Baby, you didn't have to do that. This amazing dinner was enough."

Taking out the box, I handed it to her. "I wanted to. Go ahead, open it," I urged. Sweat began to line my forehead as I waited for her to open it. *I hope she likes it.*

Her gaze left mine to look at the box. Slowly, she took off the top before taking out the small, velvet pouch inside. She carefully removed the bracelet from the bag before examining the piece of jewelry with both hands.

"I hope you like it. It took me so long to decide what charms to get for it."

Her eyes watered as she darted them back and forth between me and the bracelet. "It's perfect," she whispered. Even though her voice was soft, it was still full of emotion. "I love it."

She looked at it a few seconds longer before asking me to put it on her. After I clasped it around her slender wrist, I admired how it looked on her. The charms I had chosen all signified something, showcasing our relationship since it began.

The one closest to the clasp was a martini glass. I ran my finger over it as explained, "I got this one to symbolize our first kiss and first date since alcohol was involved in both."

She chuckled and shook her head. "Almost all of our dates involve alcohol." She pointed to the charm a few links away, a seal. "And this one?"

"This one is for our trip to the aquarium. My favorite of all our dates."

She sniffled and smiled up at me. "Mine too."

The third was an open book. "I know you love to read, that it helps you escape sometimes." She had told me that when thoughts of Kaleb overwhelmed her, sometimes she read to help get her mind off him.

Her voice was choked by emotion as tears began to rim her eyes. "This one."

She was pointing to the charm on the opposite end, a pair of boxing gloves. "Ah, this one… this one is my favorite. I picked it because we got closer once you started taking self-defense." I tucked a loose curl behind her ear as I looked into her eyes. "I don't know where I'd be if you hadn't walked into my class."

"I'm glad I did," she whispered.

My fingers moved to the script letter K for her name. "This one explains itself."

The last charm was in the center, a heart that I had engraved with the word "Warrior." I gripped it as I spoke, "This one signifies that you'll always have my heart. I'll never be the same without you, Warrior."

My eyes traveled up to hers, and I wiped the tears off her cheeks. "I'm not going to buy you presents if you're going to cry. I hate to see you cry."

Kaiya laughed softly as she leaned into me. "They're happy tears. I really do love it. Thank you."

Pressing her lips to mine, she softly kissed me. My hand glided around to cup the back of her head as my tongue parted her lips. Chocolate and wine still lingered in her mouth as I massaged her tongue with mine.

"The check whenever you're ready, sir," our server interrupted.

Neither one of us pulled away, too wrapped up in one another to care. I almost waved him off, but I was too focused on Kaiya, enjoying the feel and taste of her. When we finally parted, her lips were swollen and her cheeks were even more flushed.

"Ready to go?" I asked, pulling out my wallet.

Kaiya nodded as she scooted out of our booth. I left cash on the table, not wanting to wait to get my card back. I was already ready to take Kaiya home, and we hadn't even gone to the club yet.

After we left, we drove to a parking garage near the club. As we got out of the truck, Kaiya commented, "Dinner was amazing. Everything was perfect—the music, the wine, the food, your gift." She looked down at her bracelet before looking back up at me. "Thank you so much."

"You don't have to thank me, baby. I enjoy spoiling you." I threaded our fingers together and guided Kaiya to the elevator. The club was about four blocks up from the garage, and by the time we got there, the line was around the side of the building.

Kaiya sighed in disappointment. "We're never going to get in if we have to wait in that line."

Smiling reassuringly, I stroked the back of her hand with my thumb. Passing the line, I gave the bulky bouncer my name, and after looking at his list, he ushered us in. I heard several people cursing and shouting angrily as we walked through the doors.

Hip hop music greeted us as we entered the main room of the club. Leading Kaiya to the bar, pushing through masses of people, I ordered our usual drinks.

As we waited, Kaiya began moving her hips to the beat of the music. The only good part about taking her to a club was that I got to have that fine body rubbing against me.

"Hey, sexy. Wanna finish what we started the last time we were together?" The annoying voice was sort of familiar, but I didn't place who it was until I turned to look at her. *Shit.*

The chick that I'd hooked up with when Kaiya had stopped talking to me sidled up next to me, ignoring the fact that my arm was draped around Kaiya on my other side.

Trailing her fingers down my chest, she spoke again, "I know I do. I still remember how good your dick tasted in my mouth."

"Ryker, who the fuck is this," Kaiya asked accusingly, her eyes narrowed and lips curved in a snarl. I could feel the anger wafting off her in waves.

Before I could diffuse the situation, the stupid blonde retorted, "Who the fuck are you?"

Fuck, this is about to get bad. "Baby, let's—"

Kaiya moved in between us, getting in Blondie's face as she interrupted me, seething. "I'm his girlfriend, bitch. Fuck off."

My warrior was so fucking hot when she was pissed and jealous, but I couldn't focus on that, not when shit was about to hit the fan.

The other woman smugly replied, "Oh, you must be new. I don't remember him having a girlfriend when we hooked up."

Kaiya was fuming as she pushed the blonde bimbo, snapping, "Well, he does now, so go find someone else to open your legs for."

Blondie's eyes narrowed as she lunged at Kaiya. Big mistake. With her training, Kaiya could seriously hurt the unsuspecting girl. And by the look in her eyes, she planned to beat the crap out of her.

Stepping in between them, I moved Kaiya backward before leading her outside. She snatched her arm out of my grasp and stormed away from me, drawing the attention of people still waiting to get inside the club.

"Babe, stop. Let me explain," I said as I followed after her. In the past, I would've never chased after a woman who walked away from me; I would've just moved on to the next one.

"Who the fuck was that?" she spat as she whirled around to face me.

"Nobody. Some chick that I almost hooked up with."

"What do you mean almost? She seems to think that you two hooked up. And when did this happen? Before or after we started having sex?"

I really didn't want to discuss all that, but I wasn't going to lie to her. She meant more to me than that. She deserved honesty.

"When you stopped talking to me, I went out with Drew and got drunk. That chick was there, and I was trying to forget about you, so we went back to her place. But we didn't have sex. I couldn't go through with it."

Tears blurred her eyes, making them shine in the light of the streetlamp overhead. "What did you do?" she gritted through clenched teeth.

Sighing, I ran my hand roughly through my hair. *Here goes nothing.* "She started sucking my dick, but I made her stop. Then, I left."

The look of betrayal on her face tore up my insides. "But, she still sucked it. You still hooked up with her."

"We weren't even together, Ky. It doesn't matter," I defended. I knew that I'd said the wrong thing as soon as the words left my mouth. *Fuck.*

Her eyebrows rose incredulously. "It doesn't matter?"

"You wouldn't even talk to me. I thought we were through," I replied, trying to justify my actions.

"So, I don't talk to you for a week or two after we get involved, and you try to find the next pair of legs to get between?" She crossed her arms over her chest and glared at me.

"Ky, you're overreacting. I—"

"Overreacting? I'm overreacting? Do you know how hard it is to trust someone after everything I've been through?" She thrust her arms toward me. "How can I trust you not to do something like that again?" she screamed as tears ran down her face.

"Baby, I'm sorry. Don't cry," I pleaded, opening my arms to embrace her.

Moving away from me, she threw out her hand to stop me. The gesture felt like a punch to my gut.

"Don't. I can't do this right now. I need time to think." Her words were pained, her expression torn between anger and sadness.

"What are you saying, Ky?" *Shit. No, no, no.*

Ignoring me, she walked to the edge of the street, sticking her hand out as she waved at an oncoming taxi.

"Warrior, talk to me. Don't do this." My heart beat frantically as my pulse pounded. *I can't lose her.*

The taxi slowed as it pulled over to the curb and came to a stop. Kaiya looked at me as she opened the door, that sadness that I was so close to erasing back in full force all over her beautiful face. "I just need some space right now. I need to figure out what this means for us."

"It means nothing. She meant nothing. Don't do this, baby. I lo-"

She shut the door before I could finish. Tears burned my eyes as I thought about losing her, of not being with her ever again. Inhaling deeply, I pushed them back as I watched her drive away. *What the fuck just happened? The night was perfect until a few minutes ago.*

Stalking angrily back to my truck, my mind was all over the place. *Do I go after her? Give her space? I didn't even do anything wrong. What the fuck do I do?*

Once I sat inside my Chevy, I furiously pounded the steering wheel with my fists and roared my frustration. *She's so fucking stubborn. Well, two can play that game.*

Making my decision, I started the engine and peeled out of the parking garage.

Chapter Twenty-Five

Kaiya

"Kam, I'm home," I announced as I kicked my shoes off by the front door, trying to sound like everything was okay, even though it really wasn't. I was upset with Ryker, and I didn't know where things were going to end up between us after our fight. *I knew things were too good to be true.*

Kamden didn't answer—usually he replied back to me, even if it was just a grunt or single word. His door was closed, so he might have already been asleep, but I decided to check after changing out of my constricting dress.

After slipping into my sleep shorts and a comfy muscle shirt, I walked to Kamden's bedroom. As I knocked, the door crept open, and I caught a glimpse of him unmoving on the floor. "Oh my God, Kamden!"

He was so still—*no, no, no. What happened?* Pushing open the door, I rushed to his side, laying my head on his chest, searching for a sign of life. *Please don't be dead.* I heard nothing; just overwhelming silence so ironically loud that it deafened my ears.

My cheeks were soaked with moisture as I wrapped my arms around Kamden. Pressing my head against his chest, I sobbed into him. Then, I heard it—one of the most beautiful sounds I'd ever heard. It was faint, but it was there—his heartbeat. *Thank God.*

I noticed the small amount of blood pooling under his head as I was yanked away and trapped against a larger body.

"Miss me, love?" The words brushed against my ear, causing me to instinctively cringe. I hadn't heard that voice in so long, but I'd never be able to forget it. It haunted my dreams and tainted my memories. Kaleb. Pure and utter fear seized my body, choking the air from my lungs and clenching my muscles. *No.*

I couldn't move, couldn't do anything as Kaleb dragged his nose across my neck, inhaling my skin before repeating the path with his tongue. "God, I've missed you. You know how much I've thought about you over the years? About touching your skin? Tasting your sweetness? I haven't been able to think about anything else."

"How'd you get out?" My voice shook weakly as I spoke, my body petrified with fear.

A sinister chuckle vibrated against my neck. "Do you really think I could stay away from you?" He nipped my neck as he ran his hands along my arms. The familiar touch made bile build in the back of my throat. One hand traveled up my arm and wrapped around my neck, squeezing firmly before his fingers laced in my hair and tugged my head back. "You're mine," he growled.

He kept one hand in my hair as the other released my throat, venturing down my breasts and stomach to the juncture of my thighs. The violating action snapped me out of my fear-induced paralysis. Using what Ryker had taught me, I stomped on Kaleb's instep before slamming my elbow directly into his stomach, freeing myself from his grasp.

As he stumbled back, I threw a side-kick to his groin before taking up a defensive stance. I didn't fully connect, but I could tell the impact still hurt him because he hunched over and grunted in pain. "You've learned to fight back, huh? This is going to be fun."

I should've run the second I was free, like Ryker always told us, but I couldn't leave Kamden. I didn't know what Kaleb would do to him without me there to focus on. Kaleb charged at me, but I ducked and threw a back-fist into his shoulder. Each time I connected with his body empowered me, making me feel less weak and helpless. I was not a frail, little girl anymore. I was a strong, powerful woman.

Kaleb angrily whirled around with a snarl before coming at me again. I landed a roundhouse to his ribs, but he caught my leg, caging it against him as he backed me toward Kamden's bed. *I can't let him get me on the bed.* My training flew out the window, suddenly forgotten as panic took hold. I swung my arms wildly, trying to hit Kaleb anywhere to get him to let me go.

I made the biggest mistake—I left my face open. Kaleb took advantage, backhanding me in the jaw. The hit stunned me, sending me falling onto the bed. Kaleb had me pinned instantly, crushing me with his weight as his legs opened my thighs. My sense of power began to fade as Kaleb turned the tables. *Keep fighting. Don't give up.*

Struggling against him, I pounded against his arms as he tugged at my clothing. My shirt tore from the shoulder down across my chest, exposing my bra. I started to scream, hoping someone would hear me and call the cops, but Kaleb slapped me across the face, silencing me as the sound of the smack echoed in Kamden's bedroom.

Bringing my arms up to cover my face, I blocked his next hit, but I didn't expect the punch to my ribs. The air was sucked from my lungs as pain assaulted my body, the intensity of it making my eyes blur.

Kaleb pushed my arms out of the way, the movement causing more pain to slice up my side. He pulled down my bra, revealing my breasts before grabbing one in each hand and slowly kneading them with his fingers.

Don't let him do this to you. You have to fight! Don't be weak! Kaleb was focused on my breasts, the vacant look in his eyes telling me he was lost to his darker side. Shoving my arms forward, breaking his loose hold on me, I braced my hands against his shoulders as I readied to execute the rest of the first technique Ryker had ever taught me.

One foot pressed against his hip, then two, as I fluidly performed the move. My hands slid down to his wrists as he pulled back, just as Ryker said an attacker would. Immediately, I began kicking upwards, landing a few kicks to Kaleb's face before he fell off of me, landing on the floor with a thud.

Springing off the bed, I headed for the door as a hand wrapped around my ankle. Losing my balance, I fell to the floor, breaking my fall with my forearms. I struggled to free myself, but Kaleb was much stronger than me, always had been.

Kaleb climbed up my body, grasping at my shorts and pulling at them. *No!* I repeatedly began kicking him in the face, causing more blood to surface from the wounds I was inflicting. *Take that, asshole. I hope it hurts as much as you hurt me.*

Instead of slowing him down, everything seemed to amp up his rage and power as he yanked my bottoms off with ease. I tried to crawl away, but Kaleb latched his hand around my ankle and dragged me back to him.

My body went into survival mode, ignoring the pain spiraling outward from my ribs through me as my arms and legs struck out, hoping to hit anything and stop him.

Then, he was on me again, in between my legs despite my efforts. My chest heaved raggedly for breath as exhaustion began to weigh me down. I forced my thighs shut, but he pried them apart, digging his nails into my flesh and drawing blood as he opened them again.

As he reached for my underwear, wanting to remove the last barrier I had protecting me from him, I thrust a palm strike right to his nose, causing him to grab it instinctively as blood began to stream from it.

Squirming out from under him, I flipped over and pushed up on my knees in preparation to run for the front door. Kaleb swept my legs out from under me just as I stood, sending me back to the hardwood floor. Reacting too late, my face slammed into the unyielding ground before I could brace myself. Stars shot into my vision as the iron tang of my blood filled my mouth.

Kaleb rolled me over and mounted me. I weakly tried to push him off me, but he reared back and slapped me with so much force that my ears rang. My eyes began to shut on their own accord as he pulled his shirt off. I just lay there, practically defeated, unable to find the strength to fight back anymore as pain smothered everything else. *I'm not strong enough.*

"I finally get to finish what I started all those years ago," he mumbled in a lust-laden voice.

Never give up, Warrior. Always fight back. Ryker's voice played in my mind.

I weakly brought my knee up, connecting with his crotch, but it barely affected him. *I have no fight left. He always wins.* Tears began to trickle down my face before I began to numb myself, hoping to withdraw internally enough so I wouldn't feel anything that Kaleb was going to do to me.

Then, pounding on the door startled both Kaleb and me. He stilled with his hands on the button of his jeans, then snapped his gaze up to mine. His eyes gave a silent threat, but I opened my mouth to scream anyway before his hand slammed down and muffled my cries.

A dull voice yelled through the door. "Kaiya, it's me. Please come talk to me, baby."

Ryker! Oh, thank God! My brief happiness was extinguished as Kaleb leaned over me, whispering in my ear. "Don't make a sound."

As I was about to ignore him and scream for Ryker, I felt cold, hard metal digging into my side. *Where did he get a gun? Oh my God, did he shoot Kamden?*

Fear penetrated my being, instantly silencing any form of protest as I froze in place.

Ryker continued to bang on the door. "I know you're in there. I'm not leaving until you come talk to me—I'll stand out here all night if I have to."

Tears watered in my eyes at the thought of Kaleb hurting Ryker. *Please leave.*

"I mean it, Ky. I'm not going anywhere," Ryker yelled as he knocked harder.

Kaleb cursed under his breath as he stood, pulling me up with him as he kept the gun pressed to my side. He walked us to the door as he quietly threatened, "Make him leave or I'll kill him."

My heart clenched at the thought of Ryker dying, especially because of me. I never should've gotten involved with him, never should've entangled him in my web of issues.

When we reached the door, Kaleb dug the gun deeper into my injured side. A small yelp of pain burst from me, but I smashed my lips together to stop it so Ryker wouldn't hear. I wasn't sure if Kaleb would kill me, at least not until he had raped me, but I knew without a doubt he would kill Ryker. I needed to protect him, even if it meant breaking my heart by pushing him away.

"What do you want, Ryker?" I asked, trying to keep my voice even.

"Baby, let me in. I want to talk to you," he pleaded. The pain in his voice tightened my chest.

"That's not a good idea. You should just leave," I snapped as I fought back tears.

"I'm not leaving until you talk to me." His tone was firm, the one he used when his mind was made up.

Damn it, he's so stubborn.

"I'm talking to you, now go!" I yelled as my tears broke through. *Please just leave.*

"Why are you acting like this, Warrior?"

I set my forehead against the door, wondering if Ryker was doing the same on the other side. Kaleb twisted the gun, reminding me of my task. I hissed loudly in pain as I gritted the lie. "I don't want to see you anymore."

"Don't do this, Warrior. I can't lose you. Tell me what to do to fix this."

Tears rolled down my cheeks. My vision blurred from a combination of the moisture in my eyes and pain from the barrel digging into my ribs. "I can't be fixed. Some demons just don't leave you alone. They haunt you forever," I eluded, hoping Ryker would understand what I meant and get help once he left. But even if he did, they probably wouldn't make it in time.

He didn't respond for several seconds, and I thought he had left. Then the silence broke when he said, "I understand. I'll give you some space tonight, but I'm coming back over here tomorrow to straighten everything out. We can face those demons together."

I heard his footsteps going down the stairs as Kaleb pulled me away from the door, leading me to my bedroom instead of Kamden's. He tucked the gun in the back of his pants as he tightened his hold on my arm, driving his nails into my skin.

Then, chaos erupted as Ryker burst through the front door. Kaleb reached for his gun, but I threw my weight into him, sending both of us crashing into the wall as Ryker neared us.

"He has a gun!" I warned.

The impact caused Kaleb to lose his grip on me, but also made me lose my balance, sending me stumbling back into the opposite wall. Ryker slammed into Kaleb, tackling him to the ground. They rolled on the floor several times before Ryker finally pinned him, and started elbowing him in the face.

The gun flew backwards from Kaleb's hand and went off as it hit the floor. Ryker stilled, then snapped his eyes to me, making sure I hadn't been shot, which gave Kaleb the opportunity to punch him square in the jaw.

Stunned, Ryker wobbled slightly before Kaleb hit him twice more, causing him to fall to the floor. Kaleb darted for the gun on the ground a few feet away from me, but Ryker grabbed his leg, making him stumble and crash to the floor. Kaleb used his other foot to kick Ryker in the face several times. Blood streamed down his face as he let go and lay dazed against the floor. *No.*

Kaleb rushed for the gun again, and I knew I couldn't let him get a hold of it. I couldn't let him shoot Ryker. I threw myself at the weapon, causing it to skid away from me when I hit it. Frantically crawling, I stretched my arm out to grab the handle, but Kaleb's foot came stomping down, crushing my hand beneath his boot.

Yelping, I pulled my hand back, clutching it to my chest as I watched Kaleb reach the gun. *Shit.* I scooted back, desperate to get to Ryker, to protect him.

Ryker groaned when my hand brushed against him. Tugging on his bicep, I helped him sit up as Kaleb picked up the gun. I draped his arm around my shoulder before struggling to pull him to his feet.

Kaleb pointed the gun at Ryker, so I stepped in front of him, blocking as much of Ryker's bulky body with my much smaller one. All I cared about was him—Kaleb could do whatever he wanted to me if it meant that Ryker would be safe.

Kaleb's eyes blazed in anger at my action, obviously pissed that I was protecting Ryker. "Move, Kaiya," he growled.

I silently shook my head, fearing my voice would waver if I spoke. Kaleb cursed and threatened, "Don't make me do this."

I didn't respond—inside I was screaming, the frail, weak part of me begging me to move out of the way. But, something else was keeping me there, something stronger than fear—love.

Tears burned my eyes—we were probably going to die and Ryker didn't know how I felt, that I loved him. *Oh my God, I love him.* There was no doubt or question anymore. The reality of it had finally sunk in. I knew with every fiber of my being that I was in love with Ryker.

The click of the gun snapped me from my thoughts. Everything happened so fast after that—Ryker pushed me out of the way as Kamden stumbled out of his bedroom and threw himself at Kaleb.

The gun was pointed straight at me when it went off from my brothers fighting over it. My body froze at the sound, the only movement being my eyes shutting tight in fear.

I expected excruciating agony, but the burning that I felt in my chest was not what I anticipated. My eyes snapped open to Ryker's bloody face; his eyes were scrunched in pain as sweat trailed down his skin. His arms were tightly wrapped around me, his chest pressed against mine.

Looking down, I was utterly unprepared for what I saw. A bullet was sticking out of my blood-splattered chest, right over my heart. But that wasn't even the worst part.

My breath caught in my throat as I focused on the bloody bullet hole in Ryker's chest in front of me. Realization clicked at what just occurred. "You saved me," I whispered in shock.

Wincing, he forced a smile. The pained expression didn't look right on his beautiful face. "I told you that I always would," he croaked.

Tears trickled down my cheeks as he slumped against me, forcing me to bear his weight. My legs gave out, unable to hold the both of us up as I fell to my knees.

Shifting Ryker to cradle him in my lap, I pulled off my ripped shirt, balling it up and pressing it against Ryker's wound. He clenched his eyes shut as he hissed in pain.

"I'm sorry, baby. I have to stop the bleeding," I choked, my tears now falling like a torrential downpour.

Sounds of a scuffle reached my ears, causing my head to jerk up. Kamden and Kaleb still wrestled over the gun about ten feet away from me. Then, Kamden finally ripped it from Kaleb's hands before pointing it at him.

Sirens sounded in the distance, probably from a neighbor calling to report the yelling and gunshots. *I hope an ambulance is coming with them.*

Kaleb stepped closer to Kamden, who threatened, "Don't come any closer."

Kaleb curled his lip up before spitting blood on the floor. "We both know you won't shoot me, brother. You're too weak, just like you were too weak to protect Kaiya from me all those years."

Then, Kaleb threw himself at Kamden. Struggling over the gun once again, it fired, the sound making my stomach clench. Both my brothers fell to the floor, and I couldn't tell who had been shot. *Please don't be Kamden. Please don't be Kamden.*

Neither one moved as my heart pounded wildly in my chest, my adrenaline lacing my veins and making me feel like a charged up live wire. Kamden finally groaned before starting to get up, and I exhaled a huge sigh of relief. *He's alive. He's okay.*

Kaleb didn't move. Even though he had tormented me for so long, a little piece of my heart still hurt at the thought of him being dead—he was my twin, after all. Even after everything he did to me, I still felt a small part of that special bond that only twins have, which had made all his abuse so emotionally damaging.

Ryker moaned softly, drawing my attention back to him. His hand clutched mine, which was still holding my shirt against his chest. Tears fell from my face onto him as he stared up at me through half-lidded eyes.

His hand reached up to swipe the tears from my face before he rested it there, cupping my cheek. I leaned into his palm as I brought my free hand to rest atop his. *Tell him.*

Just as I was about to speak, he mumbled, "Kaiya, I—"

His hand went limp, falling from my face as his eyes shut.

No. "Ryker! Ryker, wake up!" I shrieked as I lightly smacked his face, trying to wake him. "Don't leave me!"

The stomping of multiple pairs of feet sounded behind me, but all I could focus on was waking Ryker up.

"Open your eyes! Damn it, look at me, baby! Please!" I desperately screamed.

I heard voices, but I couldn't make out what they were saying. Hands grabbed me and pulled me away from Ryker as two people took my place next to him, sending me into a fit of crazed panic.

"No! Ryker! I need to be with him! Please! Don't take him away from me!"

Thrashing wildly against whoever was holding me, I screamed until my throat was raw. I didn't know how I was able to move due to all my injuries, but the only pain I felt was my heart ripping apart as I thought about Ryker being dead.

More hands gripped onto me as another person came into my view, but my eyes were so blurred with tears that I couldn't see who they were. Despair sucked the air from lungs, suffocating me as I continued to struggle. Other sets of hands grabbed me, holding me still as I felt a sharp sting in my arm.

Still fighting, I kicked and flailed until my body began to feel boneless, my vision swimming as my eyes suddenly became heavy and dizziness swarmed me. I slumped against someone right before blackness blanketed me.

Annoying beeping woke me. I groaned as pain assaulted me everywhere, making me wish I'd stayed in the black void I'd been in. *Where am I?*

"*Sorella?*" a tired voice spoke. "Are you awake?"

"Ugh, why are you yelling?" I mumbled groggily.

A sigh of relief followed by a strained chuckle met my ears as a hand squeezed mine. I struggled to open my eyes, which felt like they had been sealed with superglue. I managed to open one as I turned my head toward where I heard the voice.

Kamden gave me a small smile as he stood and kissed my forehead. "Are you thirsty?"

My mouth felt like someone had stuffed it with cotton after buffing my throat with sandpaper. "Yes," my voice cracked hoarsely.

Kamden handed me a cup with ice chips. When I finished, he set the cup back on the bedside table, I took in my surroundings—I was in a hospital room, which explained the annoying beeping of the machine hooked up to me. Memories of what happened with Kaleb rushed back, and I gripped Kamden's hand tighter. "Where's Ryker? Is he okay?" I asked as I fought back tears. *Please be alive.*

"He's fine. He's in the room right next door. They had to sedate him because he kept fighting to get to you—he ripped open his stitches."

I exhaled a huge sigh of relief. *He's alive. Thank God.* "When can I see him?"

"I don't know. We'll have to ask your doctor. You have some fractured ribs, as well as some small fractures in your right hand and face. He said your gunshot wound wasn't that extensive; the bullet came out fairly easily. You were very lucky— Ryker took the brunt of the impact and slowed the trajectory, otherwise, it would've…"

Kamden choked, unable to finish his sentence. The tears I'd been holding broke free then, the severity of what happened almost strangling me. "He saved me."

"He loves you," Kamden said softly with a knowing smile.

My head snapped up to his, and I winced from the sharp throb that resulted. "He said that?"

"No, but no one takes a bullet for someone unless they love them. I saw how you protected him—you love him, too, don't you?"

"Yeah, I think I do," I replied softly.

"You do. I can see it on your face."

I changed the subject, not completely comfortable with discussing how I felt about Ryker with Kamden yet. I needed to talk to Ryker first, see if what Kamden was saying was true. "How about you?"

"I suffered a small concussion and some bruises, but nothing major like you."

"Kaleb?" I hesitantly asked.

Kamden's face tensed as his eyes watered. He shook his head, unable to voice what happened. I couldn't imagine what he was feeling, but I knew it wasn't good. My heart became heavy for him. He had to kill our brother for something that should've never been an issue between the three of us.

"I'm sorry." I squeezed his hand.

His eyes met mine as he nodded, sorrow etched into every feature. I wanted to comfort him, to take away his pain, but I knew that look; he wasn't ready to talk about it yet. I would be there for him when he was, just as he had always been for me.

The door opened, and a man who looked to be in his forties walked in wearing the traditional doctor's coat, holding an iPad.

"Ah, good, you're awake. I'm Dr. Wright," he introduced as he walked to the side of my bed, opposite of Kamden.

I gave him a polite smile, then impatiently asked, "When can I see Ryker Campbell? He's the patient next door to me."

The doctor laughed softly. "First things first. Let's get you checked out before we move on to anything else."

After he checked my vitals and all the other routine crap they have to do, he lifted the gauze covering my wound to examine it. "No sign of infection, and your stitches look good. But, I still want you to stay a week or so just to be safe."

"Can I get up and walk around?"

He responded with a knowing smile. "Yes, just don't exert yourself too much. You just got shot, plus you have multiple fractures and bruising all over your body—you need to take it easy. Give your body time to recuperate."

"I will." *After I see Ryker.*

Dr. Wright nodded as he typed something on his tablet. "I'll be back to check on you tomorrow."

Kamden and I both thanked the doctor before he left. "Help me up," I requested as soon as the door shut. I wasn't wasting any more time. Being away from Ryker was eating me up inside. I needed to make sure he was okay. I didn't care how much it would hurt.

Kamden gave me his disapproving big brother look. "Ky, you heard the doctor—you need to take it easy."

Narrowing my eyes, I threatened, "Help me up, or I'm going to get up without you, and I'll probably further injure myself."

Kamden sighed in defeat. "Fine. You're such a brat."

In true brat-like fashion, I stuck my tongue out at him. He pulled me up by my arms since one of my hands was in a splint and helped me scoot to the side of the bed. I winced in pain from the movement, and the side where my fractured ribs were seared me in agony, making me squeeze my eyes shut and grit my teeth.

Kamden stopped and let me go. "Ky, this isn't—"

"I'm fine, now help me stand," I demanded, my voice leaving no room for argument.

He mumbled something indiscernible under his breath, but I was able to hear a few choice words as he complied with my request. My whole body hurt as I strained to stand, but I fought through the pain, needing to see Ryker.

I hobbled like a ninety year old grandma with arthritis as we made our way from my room to Ryker's. Kamden used one hand to brace my arm the entire way, keeping me from losing my balance and falling while he pulled my IV stand with us.

It felt like it took hours to get to Ryker's room. I was about to bust out of my skin when Kamden opened the door and slowly led me in. I had to stop myself from pulling away and running to Ryker's bed.

"Hurry, Kam," I urged when Ryker came into view.

He was sleeping when I finally reached him. Kamden steadied me before pulling up a chair behind me for me to sit in, but I stayed standing as I threaded my uninjured hand with his. Tears trailed down my face as I assessed him—he had a black eye, his lip was busted, and multiple bruises and cuts marred his beautiful face.

I squeezed his hand before bringing it up to my lips and gently kissing it. I didn't know when he would wake up, but I wasn't leaving until he did.

Letting go of his hand, I awkwardly struggled to push the rail on the side of his bed down, planning to climb in next to him. I needed to be as close to him as possible, to feel his chest rise with breath, hear his heartbeat, and feel the warmth of life in his skin. I didn't have enough strength to lift myself in, and tears started to rim my eyes.

"Kamden, help me," I cried softly.

"Kaiya, I—"

Interrupting him, I begged, "Please, Kam. I need to be near him right now."

Kamden never did well resisting when it came to me. He gingerly helped me get into the small bed with Ryker. All of my efforts had exhausted me so much that as soon as I rested my head against Ryker's chest, right over his heart, sleep took me away.

Chapter Twenty-Six

Ryker

When I awoke, the faint smell of strawberries and vanilla filled my nose as I inhaled deeply, causing a smile to spread on my face. *Kaiya.*

My eyes snapped open before my gaze traveled down, focusing on hair the color of dark chocolate, porcelain skin, and a small, familiar body—Kaiya. *How did she get here?*

"As soon as she woke up, she made me bring her to you," a voice answered my unspoken question.

My eyes met Kamden's, who sat in a chair next to my bed. He looked like he had aged years since I saw him last, and exhaustion laced his face. Deep, purple bags rimmed his eyes, and his skin looked pallid. "Sounds like her. She's so stubborn," I chuckled, then winced from the resulting pain in my chest.

"You okay? Do you need me to get a nurse?"

I looked down at Kaiya's head on my chest, and smiled. "Nah, I'm good now."

"You love her?" Kamden abruptly questioned.

I looked up at him. After what we had gone through, after what I'd done for her, I didn't have to even think about my answer. "Yes, I love her."

He gave me a small, but genuine smile. "Thank you for…" He cleared his throat as his eyes watered. "For saving Kaiya. I don't know how I can ever repay you, but I'll find a way."

"You don't have to do anything. I have everything I need right here." I gestured to Kaiya in my arms.

His smile widened as he wordlessly stood and walked to the door. When he grabbed the handle, he looked over his shoulder. "I'll be outside if she needs me."

Focusing back on the amazing woman next to me, I softly ran my fingers through her hair as I quietly spoke, "Wake up, my Warrior."

She began to stir as I continued to run my fingers through her long locks. I probably should've let her sleep, but I needed to see her, needed to make sure she was really okay, especially since I hadn't completely stopped the bullet. I didn't know if I'd ever be able to forget the image of it embedded in her skin.

Her head shifted as she looked up at me. Those gorgeous eyes captivated me as they met mine, making me lose myself in her as I sank into them.

"Hi," she murmured as her lips tipped up in a soft smile.

"Hi. How are you feeling?"

"Sore, but better now that I'm here."

"I heard you fought your way over here."

"Me? What about you? I heard you ripped your stitches open trying to get to me," she countered as her mouth quirked up playfully.

"They told you that, huh?" I glanced away, slightly embarrassed by my behavior.

"Yep," she replied, putting extra emphasis on the P as she gave me a teasing grin. "Now, why would you do something crazy like that?"

"When I want something, I have to have it. You know that."

She scooted up a little, bringing our faces closer together, maybe only inches apart. "So did you get what you wanted?"

Closing the distance between us, I tenderly pressed my lips to hers, ignoring the light pain it caused in mine. "Now, I did." I set my forehead against hers.

"Don't ever do something like that again," Kaiya scolded as she gripped onto my hospital gown, her playfulness from moments before gone. The tone in her voice told me that she was crying, so I pulled back to cradle her face in my hands. The sight of all the cuts and bruises, along with her tears broke my heart—I hated to see her hurt.

"I'd do it again if I had to." I grazed my thumbs over her cheeks. I'd take a bullet for her no questions asked.

Her watery eyes locked on mine. "Why?"

We'd never talked about love before, both of us afraid of what it signified. Our pasts had made us scared to love, but after almost losing her, I wasn't going to take what we had for granted anymore. "Because I love you."

Her lip trembled as more tears flowed from her eyes. "I love you, too," she sobbed before bringing our mouths back together again. Our lips caressed each other, embracing softly as our tongues lightly laced together. Passion was evident in every movement, present in every breath as we demonstrated the love that we had just spoke.

When we finally broke apart, Kaiya's lips were swollen and her skin flushed beneath the bruising. Her cheeks were stained with tears as she looked at me.

"So, all I had to do was take a bullet for you to get you to tell me that you love me? Why didn't I do that sooner?" I joked.

She rolled her eyes at me as she lightheartedly retorted, "I've never been in love before—how was I supposed to know what it felt like?" She poked a finger into the uninjured side of my chest. "You, on the other hand, have loved someone before, so why didn't you tell me?"

"That's exactly why—I've been in love before, and I got hurt because of it. The way I feel for you is so much stronger than I ever felt for her, even when I thought she was pregnant with my kid. So you could hurt me way more than she did—I'd never recover from you."

More tears trickled down her face as our eyes locked. "Me neither. I'm trusting you with those tiny, broken pieces of my heart, everything that's left of me. There'd be no way to put them back together after you—you're the only one who knows how."

I smiled at her; I'd been waiting for this moment, waiting for Kaiya to fully trust me. I couldn't even explain how it felt to have the woman I loved love me back, to trust me after everything she'd been through. Spectacular didn't even come close.

As she settled on her side next to me, I leaned my forehead against hers. From that angle, I could see the gauze covering her injury through the opening in her hospital gown. I slowly pulled it back, wanting to see the damage done by the bullet.

A small, jagged circle sat right over her heart. I couldn't believe how close I'd come to losing her. *Thank God I stopped it.* Her skin was bruised around the injury, which was puffy and red, but it wasn't that deep.

She did the same with mine, pulling the gauze back to look at my wound, which mirrored hers the way we were facing one another. Mine was bigger and more inflamed, probably from ripping out my stitches and the severity of the trauma, but it was almost exactly in the same spot as hers, just on the opposite side.

More tears dripped from her eyes as she looked over my injury. I brought my hands up to wipe them away before lifting her face to look at mine.

"Stop crying, Warrior. We're both still alive."

"I don't like seeing you hurt, especially because of me." She traced the tattoos around the injury softly, careful not to get to close. "It's going to scar—it'll mess up your beautiful tattoos."

"I'll bear any scar for you, Ky. Plus, scars are sexy," I said with a smirk, trying to lighten the mood.

Kaiya wasn't amused, her face still marred by a frown. "Not on women they're not."

"Yours will be incredibly sexy because it matches mine. Both will always remind me of the moment I realized I couldn't live without you, that I was completely in love with you."

My words turned her lips up into the beautiful smile that I loved, but also caused more tears to flow. "You're kinda perfect, you know that," Kaiya said as she looked at me, her voice full of emotion.

"So are you, baby. Absolutely perfect for me." I kissed her forehead, letting my lips linger as I breathed in her scent.

When I pulled back, Kaiya settled next to me, laying her head on the uninjured side of my chest. We lay there in peaceful silence, both of us emotionally and physically exhausted. I drifted off to sleep, content with the love of my life in my arms.

Epilogue

Kaiya

People say that time heals all wounds. I still call bullshit. I've learned that even the deepest scars can be healed by the right person but not because of time.

The saying should be rephrased to say that love heals all wounds because that's what's been healing me over the past few months. I'm not completely healed, but I'm getting there—I make progress every day.

I had to stay in the hospital for a little over a week, but Ryker had to stay almost three because of his injuries. The bullet had gone clean through him before it hit me, so his surgery and recovery were more extensive. I stayed by his side every day until visiting hours ended, and came back first thing the next morning when they opened again.

I took a leave of absence from work to deal with the aftermath. After everything that happened, I changed; we all did. Even though Kaleb is gone, the pain and scars from what he did to me still remain, but Ryker heals them more and more every day.

Kamden has his own scars to deal with following the shooting. Killing Kaleb haunts him, even though it was in self-defense. He's seeing a therapist regularly to cope with the backlash of the incident. Therapy is definitely not my thing, but it's working for him, and I hope it helps his healing process.

Ryker started physical therapy because some of the nerves in his chest that connected to his shoulder were damaged by the bullet. I worried that he would never be able to train or work out again, but he's determined to make a full recovery. And he will—he always loves a challenge.

I don't know what I'd do without Ryker. It's amazing how someone can just come into your life, completely flip it upside down, and make you wonder how you ever lived without them before.

Ryker insisted I move in with him, but that was too much, too soon for me. Even though I love him, being in a committed relationship is definitely an adjustment for me. Plus, I couldn't leave Kamden alone, especially since he's been having trouble dealing with the repercussions of that night.

We compromised—Kamden and I moved into Ryker's apartment complex, only one building away. There's no way we could stay in ours after what had happened there.

I alternate between sleeping at Ryker's place and mine, but Ryker usually ends up at my apartment on nights that I don't stay with him. We were both used to sleeping alone, but now I wouldn't be able to sleep without him.

We've been suffering from nightmares for the past several months, waking up in cold sweats and struggling to breathe. But we're there to pull each other through each one, saving the other from the suffocating darkness. I have no idea how long they'll last, or if they'll ever go away, but we'll get through it. We'll always save each other.

Every night before we go to sleep, Ryker presses a kiss to the scar on my chest, showing me that not all scars are bad. Some are beautiful despite their ugly appearance, the meaning underneath what's important. I've learned that all my scars, even the ones left by Kaleb, have made me who I am, have taught me valuable lessons. But that one, the one that Ryker and I share, means the most to me. It symbolizes love, a love I'd never thought I would have, a constant reminder to never take it for granted. And I never plan to.

Nikki Sparxx

the End

Acknowledgements

First off, I would like to thank my family for their support in this next step of my journey. They've never discouraged me from following this amazing dream of mine, and their support means so much to me.

Thank you to my beta readers, Vanessa, Natasha, Ena, Nicki, and Stephanie for their invaluable feedback. They helped make *The Scars of Us* what it is, and I'm so grateful for their input.

To my editor, Ana Zaun, for pushing me and helping me take my writing to the next level.

To Kari at Cover to Cover Designs, thank you for putting up with my OCD demands when it came to my cover—it came out gorgeous and I love it.

To my muse, Andrew England. Thank you for being the perfect inspiration for Ryker, and for being so easy to work with. I look forward to working with you on my upcoming projects in the future.

To Simon Barnes for the amazing photo used for the cover. I loved working with you and Andrew, and can't wait to see what we come up with for my other books.

I want to give a huge thanks to my self-defense instructor, Master Philip Lobo at Wolfpack Fighting and Fitness Academy. I really wanted the self-defense maneuvers that I used in the book to be actual, effective techniques, and he answered all my questions and demonstrated each and every one for me. His teachings were priceless, and I'm so thankful to have learned so much from him.

And most importantly, to the readers. Thank you for reading *The Scars of Us*. Time is precious, and I'm beyond grateful that you spent some of your time to read my work. I hope that you fell in love with Kaiya and Ryker, just like I did when I wrote their story.

Made in the USA
Monee, IL
05 May 2023